Mystery novels uniquely subtle means by which the real powers of darkness interact with human society. This is not so with Smitherman's *Engaging the Sons of Darkness*. The human characters will seem familiar to the reader because they will closely resemble some they have known. The supernatural characters will be equally familiar, being those revealed in the Bible. Though written as fiction, the truth behind the basic plot line is very real. Those who appreciate the power of mystery to weave truth into reading will not be disappointed with *Engaging the Sons of Darkness*.

> Dennis D. Frey, Th.D., President, Master's International School of Divinity

This is a riveting, thrilling page-turner for a first time writer. Barbara Smitherman has got the right combination of thrills and suspense in this tale of spiritual and worldly warfare. I can't wait to read more from her.

> Doris Rhone, Elder, Tabernacle of Praise

This book is a "must read" in light of the time we are living in. I found it to be a brainteaser and kept me wanting to skip ahead to see if I identified the correct characters insinuated in each chapter. Kudos to the author!

> Constance McGinnis, Supervisor of Admissions, McAlester Regional Health Center

This was a riveting novel, which kept me interested and curious at all the plots and powerful underlining messages. From beginning to end, there were so many "teachable moments" about the bigger picture of Christianity and the true spiritual warfare that is going on everyday and everywhere we go. I was blessed and challenged to better stay on my "spiritual post" and better direct my prayers for victory in my life and my surroundings. This is a great book and gives a strategic insight into the spiritual realm, which I would recommend every believer to read.

Rev. Dr. Vanessa Weatherspoon, Gathering
Of The Eagles Ministries

ENGAGING THE SONS OF DARKNESS

What Happens When Unseen Forces Envelope the Jack Fork Mountains?

ENGAGING THE SONS OF DARKNESS

BARBARA SMITHERMAN

TATE PUBLISHING & *Enterprises*

Engaging the Sons of Darkness
Copyright © 2009 by Barbara Smitherman. All rights reserved.

No part of this publication may be reproduced, stored in a retrieval system or transmitted in any way by any means, electronic, mechanical, photocopy, recording or otherwise without the prior permission of the author except as provided by USA copyright law.

All Scripture quotations are taken from the Holy Bible, King James Version, Cambridge, 1769. Used by permission. All rights reserved.

The opinions expressed by the author are not necessarily those of Tate Publishing, LLC.

Published by Tate Publishing & Enterprises, LLC
127 E. Trade Center Terrace | Mustang, Oklahoma 73064 USA
1.888.361.9473 | www.tatepublishing.com

Tate Publishing is committed to excellence in the publishing industry. The company reflects the philosophy established by the founders, based on Psalm 68:11,
"The Lord gave the word and great was the company of those who published it."

Book design copyright © 2009 by Tate Publishing, LLC. All rights reserved.
Cover design by Janae J. Glass
Interior design by Nathan Harmony

Published in the United States of America

ISBN: 978-1-60696-011-0
1. Fiction: Christian: Fantasy
2. Fiction: Suspense
09.01.06

I

The June air was humid; darkness enveloped the small town of Evansville, a town sat upon an imaginary throne, isolated in time, a long forgotten relic. Scattered throughout the landscape a few glimmering lights could be seen coming from the scarcely populated town that was closed up tight. As the town lay in its morbid silence, a slight movement coming from the underbrush was stirring the leaves, a sound so faint it could easily go unnoticed. Being aroused from a peaceful nap, a lone tan dog, sensing danger, suddenly raised its head, let out a deep growl, and moved onto the safety of the porch, as the dark shadowy figure moved closer into the town.

Standing on the edge of the town surveying the landscape, a newcomer—a strange figure of a man—was watching the actions of the night unfolding as if it were a scene in a play.

On the east end of the main street, the shape of a tall steeple attached to a white building in desperate need of painting could be seen. This would serve as the house of worship to the fifty more or less citizens that regarded themselves to be devoted followers of John Wesley. Approximately two hundred feet to the right, stood the town's only grocery/general store and gas station. It was inside the general store that a single beam of light penetrated the darkness surrounding the building. No other building on the town's main street showed any sign of life or activity.

With what would appear as a form of time travel, the stranger was standing in front of another of the town's establishments set off the main street on a side road closer to the opposite end of town. One could hear, coming from the inside, the sound of clicking as a white ball made its way across a table and made contact with one of the several other balls of differing colors. The voices had a type of gaiety as the people inside were engaged in their own unique type of recreation.

Approaching the entrance, the stranger was hindered from entering the building by the sentry. With eyes that were cold and unwavering, the sentry was waiting to attack this stranger if he made an attempt to enter. After several minutes of visual combat, the stranger made his way away from the door. He knew that he alone was no match for this large imposing figure. The stranger was all alone in this town that time had forgotten. Until his own accomplices arrived, he knew he better not attempt to invade the territory that had been claimed by those that were permanent residents here.

This was going to be a harder assignment than he ever imagined. He, of course, was used to doing hard jobs and dirty work, but this was one job that was going to be harder than anything he had previously undertaken. He hadn't been in the town more than fifteen minutes and had already encountered heavy resistance. Why had he been commissioned to come to this place? *What was so important about a town that the rest of the state and the world never even gave a second thought? What could possibly be the benefit of this place?* There had been a slight hint, before his departure, that this place would be instrumental in changing the world. This was not a probability that was evident to him at this time. Continuing through the small town, he knew it was imperative that he locate the person or persons that had been instrumental in his being sent to this place.

He had been instructed that there was a person there anxiously awaiting his and his crew's arrival to begin working on the improvements and renovations of this town. He had been told that, unlike so many other places in which he had to search endlessly to find a particular person and place, he would not have that much difficulty here. There were so few people here that truly wanted change, so few that would accept change. But he had been assured; there were a few that were desperate for change, that there was one in particular that longed for this to happen. He had also been personally informed that it would take some time but the other citizens would come around to accepting and appreciating the change.

Most of the citizens of Evansville had come to believe that this was the way things were and nothing could change them. Others had just grown to believe that everything was the way it was *supposed* to be; they had grown complacent. Then there were those that thrived on the way things were. They actually prospered in the present state of affairs.

The stranger went from one end of the town to the other and back again. He went up and down every alleyway. He searched up and down every back road and checked inside every available structure. Making sure he had looked under every nook and cranny, there just didn't seem to be anyone who remotely had any interest in his presence or his ability to change the town into a prosperous, world-changing place.

Everyone that had seen or recognized his presence only gave him threatening stares and gestures; he believed it was time to call in to the head office to get more precise directions on what to do next. He knew that there really was someone that he was supposed to meet and work with, but as yet that person had not materialized. There was no clue as to their location; there was no hint as to where to look. He didn't know the name or where the person lived in this place.

The obvious places had not been the place, now he had to depend on them to reveal themselves. He hoped this wouldn't be too long. From what he had already seen, there wasn't much time before the whole town would be beyond the point of no return. Before long, it would only be a memory. This town was like a person in the terminal stages of a deadly disease. It was gasping for air, and the sense of touch had long since left. It was now just a matter of time until the heart stopped pumping, being choked out by the disease that had it held captive.

Maybe the contact person or persons didn't know that he was coming. *That couldn't be right,* he considered to himself. Had they not contacted headquarters asking them to come? Did they not make the necessary arrangements for their arrival? How could they not know that he was coming? Maybe they didn't realize that he would be sent ahead by himself to survey the conditions and begin the process of renovation. Maybe they expected a large workforce to come in all at one time, bringing all the necessary equipment and machinery that it would take. Maybe they had given up altogether since his arrival had been so long in coming. However, if they were familiar enough with headquarters that they could contact them directly, they should have known that it would not come in the expected way. There were certain techniques that had to be set up; an established plan had to be in place before the actual work could begin.

This was not your average run-of-the-mill operation; this was not a company that would come in, do a cosmetic face-lift, then leave. The company that he worked for would come in, tear down, rebuild, and stabilize the whole town. Major improvements would be made that would benefit all the people within the town.

⚡

"I was just checking in. I have arrived in Evansville, and I have not yet been able to locate my contact person," the man reported to corporate headquarters.

"Just be patient. They will reveal themselves shortly."

"Can you tell me a little about who I'm looking for?"

"No, but you'll know who it is; after all, there are only a few that really want our help, but there is one who is truly determined to bring about a change to the place."

"I went to the most obvious place, but it was locked up tight without a sign or clue that the person I was to meet had ever been there."

"Now, you know that in our job the obvious place is usually the last place to find what you're looking for."

"You're right. I'll just be patient and look, watch, and listen. I'm sure that they will make themselves known to me soon."

"Fine. Once you have everything prepared, just let us know. Then we will send out the crew."

"I will. Thank you."

All that was left now was to wait. This was going to be a very tedious time. He knew that time was of the essence—not for his sake, but for the sake of the town and its residents. He sat quietly on the steps of the city hall, waiting for his contact to reveal him or herself.

Sitting in the silence of the night, the sounds of loud chattering, growling, and hissing were all around and were coming closer and closer to where he sat. He never gave any indication that he had heard, nor did he acknowledge the direction from which these sounds were coming.

He sat very still and quiet, just listening, being prepared to go and meet with the contact person. A growling, throaty voice broke the silence as the stranger sat and waited.

"What are you doing here?" the voice wanted to know.

"That really is none of your business," he replied.

"Don't you see that we have everything under control here?"

The stranger never returned with an answer to the ominous figure, a tactic that enraged his confronter.

"I don't know what you assume you can do here all by yourself. What, your head office got a shortage of workers or something?" Still there was no answer from the stranger.

"Well, I tell you what. You can stick around here if you like, but you truly will be sorry. There is nothing here for you; no one will come to your defense or support you in any way." Staring at the strange man, the figure interjected, "You will only be wasting your time. Besides that, you look a little weak. You got a problem? Your energy run down? On the other hand, maybe you been working too hard lately," he amusingly snarled.

The stranger never acknowledged the presence; he simply continued to wait patiently for his contact. Realizing that his efforts at this point were useless, the growling figure crept slowly away from the stranger, not removing his glare until he was well out of sight. He had to get to the office and report his finding to the management team.

There was a major threat brewing. There was a new company in town, a company with the plan of coming in and tearing down everything that it had taken his company decades to build up. Although the worker had only seen one for now, he knew from everything that he had been told that before long there would be a whole crew working endlessly to change the whole town.

This was news that the higher-ups would not be happy with. Things had been going so well; everything was working the way they had planned. It had taken years to get this town and its people the way they wanted. Everyone, or so they believed, was getting used to the changes and was following along with the major scheme of things. Now that it was just right, somebody had called in these troublemakers to rearrange things.

The outer office was full of workers relaxing and chattering among themselves. Some were reclining on the sofas; others were sprawled out across the floor. These were the common laborers that maintained the Company's general operation, making sure that everything was running according to the plan and all elements were working effectively. Management had done such a good job that the workers often had a lot of spare time on their hands. Of course, there was the occasional malfunction but nothing that couldn't be handled swiftly by one or two workers at the most.

Entering the next alcove of the "office," the worker came into the room where the upper management team gathered. There they were busy working out new strategies and schemes, putting forth new policies, and developing new ways of operating that would make the work of the laborers more effective. This truly was an effective operation. There were ways and means committees that set up new ways to better the company operation. There was a quality assurance division that decided whether the current techniques were being effective. This company was the best-run company on the planet. The office was damp, dark, and musky, but that neither hindered nor affected the Company personnel.

"Hey, boss," the worker shouted, "we got us a real problem,"

"And just what might that be?" The tall muscular dark figure sitting behind the desk inquired nonchalantly.

"Well, I was going up and down the streets tonight, making sure that everything was going right. Then lo and behold, right on the steps of the city hall, right out in plain view, there he sat. Sitting there just like he owned the place, looking around, and listening."

The boss sat up with a start and stared at the worker with a look of disgust and hatred. The words that would come out of his mouth were putrid and vile. "There who sat?" he seethed.

"One of them...you know...from that other company. The one you said would try to show up," he continued. "The ones that you said always showed up after all the work has been done."

"What did he look like?"

"Well, he was big like you, sir. He had long hair that was kind of red. He looked like he had spent the last few decades working out, but..."

"But what?" the boss asked.

"Looked like he was real tired, like he had to stop because he didn't have enough energy to keep going, so I let him know I saw him and told him he was wasting his time here."

Not hearing the last of the worker's statement, the boss was worriedly considering what this would mean. Did headquarters know that he was in town? Was he the only one here? *He has to be the only one. If there were any others, they would have been close by and the worker would never have gotten a chance to get close to him.* With his countless dealings with them in the past, he was aware of their untiring tenacity.

It had been, from experience, a very difficult task to overtake them. They always managed to outwit and outmaneuver his crew. This group would come in and some way or another, convince the town that things could and should be better, that there were better ways of doing things. There were new things to be carried out and new areas that could be built up. However, this time he vowed it would be different. His company had this town totally sewed up, and there was no way any other entity would have a chance at undoing what they had achieved to date.

The little worker was standing there, feeling quite proud for bringing this crucial information to the boss. This information stood to prove he was on his job.

"Gather up all the workers immediately, and bring them into the briefing room," the boss instructed the ways and means supervisor. "There is a matter of extreme importance that must be addressed immediately."

⚡

Meanwhile, sitting quietly on the city hall steps for what seemed like an eternity, the newcomer caught a faint sound, a sound that he instantly recognized. This was the sound he had been waiting for. This was the first revelation of the person and the place where he was commissioned to be. Instantly rising to his feet, he followed the sound that was so faint and weak that only he would have been able to hear. Instantly, he began to feel energy returning to his being, an energy that had slowly been depleted over the last few days.

At the far west end of town, there was a well-manicured lawn, in the middle of which sat a white doublewide mobile home. Out front of the home, a small flower garden enclosed with a white plastic fence added a sense of hope to the neighborhood. On the front of the home, was a large deck with a plastic picnic table, chairs, and a gliding swing. The light was on in the back room. By receiving his recent invitation, the newcomer silently entered.

Looking at the person whom he knew to be one of his contact persons, he was not surprised to find that he was entirely as he had imagined him to be. The man was approximately thirty years old—a fact that his physical appearance belied. He looked to be much older; his face had the deep creases of worry across the forehead, dark circles under the eyes that were evident of a lack of rest, a true state of sleep deprivation. The hair on his head was beginning to recede, and there was a sprinkling of gray throughout.

Sitting at the desk in the converted office, the man poured over countless numbers of newspapers from the past. Several were neatly folded to one side, and others were just laid across the chair or piled on the floor. The man's attention was being absorbed by an article dated July 22, 1989.

Remembering back, a feeling of sadness came over the newcomer. He now understood why he had been commissioned to this place. That article told of an event that had a major effect on Evansville. This was about the time that the Company that he was appointed to come and put out of business had taken over and turned Evansville into their model city, a city to be used as the prototype for all future towns and cities across the nation. Now he was beginning to understand how this little town would be the catalyst that could and would change the world for either good or bad.

There was much planning to be done, a lot of materials to be gathered, and a lot of workers needed to bring this project into focus and a final realization. Not only did the newcomer need his strong crew of workers, he also needed to enlist dedicated volunteers ready to stand up to the challenge. This truly was not going to be an easy task. The work was going to be hard, and there was a critical time limit to be adhered to.

II

Phillip Fields had always been an intuitive child growing up in the city of Longview Texas, a town about two hours east of Dallas. One of his biggest desires was to understand how things worked—how they came about, what was the cause and effect of its existence. Phillip would spend hours reading, trying to understand exactly where everything on this earth had originated. In his high school Biology class, it was hard for Phillip to understand the idea how everything on the earth had just evolved from some higher life form. If this was actually how everything came about, then where did the original life forms come from that everything else evolved? Phillip could not seem to understand or believe this theory.

Phillip's family was in the average working class; his mother, Mary, was born and raised in Longview. She had attended and graduated from Star College of Cosmetology and received her state license to practice the art of cosmetology. She had opened her own beauty salon, a salon that over the years had grown to include six stylists, two shampoo girls, three nail techs, as well as a tanning booth. By the standards of the day, she was quite successful; her business was thriving, and her home life was by all outward appearances happy. Phillip's father, Kevin, also a Longview native, had attended Texas State Technical College after high school and received a certificate in heavy equipment repair. Kevin had begun as a diesel mechanic for the local truck stop, but after working for four years at the truck stop, he took an unprecedented leap and opened his own diesel engine repair business. It took a while, but now it was beginning to pay off, as he would say.

Kevin Fields had a plan for success from the very beginning; he went to the very school from which he had graduated, convinced the school that the students would learn better in an actual work environment and had succeeded in the recruitment of students to assist him in his business. This arrangement would prove valuable to both him and the school; the school had a place for the students to practice their clinical skills. Kevin in turn had cheap labor.

Phillip was the oldest child in the family. He had a sister Carrie, three years his junior. As far as anyone knew, she had no sense of direction; she just went along with the flow, no matter where that flow managed to lead. By the age of fourteen, Carrie had somehow decided that she must have been adopted and no longer felt she should follow the rules of this foreign family (though this is not what she actually stated in words, her actions would quickly give anyone caring to watch that impression). Carrie's actions and attitude were a great stressing point for Mary and Kevin Fields. After all, they were pretty successful people. What would the people in town believe about their rebellious daughter? Not only were they disappointed in her, but her actions were a major source of embarrassment—the nose ring, belly ring, tongue ring, and the jet black hair of her gothic lifestyle. By her nineteenth birthday, Carrie had tattoos all over her body—areas that could be seen and those that couldn't. Her entire wardrobe was black except for the occasional red item.

There were times Phillip felt as though he was in the world all by himself. With his parents constantly worrying about Carrie and trying to keep on top of their respective businesses, there really didn't seem to be time for Phillip. Phillip soon began to understand being the good kid had its innumerable drawbacks.

It was during his junior year of high school right after the Christmas break that a new student entered Longview High School and sat beside him in his Algebra class; her name was Sherri Johnson. Sherri Johnson had transferred to Longview High School from a small school in Hugo, Oklahoma after her father was relocated to Longview.

Although for Sherri this had not been a distant move (Hugo was only about two and a half hours away from Longview), it seemed to be a continent away. Hugo was a city in southeastern Oklahoma's Choctaw County with a population of about 6,000. The most exciting thing about Hugo was it served as winter quarters for some circus performers and animals. Hugo was also the county seat of Choctaw County, located in a cultural area of the state known as Little Dixie and the tourist area for Kiamichi Country.

The largest classroom, student-wise, in which Sherri had ever been, was thirty. All thirty students had started school in kindergarten together and continued on through graduation. There was never a question at the beginning of school of who you would have in your class; you already knew. They had been the same every year. To move to Longview, a metropolitan city in comparison to Hugo was a big step, one that carried a strong element of fear.

Phillip couldn't help but notice the new girl at school; after all, she sat right beside him in Algebra class. She was different from any of the other girls he had met in school— or anywhere else, for that matter. Sherri had long golden brown hair and fine, delicate features that a sculptor would die to create. She had a smile that you only saw on television. It made one wonder if she had to wear braces for about ten years to have teeth that straight and white.

Her hazel eyes appeared to speak without her mouth ever moving. Phillip could tell that she was a little nervous, but she had no difficulty fitting right in with the routine of Longview High. *Maybe, just maybe*, Phillip daydreamed, *he could ask her to the junior-senior prom*, but he had better act fast. Just give it a week, and one of the school jocks would have her wearing his letterman's jacket and taped-up class ring. This was a dream that Phillip couldn't really see as a possibility. Just why would a girl like her ever consider going out with him? Who was he? Phillip Fields, the local geek, the loner, the one who is so nonathletic he doesn't even know what side of the gym to sit on for the home basketball games.

"Hi," the sound of the voice broke into Phillip's self-pitying thoughts.

"Oh, hi." *That was dumb,* Phillip reasoned. *Couldn't you come up with something more original than that?*

Three months passed. The junior-senior prom was only three weeks away, but to his knowledge, Sherri didn't have a date. As matter of fact, Phillip had not noticed Sherri being overly friendly with any boys at school. Therefore, today was the day that he had decided to ask Sherri to the prom. *But what if she says no? What if she laughs at me or says something like "You got to be kidding?"* These thoughts were constantly occupying Phillip's mind.

Phillip had a real fear of rejection and ridicule. He would avoid conflict at all cost, which is one of the reasons he would never attempt to go out for any type of contact sport. Not to mention the fact that he couldn't play. In going out for sports, he knew there would be conflict; he had heard his father say time and time again that a good player had to have a win or die attitude.

He didn't want to face the ridicule involved during the training and practice periods from the coaches and other players. Phillip had long felt it was on account of his non-athletic ability that there was a strain in his and his father's relationship. In high school, Kevin Fields had been the team's star running back, an accomplishment that *could have* taken him to high places. However, in his senior year, Kevin had messed up his knee and was not able to play football again, not seriously anyway. Kevin had always dreamt that his son would follow in his footsteps and quite possibly be a first round draft choice for the NFL. Phillip was just the opposite—a book worm, a wonderer, always trying to figure out the how and why of something. Instead of carrying the ole pigskin, Phillip was more likely to be finding ways of cloning a skinless pig.

Asking Sherri to the prom was one of the scariest things that he had ever done. He had practiced in front of the mirror at least three dozen times a day, preparing for the actual occurrence. Phillip not only practiced the invitation, he also practiced what he would say when she refused. He used every turndown he knew and practiced his facial expressions and his comeback. He knew that she would probably say no, but at least he would have the satisfaction of asking her.

The day was finally here. Phillip had decided to ask Sherri to the prom. After Algebra class, he lingered around the door of the classroom, waiting for Sherri to come out. A wave of nausea was creeping up in his stomach; his hands were shaking so hard he caught himself clinching his books as if they were a newfound treasure.

"Hey, Phillip," Sherri said as she came out of the room. "Did you leave something in the class?"

"Huh? Oh, no, actually I was waiting on you." *Okay, that's it. You got to ask her now because if not, then you will have to explain why you were waiting on her.* Fear clinched Phillip like a vice.

"Oh, that's sweet," Sherri replied. "Why?"

"Well, I was just thinking... You know that the junior-senior prom is in a few weeks, and I was wondering..." Sherri, sensing his nervousness, lightly touched his hand.

"I'd love to go with you," she remarked.

"But I would understand..." Phillip started to reason. "What did you say?"

"I said I would love to go to the prom with you, silly. Actually I was hoping that you would ask me."

"Really?"

"Yes, really."

This was more than Phillip could have ever dreamt; he had actually asked (or at least started to ask) and gotten a date with Sherri on the first try. *Okay*, he reasoned to himself, *don't act excited…just be normal. Wait, what do I do now? Do I just say well I'll see you tomorrow or what?* This was all so very new to Phillip. However, he didn't have to worry about it long. It was Sherri who suggested they meet after school and make plans for the prom, what they would wear, and the other details.

Phillip went on to his next class in a state of awe, a dreamlike trance. This would prove to be the longest day ever; all he wanted was for the three o'clock bell to ring so that he could meet Sherri. Phillip felt better than he had ever felt in his life. Life truly was good.

After that first date (though it was more like a meeting), Phillip and Sherri became constant companions at school and after. They would talk frequently on the phone.

There was something about their chemistry, something that just bonded them together. It must have been fate that had brought Sherri to Longview, and karma that drew them together.

⚡

The blue shirt with the white collar no, maybe I need to just wear a nice button-down shirt. Phillip was having a hard time trying to decide what to wear, and this was an occasion of the highest importance. It was one week before the prom.

Sherri had invited him over to her house for dinner and to meet her family. Phillip was as nervous as a cat on a hot tin roof; he had never been invited to meet a girl's family before. His mother had told him that this was a very good sign that Sherri must really like him, or she would have never invited him to dinner. It seemed as though he and Sherri really had a special relationship. He felt very comfortable with her, more so than he had felt with anyone other than his family. *Oh well, the blue shirt with the white collar will do fine.* He wasn't trying to impress her folks with his clothes. He wanted to impress them with who he was, but he still wanted to look right. *You only get one first impression.* Looking himself over, he made a mental checklist—hair combed, clean shaven, no zits. *Okay, that will have to do.*

The drive across town had given Phillip the time to practice his conversation with Sherri's parents. He just couldn't blow this date. Following her directions, Phillip pulled up to a red brick ranch house. The yard was meticulously manicured. A climbing red rose brush was attached to a white trellis with the first buds of roses beginning to bloom. To the south of the house was the True Light Christian Center Nondenominational Church. The only thing that separated the church and the house was the church parking lot.

To Phillip that was a little odd; he didn't know anyone who had a church in the front yard. *Oh well, maybe this was the only house they could find when they first got here.* He was sure this was only a temporary arrangement.

Before getting out of the car, he did a last-minute inspection of his appearance. Let's see, flowers for Mrs. Johnson and a small box of chocolates for Sherri. Were chocolates a good choice? Suddenly, a feeling of apprehension hit Phillip. He hoped she was not allergic to chocolate. Next week was the prom. He surely didn't want anything to mess up—not now; it was too close.

When Sherri answered the door, she looked exceptionally beautiful in her light blue sundress and white sandals. Phillip felt quite proud of himself for picking out the blue shirt. *It must be karma again*, he thought to himself.

Meeting Mrs. Johnson, Phillip got a glimpse into the future; she was a twenty-years-older version of Sherri. Sherri's resemblance to her mother was uncanny. Sherri had three brothers: Mat, fifteen, Jimmy, thirteen, and Ben, ten. The youngest one, Ben, sat across the room from Phillip, staring at him, not saying a word, making Phillip very nervous. In a failed attempt at trying to ignore Ben, Phillip smiled at him then pretended to watch the action of the game that Mat and Jimmy were playing on the Nintendo.

Throughout the entire room were various types of religious memorabilia. Plaques with Bible inscribed verses, angel figurines, and crosses adorned every table and wall space. This was something Phillip's house was totally void of. It was during his time of his visual surveillance of the room that Sherri came in.

"Phillip, would you like something to drink? We have orange juice, tea, or water."

"A glass of tea would be nice."

"All right, dinner will be ready in a few minutes. My father is on his way from the office, and then we can eat."

"Oh, your father has to work on Saturday too? My father does too."

"Oh yes, actually Saturday is the busiest day for my father."

Before Sherri could explain why it was his busiest day, her father came through the front door. "Oh, there he is now. Hi, Daddy. This is Phillip."

"Hello there, Phillip, I'm Sherri's father, Reverend Robert Johnson."

The introduction surprised Phillip. Sherri's father was a minister; now everything began to fit into place—the emphasis in the house with all the religious items. That's also why they lived next door to a church; they had to relocate here because he was the preacher. It all made sense now.

Phillip's knowledge of church and the Bible were very limited; of course, there was a Bible at his home. It was on the bottom shelf of the entertainment center. He could remember when he and Carrie were small, his mother would read the nativity story to them at Christmas time, but as far as ever having any affiliations with any type of organized religion, they didn't. He was almost certain though that his parents believed in God, because they would refer to Him at times. Nothing that would ever suggest that they *didn't* believe. Things like, "The good Lord helps them who helps themselves" or "Cleanliness is next to godliness"—were said around the house frequently. His family probably never attended any church services on account of his parents' busy schedules. Sunday was usually the only day they had to rest with running businesses and sometimes his father even having to work on Sunday.

For some reason, Phillip was beginning to get a feeling of guilt, the kind of guilt that he always got when he knew he should have done something and didn't, or that he shouldn't have done something and did. In his mind, he was making excuses for his parents and himself for not taking part in a religious tradition. Could this cause a problem in his and Sherri's relationship? Phillip began to worry. What if his nonreligious status caused Rev. Johnson to forbid his seeing Sherri? For the life of him, he could not understand why he was having these feelings. He couldn't attribute it to karma. *That is just plain silly.*

Dinner had gone well; the Johnson family was unlike any other family that Phillip had ever known. There was a perfectly set table. Reverend Johnson offered a prayer before the meal, something Phillip could never remember happening at his household. Reverend Johnson had given thanks for the food and for the person who prepared the meal. It was the most relaxing and pleasant atmosphere that Phillip could ever remember at a family meal. He really couldn't remember a time when his family had actually sat down and had a meal as a family. This was something Phillip could get really used to doing.

⚡

The months had flown by; it was now two weeks before graduation. Phillip had become very close to Sherri and her family. By all accounts, the senior year had been a very trying year. There was the big decision of what school to attend, what to major in, and what he would do with his life after college. There was one thing that Phillip was very sure about: wherever he went, whatever he did, Sherri would be right there beside him. He and Sherri had become *unofficially* engaged during the summer of their junior year.

He was happier than he had ever been in his life. After the

long evenings sitting in the office of Reverend Johnson, he finally had found the answer to the origin of all things. These evenings had given him an immediate love for the Bible and what it said. Now the problem was how he was going to break the news to his parents that he had decided to go to LeTourneau, the Christian university, and study theology.

Phillip had finally found rhyme and reason to the origin of the universe and all things in it. He now wanted to share this information with as many people as he could. He knew there were others out there that had been as confused as he was. He had no doubt this was not something that his parents would be overjoyed about. He was sure that it wasn't that they didn't believe that there was a God; they could not see the advantage or the benefit of being a preacher. They had the impression that preachers were too lazy to work and had to depend on the handouts of the members of the congregation to feed them. However, regardless what they believed about his choice, he was going to follow the calling that he felt was before him.

III

This was getting to be a bigger burden than anything Jack had ever undertaken. It seemed that Jack was spending more sleepless nights than ever in his life. Tonight the humidity was stifling; the small window air conditioner proved useless in this June heat. It appeared that it had gotten hotter quicker this year than any other year he could remember. The clock over the office door recorded that it was ten thirty. Jack, with painstaking diligence, was going over the books from the One Stop grocery and convenience store. After going over the last few months' transactions, it became apparent there was a lot more outgoing than there was incoming.

It was a major cause of concern for Jack; if things didn't start to improve soon, he would have no choice but to close the store and move his family to another town.

The store had been in Evansville for the better part of sixty years. It was first opened as the Sims Mercantile by his grandfather, William Sims, to supply the needs of the coal miners and their families during a time that Evansville was booming. The store later passed to Jack's father, Nathaniel. Now it was passed to him after his father's death eight months prior.

As a child, Jackson "Jack" Sims had always put himself in a position of superiority. This came from pride in that his family, so he believed, was the most prosperous of all the people of Evansville. They owned the only store and gas station in town. Whatever anyone needed had to come from the Sims store. This would include the schools and the two churches in town. No major event, activity, celebration, or festival could be achieved without the One Stop grocery and general store. This afforded Jack the luxury of his boastful arrogance, which often got him into trouble in his teenage years, trouble that would be swiftly slid under the rug due to his family's high standing in the community. One could say that Jack was—or at least believed he was—above and better than anyone else in this small community. Jack also believed he was above the law, that he truly ran the town. He was, in his own eyes, a big duck in a small pond.

After returning from living in Dallas to take over the family business after his father's death, Jack was prepared to resume his position as the "Big Duck" but quickly found out that in reality the citizens of the town actually owned more of the store than he did. There were overdue balances for practically everyone in town; it appeared that his father had been extending credit to everyone and only receiving meager payments, if any at all.

The store was indebted to all its suppliers. Some, like

Allied Foods, were getting ready to pursue legal actions for the uncollected debts.

Tonight Jack was methodically arranging all the delinquent accounts, adding the appropriate late charges in preparation to mail out overdue statements. He had talked with an attorney friend of his in Dallas and had been counseled to demand payment on these accounts or potential legal action would be taken.

Jack had graduated from the University of Texas with a bachelor in business management, where it was taught that it was good business to take care of business. What if he stepped on a few toes and hurt a few feelings? There was no way he could support himself and his growing family or continue to pay the expenses for the nursing center, where his mother was now a resident, if people didn't pay their bills. This was the One Stop Store, not the Come Get It Free Store. Jack was not about to ruin his whole life through legal battles created by his father's lack of business sense and overzealous generosity. No, sir, not this kid. The people of Evansville had to realize they were living in the real world; this was not the Land of Oz, and he was not the wizard.

Evansville was set far back in an area of southeast Oklahoma known as Jack Fork Mountains. There were several little communities in this area, but Evansville, founded by Cleon Evans, owner of the Evans Mining Company, was the largest 'town' in the area. During the 1940s there were almost 5,000 people living and working in Evansville. Those who didn't work in the mines had other prosperous enterprises. There were carpenters, auto mechanics, and a seamstress. There were two local cafés that catered to the single working men, and of course, there were the local bars, taverns, and houses of ill repute. Everything that the miners needed could be found in Evansville. Mrs. Wilson owned a small boarding house. There was even a seventeen-room motel, The Dew Drop Inn. During the early years, it had been projected that Evansville was going to grow to the size of maybe Fort Smith, Arkansas, or Longview, Texas. Yes, indeed, there was a great expectation for the town; all the people seemed to have a sense of pride in themselves and their little community.

In the early 1960s, things started to go bad; the coal mining business began to go under as other means of fuel were quickly replacing the demand for coal. In 1965, the Evans Mining Company closed down as a result. The men that had worked so hard building their lives in Evansville had to begin to look for work elsewhere. The town began to lose not only businesses but also residents.

The economics of the town had dwindled down to nothing. Buildings were standing empty and in time falling down completely. There were a few farms left on the outskirts of town, more of which stood empty than were inhabited. The population of the town had greatly fallen to its present number of 1,800. To all on the outside, Evansville appeared to be a quiet little community set back in the beautiful forest of the Jack Forks, a land rich in game and fish in the heart of Kiamichi Country. There were several nice gaming areas not far from the community, and every now and again, people would wander into Evansville for food and gas.

Jack first had believed it might be a good idea to add fishing bait to his inventory of supplies since Evansville was only about eight miles from Lake Hugo. Even so, how much bait did he actually expect to sell? All the hunting lodges sold everything that the outdoorsman would find themselves in need of. Furthermore, with the new super centers in the surrounding areas, people were going outside of Evansville, buying their groceries in bulk. There was no way that Jack could compete with the prices of the major stores like Wal-Mart and Target. Jack was going to have to do something to bring the store out of a hole, or it was just a matter of time before he was going to be ruined.

A sense of depression was beginning to set in; Jack did not know what he would do. The one good thing was that being the sole heir of his father's estate, he had not only inherited the store, but he now had full ownership of the family home, a large two-story Victorian house. His father had the foresight to have credit life insurance on the property, which had paid the balance in full up on his death. Even so, even if he wanted to move, what he would do with the home and the business was beyond him. There was no one in Evansville that could possibly purchase the property or who would even remotely want to.

His father had also left a moderately sized life insurance policy; after the final funeral expenses had been paid, there was about one hundred fifty thousand dollars left. Jack had first considered using the insurance money to pay off the indebtedness of the business, but in his mind, it would be just throwing good money after bad. What about his family? He and his wife, Rachael, were expecting their first child in three months, and he wanted to make sure that the baby had everything he needed. They would have to use that money to live on until he could bring the business out of the red and into the black and start making it profitable. Nevertheless, how was this going to happen? Reaching into the bottom drawer of the desk, Jack pulled out a bottle of Hennessey and a glass; it seemed of late, it was the only way Jack could get his thoughts together.

⚡

The nights were growing increasingly long for Rachael. She found herself spending more and more sleepless nights. This could possibly be attributed to the pregnancy, but then again it was more than likely the result of worry. Looking out the window, Rachael could see the light dimly burning in the office of the store. This too was getting more and more commonplace in her life. She knew that Jack was at the store trying to figure out what to do about the business or at least that is what he would say. However, once he would come home to bed, there would be the strong smell of alcohol on his breath, and he would be like a different person, one she didn't recognize. When she and Jack had first met at college, she knew that he was a little wild, that he had a little bad boy in him. That, she believed, was actually what drew her to him. Rachael had always enjoyed a good time, a little adventure.

College was a time of experimentation and exploration, a time to experience life. They had done the things that all the other college kids did. They had gone on the spring break trips to Cancun and Palm Beach; they had the all-night "Pharm" parties—not to mention the occasional close calls with the police. These were the things that kids did. Those who could manage to keep their grades up graduated with a degree in their chosen field. For Rachael that field had been paralegal studies. Remembering back, Rachael could recall college had been a wild and crazy time, a time of excitement.

It was after graduation she and Jack decided to get married and raise a family. There was no long engagement or the meeting of family; they had simply gone to the courthouse, gotten married by the judge, and started to work in their perceptive fields.

It had been Rachael's desire to open an independent office and contract her services to any attorney that needed her service. She was not going to tie herself down working for any one law firm on a salary, when she could work for as many or as few as she liked and charge a fee. She had been considering actually working from home. In the event she and Jack had children, she could still be a full-time mom and make a very good living as well.

When Jack had gotten the call that his father had a massive heart attack and was not expected to live through the night, she had a concern of what it would do to her future. She had heard all about Jack's hometown and the family business. From all that Jack had told her, she had the understanding that Jack's family was well off and that one day, he would inherit the whole thing.

The day they arrived in Evansville for Nathaniel Sims's funeral, Rachael was totally shocked at the town of Evansville of which Jack had repeatedly bragged. He had implied that his father was the closest thing to the royal king and him the royal prince. The town was run-down. Most of the houses were in poor repair; even the church where the services were held was in desperate need of repair. One could see the watermarks on the ceiling around the mock Michelangelo's Sistine Chapel masterpiece that took up the center of the ceiling. Cracks in the paper of the artwork were beginning to peel. The red carpet was worn from years of travel. The pews were unpadded and very hard; they were in such a poor repair that Rachael was afraid the rough wood would surely tear her hose.

The church itself was filled to capacity, but those paying their respects were not unlike the common people one could find in any low-income tenement housing. Where were the town's officials that one would expect to find at the funeral of one of its most influential citizens? Everyone had a strange attitude of sorts. The minister, Rev. Potter, was a man in his late sixties, maybe even his early seventies. He was a little man with a raspy voice who wore the old-time wire-rimmed glasses that sat right on the bridge of the nose.

Rev. Potter went through the service as if it was a memorized speech. He showed no emotion. He projected a very cool and non-caring attitude about the life of the man lying in front of him in a casket, a casket that probably cost more than his total earthly possessions.

The pianist, whom Rachael learned later was Mrs. Potter, seemed as though every stroke of the keys was an effort that she had long ago given up. The music was slow, dull, and boring. There was a small choir of seven people who sang from hymnals that looked to have been published in the early 1920s. *At least*, Rachael had believed to herself, *this will soon be all over.* She was sure that as soon as he possibly could, Jack would get things sewed up here, and they could continue their life in Dallas. Of course, they may have to move Jack's mother to Dallas to a care home closer to them;

she had been diagnosed with Alzheimer's disease about three years prior and since that time had not been able to recognize Jack or his father. She had to depend on the New Haven Care Home staff for her every need. Furthermore, now that Nathaniel had gone on, it would be far too hard for Jack to make regular visits to check on his mother from Dallas.

⚡

The Sims home had all the signs of a man living alone. The inside was cluttered though not dirty. Cluttered papers were strewn around the living room, dirty dishes were in the sink as if Mr. Sims just hadn't taken the time to tidy up, the refrigerator contained lunch meat, some grapes that were beginning to spoil, a half gallon of outdated milk, four eggs, and a box of low-fat cottage cheese. In the freezer compartment, Mr. Sims had a two-week supply of frozen dinners in a variety of menus. The inside of the house smelled rank, like the smell of old people. It was still furnished the same way it had been in Jack's childhood. The early American sofa and love seat were covered with thick plastic, the kind that sticks when sweated on, and sitting on it, one was definitely going to sweat.

Going around the living room and running her fingers over the tables and the mantel of the fireplace, Rachael tried to imagine life in this house in years long since gone. By all standards of the town, this truly would be considered a mansion. With a little updating, this could be a very nice home. She hoped that any prospective buyers would see the potential of this house and grocery store combination; then they could settle Nathaniel's estate in an expedited manner.

It wasn't until that night after Nathaniel's funeral while

they were in bed that Jack hesitantly told Rachael that they would be relocating to Evansville. He was going to take over his father's business. With his degree in business management, he knew that he could turn the old One Stop into a lucrative business. Besides, if Rachael planned on working from home, it didn't matter where they lived; she could still make a go of it. He explained that she could do research from anywhere. On the plus side, here they had a home that was paid for, an established business, and a town in which they did not have to try to work them selves up in; it was already theirs.

Jack was secretly excited about the prospect of resuming his position of importance in the town of Evansville. It had always been Jack's desire to be important in Dallas, a goal that he had not yet been able to accomplish, but here it had already been proven that he was important. Now that he was the sole owner of the store, he would be even more so.

It was only after two months that reality had begun to set in. Jack had become increasingly more agitated; nothing was going the way he had imagined they would. There was no money coming in; the store was going deeper and deeper into debt as a result. Jack had taken to drinking more and more, and he was becoming more and more distant. He would spend hours downstairs, sitting, just staring out the window. When she would attempt to talk, he would either ignore her or snap at her in a very hateful manner. Rachael had even noticed a look on his face that had the sheer stare of something evil; his whole face would seem to contort, and his countenance would change to something she did not like, actually something she feared.

There was something about this place and the people

that Rachael could not quite understand. There were secrets that only those who lived there knew, and since she was an outsider, it seemed they didn't want her to know any of them. She felt as though she was still in grade school and the other children were taunting her with "We know something you don't know." Some people, it appeared, gave her a look that she felt was one of sympathy. At first, she assumed this was in part as a result of the death of Jack's father, but after nine months, she knew there was something deeper that she had no clue about.

IV

Sitting on the easternmost edge of town, lights were shining through the windows of a run-down house, where the once sturdy white pillars held up a large beautiful scalloped veranda roof. These pillars were now rotting from the extreme elements of nature and the vicious attacks of hungry termites. It would appear that the slightest bit of pressure applied would send them crumbling to the ground along with the overhanging roof. There were visible cracks in the foundation and walls. The windows with their torn and rusted screens were covered with a thick plastic to provide instillation from the cold of winter and perhaps retain the cool air of the one ceiling fan and antiquated water cooler in the summer. It was here that Cherish Rollins and her three-year-old daughter had come too call home.

Cherish Rollins, as well as her parents, had been born and raised in Evansville. Her family had settled here in the early 1940s. They were only one of the several families that had come to Evansville from southwest Arkansas during the days of the coalmines. After putting forth an outward appearance of working in the mines for a very short period, the Rollins family soon realized this was work they were not willing to do. The town's people labeled them a worthless lazy bunch and had nothing to do with them. It was in the late 1940s early 1950s that her grandfather, Gabe, saw the financial benefit in making and selling corn whiskey as a way of supporting the clan. This was an occupation that further ostracized them from the good citizens of the town, earning them the title "poor white trash." Nevertheless, that they were trash was forgotten when some of the good citizens would sneak out to the old barn at the Rollins' for a drink or bottle of the sinful sauce that Grandpa Rollins could supply.

Life had always been a struggle for Cherish. All of her life, she had a hard time trying to get along with the people in her hometown. She was always in trouble with someone, but because she was that no-account Rollins girl, no matter what the circumstances were, it was always her fault. School was particularly difficult for Cherish; the other kids constantly laughed at her and called her nasty names. It was not unusual for Cherish to be involved in at least three fights a week. Because of not being able to keep up academically and the emotional strife, Cherish dropped out of school in the ninth grade going to work as a domestic servant. She would clean houses for whoever was willing or trusting enough to allow her into their homes or had the extra money to pay her. Residential housekeeping was all she knew how to do; besides that, there was no other place that she could work. Evansville's only excuse for a motel, the Dew Drop Inn, was in such a poor financial condition they could not afford to hire a full-time maid, not to mention there were never over two or three rooms that needed cleaning a month.

Cherish had learned at an early age that she was under the total and complete control of her father. Nolan Rollins was a man who possessed an extremely violent temper. There was always a reason for him to get mad and take the belt to Cherish or one of her brothers. If her mother made the *mistake* of trying to get him to stop, his anger would instantly be turned to her. It was not an uncommon occurrence that all four of them would be nursing a black eye, swollen lip, or bruised noses. One night it had gotten so bad her father had started beating her mother because she had not cooked the cornbread the way he liked it. By the time he was finished beating her, Cherish's mother had to wear a brace of sheet strips because she was sure she had a few broken ribs. Grandma Rollins assisted her in splinting the rib cage so that she could resume "her functions." Her grandmother told her mother that it was just plain wrong for a woman to sass her man, and if she did, then it was the husband's right to correct her. Cherish could only dream of a day when she would be able to leave this place and forget that it and everyone in it ever existed.

This was a dream that seemed to be shattered when, at the age of nineteen, Cherish had become pregnant. Her father was infuriated, and because she would not reveal the name of the father, her own father physically kicked her out of the house. He had slapped her so hard across the face that it felt as if a red hot iron had been placed on her face. She was knocked completely off her feet. She was now sure that if it had not been for her brother, Samuel, her father would have hurt her very badly; he had taken the stance to kick her when Sam had caught his arm and pulled him back. Instead, he pulled her up by the hair on her head, threw her out of the door, and told her to fend for herself and her no-name kid. He told her to get the daddy to take care of them; that was, if she knew who the father was.

Cherish had no money, nowhere to live, and not a clue as to what or where she could get help. Being in a complete state of helplessness, the thought of death became a very comforting thought. Running from the house, tears running down her cheeks, stumbling over rocks and holes in the road, she headed to the long covered bridge over the West River; this was the perfect place to end it all.

As she ran down the dirt road toward the bridge, Cherish got a feeling of uneasiness. It was as though someone was following her. Afraid to turn around, she ran even faster. Her heart was pounding in her chest; she could actually feel the blood rushing in her head, she was running so fast. Stopping to catch her breath, she decided, what if there was someone behind her? What difference would it make? It would be easier that way. She wouldn't have to take her own life; they could do it for her. Flashbacks of another night not so long ago began to flood her mind, a night as she walked along this road going home after working for a lady in town, a night that someone really was following her, a night that she had actually prayed for help.

The West River Bridge had one of those coverings over it that looked somewhat like a house. Looking over the side of the bridge and trying to get enough courage to jump, yet wondering in her mind, would she be in any pain before she finally died? Or would it be sudden?

With a feigned determination, she began to climb up on the crossbeam of the bridge, when suddenly things totally changed:

"What cha doin' up there, chile?" a voice said, coming out of the darkness. The voice so startled Cherish, she frantically groped for the railing to keep from losing her balance. Looking to her right, she saw Mamie.

Mamie was one of only a handful of black people that still lived in Evansville; she was elderly and had lived there as long as Cherish could remember. Her husband had been a coal miner at the number nine mine. She and her husband had eight children; all of who had either left the area to never return, or by some other means had met their end. Mamie was left all alone living in a moderate-sized house on the east end of town with nothing but a lot of cats to keep her company.

Most people in the town just ignored her and her odd behavior; others said she was a witch, but there were others who believed she was touched in the head as a consequence of losing her whole family. There were stories that Mamie could put spells on people, that she knew all the dark secrets of voodoo. Furthermore, as a result of their fears, no one bothered ole Mamie.

"Did ya hear me? I said what ya doin,' chile?"

Afraid not to answer but also afraid to acknowledge her, Cherish mustered up the courage to spit back, "What's it to ya?"

"Well, there is only two reasons I could think of that you would be standing where ya standing. Either you want to get a better view of the town or you thinking of jumping, so which it be?"

"Whichever it is, it is none of your business."

"True," replied Mamie, "but if you thinking of jumping, unless you don't knows how to swim, all ya gonna get is wet." Mamie chuckled. "That there river be about fifteen feet deep, and when you jump, you gonna go under, but then ya gonna come back up, and your natural instincts gonna kick in, and you gonna start swimmin.'"

Looking down at the river, Cherish could see the dark water below, not really knowing whether to believe this old lady or not. Cherish wondered in her mind whether this could really be true.

"How you know that?" Cherish asked in a very indignant tone of voice. "You ever jumped off a bridge?"

"Yep, matters of fact, I have. I thought nothin' in my life was worth livin' for; nothin' was ever gonna change or get no better. So I jumped in the river, and just like I said, I came to the top, and next thing I knows, I'm swimmin.' Alls I came out with was a wet body, all my problems, and plus now I had myself a new problem ya see," looking down at Cherish's feet, "I was like you. I jumped in with my shoes on, the only pair I had to my name, and I lost one of them in the water. Now I didn't even have a pair of shoes."

Thinking this all over, Cherish couldn't help but wonder if what the old woman was saying was the truth.

"Well, I guess I will just have to take off my shoes then," she said sarcastically.

"No, better yet, why don't ya just get down from there, go home, and tomorrow things will look a lot better to ya."

"If I had a home, I might, but I don't seem to have one…" The tears began to well up in her eyes; this was something she never wanted to happen. Her father always said watery eyes were a sign of what a person had in them—no blood and guts, just plain old water.

"What ya mean ya ain't got no home? I know who ya are, you that little Rollins girl. Your folks got a place out on Lone Oak Road."

"Look, I'm tired of talking to you. Things ain't gonna get no better. I just ain't got nothing to live for, so you just go away and let me be."

"That ain't so; you got a lot to live for. That baby of yours ain't even got born yet, so I know it ain't ready to die."

Those words stung deep as if a horde of bees had just landed all over her; those words were not what Cherish would have ever expected coming from Mamie. Mamie didn't know her, not close anyway, so how could she know about her being pregnant?

"How you know that? You really are a witch!"

Mamie chuckled again. "No, chile, I ain't no witch, but I do know some things, and right now I knows ya need to get down from there and come on and go with me. I'll fix ya something to eat, and then we can talk, and then after we get it all talked out, if ya want, ya can come back here and finish what ya started."

Refusing to look at Mamie, Cherish stared back down at the dark water below; she truly didn't *want* to die. What about the baby? No matter what or who, it still deserved a chance to live.

Slowly Cherish began to make her way down from the bridge railing. The thought of going with Mamie was weighing heavily on her mind. This was a woman that all her life she had tried to avoid not to get to close to, scared she would turn into a frog or something. Now she was listening to and getting ready to follow her home. Maybe it was like that story she had read in school a long time ago about the little kids getting fooled by the witch with the house made out of cookies.

What other choices did she have at this time? If she went to Mamie's house and no one ever saw her again, that would be just fine with her. What did she truly have to lose? She knew that although her father was the town's self-appointed bully, he would not come around Mamie's house. He was far too superstitious and afraid of just the thought that Mamie could put a spell on him. He felt that her supernatural powers were a lot worse than his physical power.

She would just go to Mamie's for a little while, get something to eat, possibly a good night's sleep, then she could decide tomorrow what to do. She was tired mentally, physically, and emotionally. This would give her a short break to get her mind and thoughts together. Mamie, standing, still watching Cherish make her way down, felt something move past her; it caused a shiver to go up her spine. Mamie looked quickly to the left, not seeing anything but sensing a presence, one that she had come to know very well, a slight smile crossed her lips. *I got this under control. I will win this battle.*

Cherish and Mamie talked well into the night; the stew that Mamie had prepared was the best Cherish had ever tasted. Before she knew it, Cherish had related her whole life's story to this wise old woman, only conveniently leaving out the details of her pregnancy, the identity of the father, and the circumstances of the conception. Mamie had kindly explained that those things were not important. It was the child that was important.

"The Good Book says all things works together for good." Mamie said.

That was different; the Bible was not a book that held any importance in the Rollins household. Cherish had not a clue what it said. Mamie, on the other hand, was always using words that came from the Bible. They all seemed to have a certain type of ring to them. They had a way of smoothing out any situation. Maybe Cherish would learn some of the sayings in it. Then she would feel better when things went wrong. The words probably wouldn't change things, but at least they would give her something to say instead of cussing.

Mamie had told Cherish that since she had nowhere to go; she was welcome to stay with her until after the baby was born. She could assist her a little around the house, and she would have a roof over her head and food to eat. Once the baby came and she was able, she could then go out to look for work and a place of her own.

During the two and a half years that Cherish stayed at Mamie's, she learned a lot, not only about Mamie, but life in general. Although Mamie was a little strange, Cherish quickly learned she was not a witch nor did she know any secret voodoo spells, but she did act very weird at times. There were times that Cherish would hear Mamie talking to herself; it had to be to herself because there would be no one else around. She would say things like, "Not this time you don't," or "Thought you could sneak in, didn't ya?" Other times she would find Mamie sitting up late at night with the Bible in her lap with tears streaming down her face. Cherish would just think she was feeling bad about her kids and husband. It was during these times that Mamie seemed to be totally oblivious to her surroundings; she would not even notice Cherish or anything else in the room.

There was also the strange way she would clean the house. She would take a bottle of olive oil and rub it over the doors and windowsills. She would rub the oil over the whole house—the bedposts, chairs, tables, everything. There was actually one time she even went on the outside the house and sprinkled it all around the outside of the house. She would say this was the way to keep all evils from entering the house. This must have worked, because Cherish had feared that as soon as her father learned that she was at Mamie's, he would get up enough drunken courage to come after her, but that had not yet happened.

Mamie was, to say the very least, somewhat different, but she was a very kind and loving person. She could always make you feel good about yourself. She had a way of making any bad situation look better. Cherish totally enjoyed being with Mamie; she could believe that her meeting Mamie that night on the bridge was the best thing that had ever happened to her in her entire life.

⚡

Getting ready for the holiday season was a different adventure for Cherish. Mamie was pulling down jars of fruits and vegetables, which she painstakingly processed during the summer months. She had gotten a wild turkey from Isaiah Brown about three weeks ago; she had to pay him $3.50 for the ten-pound tom. It would have cost her $7.00, but she dressed it out herself. The dressing out of the tom turkey was not an activity that Cherish could participate; just the smell caused her to become extremely nauseous. There was a kind of gaiety that Cherish had never experienced in the preparation for the holiday.

It was Wednesday, the day before Thanksgiving. They were preparing the cornbread for the dressing, Mamie was rolling out dough for her famous sweet potato pies and peach cobbler, and the jars of vegetables were standing ready to be added to the simmering pots of ham hocks, crushed red pepper, and salt. It seemed that there was going to be enough food to feed half of Evansville on this Thanksgiving Day. Mamie said, "You always cook a lot of food on Thanksgiving; that shows the Lord that you are truly thankful, and besides, somebody just might need a plate of food." Cherish later found out that Mamie would take food around to other people who didn't have anything to cook for Thanksgiving.

The Tuesday before Thanksgiving, Mamie and Cherish had gone into town to get some staples that were needed for the meal. Cherish had heard that Jack Sims had returned to town to take over the store and that he was married and expecting a child. Going into the One Stop was not something she wanted to do at this time, so Cherish decided to go over to the post office to see if there was any mail. This trip into town was a test of courage for Cherish. Her baby was due at anytime, and she didn't want to be the object of conversation around the Thanksgiving tables of the people of Evansville. It seemed that she had not been in public for years, of course, by now; she knew everyone knew she was pregnant and possibly knew that she was staying with Mamie. In her mind, she could hear the thoughts of the people, the nasty assumptions, and accusations. However, Cherish would never as long as she lived allow anyone to have an opportunity to criticize and ridicule her child; her child would not grow up in the hatred and misery that she had.

The Thanksgiving dinner was the best Cherish could ever remember in her life. Thanksgiving at home usually consisted of a two-day drinking binge and the Rollins Clan getting together, the men out in the barn, drinking, cussing, and target shooting, a sport that always sent fear through the women. They knew all the men were drunk and were afraid that someone would be shot. Of course, there was always more than one fight when the whole clan got together.

They may have a meal of rabbit and dumplings and a pound cake that Grandma Rollins would have whipped up, and sometimes they would have a special treat from Uncle Earl, Grandpa's brother. He would bring in a bag of candy for all the kids. There was never a solemn moment of prayer or thanksgiving to God; it was just a time to be them selves, and this was not what anyone with any sense would really want to be.

Cherish could remember her brothers, Sam and Brent, trying to fit in with the men, getting their first shot of corn, and learning the language of the Rollinses. The girls all stayed in the house and listened to the women talk about their men and how to make them happy.

Cherish always dreaded the holiday season because before the night was over, there was sure to be some hard feelings caused by a big argument that would last for days, weeks, and sometimes months. Nevertheless, this Thanksgiving she felt extremely happy, or as Mamie would say, "blessed" to be there with Mamie.

After they had eaten supper, Mamie started gathering up food in tins, preparing to deliver her wares to those she knew would like a good Thanksgiving meal. Cherish was to stay at home and clean up the kitchen.

Mamie had been gone about twenty minutes, and Cherish was clearing the table and taking the dishes to the sink, when suddenly she experienced a crippling pain that shot across her back into the pit of her stomach, a pain she had never before experienced. Mamie had told her that when her time came, she would know it instantly. The pain was so intense she fell to the floor, holding onto the chair; she could feel a wetness flowing from her body. The pain was like someone cutting her in half with a dull knife. It racked through her whole body. There was nothing she could do. She couldn't stand. She couldn't crawl; she literally could not move.

After what seemed hours, the pain began to subside, and she gradually pulled herself up. If she could just make it to the bathroom, she could get a towel to use as a compress to stop the water and blood that was flowing from her innermost body. What was she going to do? She was all alone. She had no idea what she was supposed to do, how she was supposed to lay, or if even she *could* lie down. The closest she had ever come to childbirth was watching cats have kittens and dogs have puppies. But they never seemed to have this much pain. There must be something terribly wrong. Another pain hit her, this one more intense than the first. She had to get to the bed; she had to make it. Crawling to the bed was an intense effort. She felt that for every inch she went forward, her whole insides were going to fall out. Just as she got to the side of the bed and tried pulling herself up, the pain became more and more intense. Then everything went black.

V

Everything was going as planned; the Company workers were relentlessly going about their daily routines. Every operation was going according to the schedule. Of course there were still some areas that had to be addressed, some projects yet to be carried out, but all in all, things were going well and were coming along right on time. The stranger had not made any attempt to interfere with progress, and as far anyone knew he may have been gone altogether.

The Company security officers had been working extended shifts to make sure that he would not cause any problems. Security had been increased at every major operation point. The number of officers to patrol the area had been increased as well. The top executives each had a team of bodyguards, and the most valuable members of the operation were under heavy guard. There was no way that a foreign company or operative was going to come in and stop the progress of this operation. The local management team had their instructions from headquarters. At all cost, this project would be completed. This was the first of a large-scale enterprise; it was the blueprint for many more to come around the world.

In making a choice for the first location, headquarters decided on Evansville because of its locality, size, and population. It was centrally located in the country, much like the heart is located in the center of the body. By actually looking at the map of the United States, Oklahoma would be centered on the map where the heart is in the body, and Evansville would be centered in Oklahoma as the SA node or pacemaker is in the heart. Once Evansville received the right stimuli, then that stimulus, like the body's blood, would spread across the nation and then from this nation to every other nation around the world. Evansville was the perfect location; the people were willing subjects for the operation to be successful, so there was no doubt the Company's plan would be a major success with the ultimate goal achieved.

The morning briefing went as scheduled, the night shift worker reporting in on the work done overnight, the day shift workers finding out what they needed to do. This was a twenty-four hour a day, seven days a week job. This was necessary because of the nature and size of the job.

The local boss, Jesse, was going over the reports of the following day and preparing the assignments for this workday when he remembered something important. "What about the stranger you saw the other night?" he asked the little worker.

"I don't know, boss."

"What do you mean, you don't know? Have you seen him or not?"

"Well," the little guy stuttered.

"Well, what?"

"I believed I saw him the other night over by the West River Bridge, but when I got to the bridge, there was nothing there."

"Has anyone else seen him or any other strangers?"

All the workers shook their heads no.

"Well, let's don't get too comfortable," he continued. "I believe I know who this stranger is, and I know the company that he works for. They don't give up easy. He has probably been lurking around, getting our company secrets, and then reporting them back to his headquarters. Once they have all our strategies and plans, they will bulldoze their way in and try to take over."

All the workers stared at Jesse with a look of terror, "Now," he continued, "is that what we want?"

"No!" the workers voiced in unison.

"Of course not. We have worked too hard and too long to let someone or something else come in and destroy what we have achieved. Therefore, let's get our assignments and get busy. Time is of the essence; we have got to get things moving at a record pace, or we can lose seven times what we have gained."

The workers all hurriedly scattered with their shift assignments in hand. Jesse sat behind the wooden desk while his chief security guard was sitting in the corner nodding off. As he sat there, idly thinking about the stranger, it seemed very odd that he had only been seen one time; that made Jesse wonder, *how long had he actually been in town? Could he have been there for a long time, just hiding and watching, or did he just get there?* Jesse knew who he was up against, and it never ceased to amaze him how they could change their way of operation from assignment to assignment.

Jesse had decided not to contact corporate headquarters about this presence. He was sure that he could handle this one alone. There was no need in getting the higher ups all in an uproar. This stranger had to be Michael. From the description the little worker had given, it fit him to a tea. He and Michael had crossed paths before, and like in any good lesson, he learned something. Jesse felt he had learned plenty from his and Michael's last encounter; he knew the one most important thing about Michael. That was his weakness. If that weakness could be capitalized on, Jesse's job would be very easy. Michael would have to face defeat and be forced to leave this town and this project alone, allowing Jesse's company to have a monopoly. Even knowing this, Jesse still had a sick feeling in the pit of his stomach.

⚡

Michael silently stood, listening. From a distance, he suddenly heard the sound of the secret messaging code, a summons, and although he was alone, he had to answer. It was coming from the east end of the city. This was not an area that Michael had been to before. He never realized that there was anyone on that side of town that would require his attention or that really wanted his help. He wasn't aware that anyone in that part of town even knew the code. Nevertheless, no matter how faint the coded summons was, it was his job to go.

This truly was a desperate plea for help from a voice that he did not recognize. Michael had been in and around the town long enough by this time to recognize all the voices of the people that were on his and his company's side. He pretty much knew the people to watch from a distance and gather information and the ones that he could count on when the big takeover would come. But this voice was a different one he had never heard. From the tone he was pretty sure that it was one that he could trust, a volunteer that could be counted on to be strong in the challenging campaign ahead. Someone that would recognize that there must be a change, that the rival company was not what it was cranked up to be. Things were not going to get better, only worse, under their leadership. They would be able to recognize that this town would be the catalyst for the future destruction of not only this state and nation but possibly the world as a whole. Making a quick call to headquarters, Michael went in search of the caller.

"This could possibly be the beginning of the battle," Michael notified headquarters. "I have just received a new summons from a different part of town."

"Where exactly in town did it come from?" The headquarters sentry asked.

"The far east end, close to the river."

"Let's see," the sentry said, looking over an area map. "Oh yes, there is a place on the east end of town. There you will find a very dedicated volunteer, a strong leader of the movement that lives in a small white house. This is the person that wants to change the worst."

"Why wasn't I told about this person sooner?" Michael asked.

"Michael, you of all people know the rules. We don't go to them; they have to come and make themselves known to us."

"Right, is there anything that I need to do at this point?" Michael asked.

"It is not yet time to reveal your self totally. Our rival

already knows that you are there, but it is not yet time for a confrontation."

"So what do I do?"

"About three blocks west of the little white house, there is a lady taking food to a shut-in lady. You are to get her to go to her home. When she gets there, she will know what to do next."

"Okay."

"And Michael, be careful that the workers don't see you. We don't want them to know just yet that we are really on the case. We want to keep them guessing. Have you seen Jesse yet?"

"I saw him yesterday, but he didn't see me. He is definitely on his job and causing havoc in this place."

"Be careful. Our time is not yet."

"I will. I have to go now. Will check in later when I have more to report."

⚡

Mrs. Mildred Wilson was all alone in her house on this Thanksgiving Day. Since her last heart attack and the rheumatoid arthritis in her hands, it was almost impossible for her to cook a meal. She mainly depended on the meals on wheels she received from the community senior citizens center, but with today being Thanksgiving, the meals would not be coming. Mildred had a son, Hank, the local sheriff, but he never really seemed to have time for her. Actually, he had even told her that he would not be having Thanksgiving dinner. He had to work, so he probably would just grab some chips and soda out of the machine at the jail. Hank said that one never knew what would or could happen on Thanksgiving, and he didn't want to get to comfortable in case he was needed. Mildred knew this was just his way of not being asked to spend time with her. There really hadn't been anything major in this town since that hot night in 1989, and she truly hoped that it would never be anything like it again.

It truly was a blessing when Mamie had knocked on her door with the delicious meal. Mamie had taken a plate of food to several people that she knew would otherwise have no meal that day. As Mildred was extending her thanks, Mamie got a strange look on her face. It was almost as though she was listening to somebody and hurriedly said good-bye and left. Mildred didn't even have time to ask her about what to do with the dishes. *Oh well*. Mildred assumed Mamie truly was an odd person. *Maybe she was a little touched in the head, but at any rate, her food wasn't touched.* She laughed to herself.

Hank would just die if he knew she was eating food that Mamie cooked; he would swear that she had some kind of potion in it. Her cornbread dressing was the best this side of the red river, and Mildred was sincerely thankful for this meal. As she was eating, an odd feeling, a sudden chill, came over her, and suddenly her appetite had left. She had only taken a few bites. Now she was having a bout of nausea; she knew if she ate one more bite, she would vomit. She started to the kitchen to throw away the food. There, she was startled by her big yellow cat Sassy, who was standing with her back arched, hissing as if she was getting ready to pounce on something.

"What in the world is wrong with you, Sassy?" Sassy's eyes were following some unseen foe toward the door; then she bolted into the other room and sat under the table, continuing to watch the back door. "Hank is probably right.

Mamie probably was trying to kill me. She probably had that food laced with some voodoo poison. That would also explain why she left in such a hurry. I don't know what came over me, to accept that plate of food and actually attempt to eat it. It is a good thing my stomach recognized the danger and rejected it," Mildred said to herself as she returned to the bedroom, crawled up into the bed, and turned on the TV. She was going to watch the all-day marathons of *Matlock*, while promising herself not to let Hank know that she had taken food from the town witch.

Hank had told her countless times to stay away from Mamie; he had said she was a very dangerous woman, and he didn't want his mother to get hurt by her. "After all, people like Mamie being touched and all can't help what they do," he had warned her. Turning her attention to the television, Mildred watched as Ben Matlock gave Tyler Hudson an update on his present case.

Mamie knew that she had to get back home. There was that unmistakable feeling of danger; then there was that little voice that had prompted her to go home. "Lord," she prayed, "let everything be all right. Please keep your hand over the situation until I get there."

⚡

Cherish was lying on the floor by her bed. Mamie could see the red liquid on the floor beside her. "Oh, Lord, please help me," she said out loud. The chill that hit her as she entered the room was unmistakable; she knew that feeling instantly. Looking around at the apparently empty room, she stated in a strong voice of authority, "Oh no, you don't.

This is not your property, and you have got to leave immediately." Checking Cherish, Mamie could tell she had just fainted probably from the pain, but she could also tell there was something wrong; there was too much blood, and the baby hadn't been born yet.

Getting Cherish's limp body up on the bed, Mamie began to do a pelvic and visual examination on Cherish. It appeared that the placenta was attempting to be born first. This could have serious implications. She had to work fast. Mamie had been delivering babies for the better part of fifty years. This was not her first time of seeing a situation like this. After moving the placenta out of the birth canal, Mamie gently cupped her hands on each side of the baby's head and with slight pressure began the ascent out of the birth canal. Cherish was beginning to arouse. She gave a muffled cry of pain.

"Push, chile," Mamie said. "Push as hard as you can. The baby is about here."

With a strong bearing down and a long push, the small, lifeless body was forced into Mamie's hands. This proved more than Cherish could handle; she once again collapsed into a deep sleep. Looking at the baby, Mamie knew that she had to work fast to get air to the lungs. She began to give the baby mouth-to-nose respiration. After what seemed an eternity but in actuality was only a few minutes, the baby began to cry and its color began to be pink up.

Mamie knew this baby girl was truly a miracle. If she had not heeded the voice that had told her to go home and if she had not of understood the message, this precious little girl and her mother would have died.

Wrapping the baby in a clean white blanket and laying

her in the makeshift crib that she had creatively made out of a laundry basket, Mamie turned her attention to Cherish. Her breathing was even and unlabored and her color was good, so Mamie knew she would be all right. She busied herself with cleaning Cherish up and making her comfortable. She probably would sleep for a while; she would sleep until time to feed the baby anyway. It was truly amazing how no matter how sound asleep the new mother was when feeding time came she would wake up.

Quietly, Mamie went into the living room, sat in her favorite rocker, and began to read Psalm 91:10 from her worn Bible, "There shall no evil befall thee, neither shall any plague come nigh thy dwelling, for he shall give his angels charge over thee to keep thee in all thy ways." Mamie was truly grateful to the Lord that all things had worked out the way He had planned. This truly was a day of Thanksgiving. She sat and prayed a heartfelt prayer that the Lord would begin to strengthen Cherish and her new baby so that they would fulfill whatever purpose He had in store for them.

Cherish and the baby slept comfortably through the night, only being awake twice for a quick feeding.

The next morning Cherish was beaming with pride. Her new little daughter was the most beautiful thing she had ever seen. Just to think that she had brought this precious life into the world. She could remember how the night before she had believed that the baby wouldn't make it, how the pain was so bad that she had totally blacked out. She could remember trying to stop the bleeding; she had just known that she and the baby were going to die. She could also remember how right before she had lost conscientiousness, she had actually asked God to help her. She remembered praying only one time before, but last night, she prayed, and he did help her.

Trying to decide what she would name her new daughter was a hard decision for Cherish. Mamie said to always remember that a person's name is the most important thing they possess; it cannot only identify who they are but can also determine their future. So Cherish named her new baby Hope. If a name could determine one's future, she never wanted her child to be without hope.

⚡

Michael stood at the edge of the house, watching the events inside, a smile slowly coming across his face. He was more energized this morning than he had been in weeks. With his energy level increased, he knew it was about time that he began his in-depth survey and start drawing up the blueprints for the operation. This had to be done before his energy began to dwindle. He had found that his energy was quickly depleted in this town, so while he had the energy, he had to get to work.

It was while he was preparing to leave that he got a message from headquarters that he needed to be at the city hall immediately. Not sure what was happening, Michael knew that things were heating up and it would not be long before the project would be in full operation. As Michael was leaving Mamie's house, a company worker quietly watched from the brush at the edge of the backyard.

So, the worker thought, *He is still here.* Wondering what he had been watching, the worker crept up to the window on the west side of the house to take a look for himself. What he watched sent a pang of anger as well as fear through his being. Scrabbling away from the window, he had to get back to the office and report what he had discovered; this was of grave importance. He knew there had to be something done about this and fast. He had to go and find out just how the management wanted to handle this situation. The worker was in a state of shock over what he had discovered. *How could this be?* He had been in control of this area, and he could not imagine how something like this could happen. This was the most secure area of town. Oh, this was not good, not good at all, and if it has happened here, how many other places has it happened in? How many people has it happened to?

VI

Breakfast was almost ready. Sherri had gotten Phil and Naomi dressed, and they were sitting at the table, waiting for Phillip to come in so they could eat. He had seemed preoccupied the last few weeks. When Sherri had tried to talk to him to find out what was bothering him, he would just say, "I'm not sure exactly. I have been trying to find out some things."

Sherri and Phillip had been married now for ten years; they had gotten married in their second year of college while Phillip had been studying theology, and she had majored in social work with an emphasis on counseling. After being married for six years, their first child, Phillip Jr., was born, who they called Phil. Two years later, they had their second child, Naomi. When they had gotten the call to come to Evansville, Sherri had made up her mind to work side by side with her husband in the ministry.

Sherri always knew that being in one's own ministry was not easy. Her father was a minister, so she understood the sleepless nights, the rough times, and the lean years. But this assignment was proving something more intense than she could have ever imagined. They had moved to Evansville a year ago when Naomi was only six months old. They had come with strong faith that this was where the Lord had sent them. They believed they were truly going to make a difference in this town, but it seemed that they had met with an unending resistance every since they had arrived. She understood that God did not make mistakes; people do, so she was wondering to herself if maybe they had made a mistake and this was not really where God had sent them.

It had been through her that Phillip had first heard about Evansville. One night, while they were lying in bed, she was telling him the stories that her grandfather had told her about the town of Evansville. She didn't even know why it had come up, but she told Phillip how her grandfather had been an inspector for the mines. Her grandfather told stories about how rough and uncivilized the people in Evansville were. He had said that there were brothels on about every corner and how the women of the brothels would actually come out into the street, grab a man, and pull him into the house. He had said there was more drinking in Evansville than in all the hills of Kentucky. It was not unusual in Evansville to be one or more shootings on a Saturday night. There were also local legends of people just disappearing from Evansville never to be seen again, although he had just figured that they got tired of the ruthlessness and moved away. Of course, there were some decent folks that lived there too. He had said that there was really some good churchgoing folk with kind hearts in Evansville, but for the life of him, he could not understand how they could just let the things go on in their town that were going on.

Grandpa Johnson had said that it seemed that every time he had to go to Evansville, something would happen. One time his gold watch that had belonged to his father had just disappeared from his room at Mrs. Wilson's boarding house. Then once while he was there, he was getting ready to enter one of the mineshafts and a coal car jumped the track, knocked him down, and he ended up with a broken arm and bruised ribs. Yes, he hated it when the time came for him to go to Evansville. He had said that Evansville truly was a dark place, somewhat sinister, hiding decades-old secrets that kept the town in a state of bondage.

After that conversation, Phillip started to inquire more and more about Evansville. He even began to have dreams about the town. He had actually had a dream in which he was preaching, and people were coming in droves, repenting for their sinful lives and getting saved. After this dream, Phillip talked with his father-in-law about the town of Evansville. Rev. Johnson had told him that while he was living in Hugo, he too had considered going to Evansville starting a ministry, but the Lord had another plan for him. Instead, he ended up in Longview at the True Light Christian Center.

Not sure that he could handle a full-time ministry, Phillip pondered what his calling to Evansville meant. His experience in ministry was limited. He had served as the associate pastor of True Light Christian Center under his father-in-law for three years. The first two years out of seminary, he served in the position as youth pastor. Nevertheless, the call that he felt he had from the Lord was for Evansville, Oklahoma. Why

Evansville, Phillip could not say, but he knew in his heart that was where he was supposed to be. There was a tug on his heart for Evansville, a tug he could not ignore.

⚡

The night before had been a long one for Phillip, looking in the mirror, he could see the signs of age creeping up. He had not come to bed until around three in the morning. Not wanting to disturb Sherri, he laid silently for about another hour, not being able to shut off his mind. He had been going through old newspaper articles trying to find a clue as to what it was that the citizens of Evansville were so diligently trying to hide. He had come across an article from the summer of 1989 that caught and held his attention; this, he was sure, was something that could possibly start to explain some things. He now had a determination to attempt to find out about the night of July 22, 1989.

"Phillip, breakfast is ready." Sherri called out, jarring Phillip out of his thoughtful daze.

"I'm coming," he answered her as he wiped his face with the washcloth.

One year ago, Phillip had been full of faith, hope, and determination, but now he was full of doubt, fear, and discouragement. This was not how Phillip had envisioned it to be. While attending seminary, he had watched the innumerable preachers that were well known across the world. They had built mega-churches, mega-homes, and drove large expensive automobiles. He had studied hard and read every book published by these superstars of Christendom and followed their entire well-laid-out instructions on how to figure out his purpose, how to reach his destiny, and how to follow the voice of God. He truly believed that God was not a respecter of persons, that he too would be able to achieve similar success in his ministry. He had truly believed that he would be able to reach a multitude of people and give them the light of God's Word. He was assured in his own mind that after all was said and done that he would be right up there with Moses, Abraham, and other great warriors of the faith.

In the beginning, Phillip had no doubt that God had spoken to him mainly in dreams that he was to come to Evansville. From the information he had gained from Sherri, relating the stories of the rough and ready town of Evansville from her grandfather, Phillip had been gung ho in going in and taming this wild uncivilized town. He wanted them to know there was a new sheriff in town. Evansville's colorful history of the houses of ill repute, the juke joints, and tales of mysterious disappearances only added intrigue to the mission. However, of course, that had been over fifty years ago; he was sure that it was a different place than Grandpa Johnson had remembered.

Now that the Lord had directed Phillip to this forgotten town, he could only believe that he was to do a great work here. He believed that there would be a great Holy Ghost revival that would far surpass the Azusa Street Revival of 1906 that had spread across the United States and Europe. He had been excited and ready to set the world on fire, a fire that would be ignited in little old Evansville, Oklahoma, and spread across the entire globe.

Phillip could remember his first time of arriving in Evansville. Driving into the town, he could feel the beginning of a kind of doubt and discouragement coming over him. His first trip here was to find suitable housing for him and his family to live. A piece of property that was adequate for a home and a church. He had planned to build a church within a year of moving here. Of course, he would need the help of his father-in-law and the Evangelical Association for the matching funds to achieve that project, but that was a task that could very easily be done. What Phillip found when he got to Evansville was a town that was slowly dying, as if a cancer was eating at its very core.

⚡

From the time Phillip entered the city limits of Evansville, uneasiness had swept over him, a feeling of dread and despair. Instinctively he had turned up the CD player in his car to allow the *WOW* gospel music to engulf the car. As he drove through the town, he could not help but notice the dilapidated condition of the town. In the center of the Main Street or downtown section was a two-story red brick building that proudly displayed the year 1922 engraved in the front. This building served as the city hall and jail. Outside were parked the four patrol cars that served the town; one was reserved for the sheriff and three for the patrol officers or deputies. The jail itself, Phillip would later find out, consisted of three cells, one cell for drunks that could hold three prisoners and the other two were six-man cells. It was a potential that Evansville's jail hold up to fifteen inmates at a time. From what he had initially observed, Phillip doubted that there were even that many people in town, let alone that many criminals.

It was in the city hall that the part-time mayor and the

city utility office were located. Across the street, three storefront buildings adjoined to each other took up the block. They housed a Laundromat in one building, the pool hall in another, and, in the last, an arcade for the youth. Across the alley from these establishments was the United States post office, a small metal building, approximately fourteen by twenty-four. A little further down, on the opposite side of the street, was a bar, Lenny's Alibi.

Continuing through the town and turning right at the corner past the post office, Phillip noticed a Victorian house with a faded out sign that read, "Memory Oaks Funeral Parlor, prop: Fred Kelley, est. 1949." This building served as both a dwelling and place of business. At the west end of this block stood the One Stop grocery store and gas station, proudly displaying two gas pumps for cars and one pump for diesel engines.

At the next corner, Phillip finally saw the place he was originally looking for, a small house converted for commercial use that displayed the sign Hometown Reality. By this time, Phillip was beginning to doubt that God had truly called him to this place. Maybe he had misunderstood; maybe God had really said Evanston, a small suburb of Chicago. Pulling in front of Hometown Reality, Phillip silently put up a fleece before God. *Lord, if this is not where I'm supposed to be, give me a sign. Let the office be closed and let me not know where else to go.* Stepping out of the car, Phillip saw a lady in her late fifties or early sixties working in her flower garden next door. Phillip nodded his head in her direction as he continued on toward the front door.

"If you're looking for Mabel, she ain't there," the woman stated.

"Mabel?"

"Yeah, Mabel, the real estate person."

A feeling of relief came over Phillip; the office was closed.

"But," the woman continued, "you can find her over at the city hall."

"Over at the city hall?" Phillip, a little confused, questioned.

"Yeah, city hall; that's where she works during the week." Sizing Phillip up, she continued, "You some kind of inspector?"

"No, ma'am."

Being very interested in whom this strange young man might be and waiting for Phillip to reveal more of his identity, the woman leaned forward on her rake.

"Thank you, ma'am. I'll try the city hall."

The feeling of relief was short-lived. Phillip wasn't quite sure what to think; at this point, the office was closed, but he did have an idea where to go. Maybe he should have just said *Let the office be closed* and not added another clause.

Phillip had remembered seeing the city hall on his way through the main street of town. It wouldn't take much to get back there; the whole business district wasn't four blocks long and two blocks wide. He was sure he could make a right turn at the next corner and be within a block of the city hall.

Pulling up to the curb in front of city hall, Phillip whipped into one of the three reserved visitor parking spaces. The building reminded him of one of the old buildings one would see in a 1940s movie; the railing on each side of the steps were made of the same brick as the building and blended in with the architecture. The front door was wooden at the bottom with a multileveled window at the top half, with the words "City Hall" painted in gold lettering. Entering the front door of the building, the floors were old faded hardwood that had not seen a shine in many a year, the kind that creaked with each step you took.

It was truly like taking a trip back into the past as you walked into the Evansville city hall; all the furniture was dated in the forties, maybe some pieces from the fifties. The receptionist's Formica-topped counter separated the room into a guest area and office. Sitting behind an old oak desk covered with a large Boston fern that was in dire need of water was a heavyset woman whose age was hard to determine—but if he had to guess, Phillip would say maybe fifty-five or fifty-six—talking on the phone, a conversation that was cut abruptly short as Phillip walked up to the counter.

"All right then, I'll talk to you later, Helen," the woman looked straight at Phillip as she hung up the receiver. "Can I help you?"

"Yes, ma'am, I'm looking for Mabel, the realtor."

"Well, you found her. What can I do for you?" Not really looking at Phillip but surveying his sky blue Buick outside. From past experience with state inspectors, Mabel had learned to look at the side of a vehicle to see if there were any state government insignias on the side. Following Mabel's gaze, Phillip looked back at his vehicle; maybe there was something wrong with it. Living in the city, he had learned that in a moment's notice someone could remove tires, mirrors, or other elements from a vehicle.

"My name is Phillip Fields and I am thinking of relocating to Evansville, and I was looking for some property."

"Oh, I see. You looking to rent or to buy?"

"I was hoping to purchase some property if I could find the right place."

Harvey Hanes, part-time mayor and city judge, exited his office to see who this newcomer might be. "Oh, Harve," Mabel nervously stated. "This here is Mr. Phillip Fields; he says he is thinking about moving to Evansville and wants to find some property."

"Is that so?" extending his hand to Phillip. "Well, hello there, young man. My name is Harvey Hanes, and I am the mayor and judge of this fine town."

"Glad to meet you." Phillip replied. There was something about this man that Phillip had some misgivings about; his hand shake was much too firm, almost a crushing squeeze.

"If you're looking for property, you came to the right person; Mabel here is the town's best real estate agent." With a sly smile and a quick glance at Mabel, he added, "Actually she is the town's only real estate agent."

Getting back to his original purpose for his visit to the Evansville city hall, Phillip directed his conversation to Mabel.

"I went to your office Mrs.... ?"

"Miss not Mrs. It's Miss Williams, Mabel Williams."

"Miss Williams," Phillip corrected himself, "the lady next door sent me here."

"Oh yeah, that was Helen. She keeps an eye on the office for me."

"Well, now, Mr. Fields, being the mayor and chief justice of Evansville and all, I kind of like knowing a little bit about the residents and prospective residents of this fine city if you will."

Phillip was beginning to feel as though he was in an

interrogation room; there had been something different about this man, the mayor/chief justice, as he had so proudly related, something he couldn't quite explain. Mabel Williams was surveying Phillip, as though she was sizing him up for a suit of clothes or maybe even a shroud.

"So, where ya from, Mr. Fields?" the mayor was continuing with his interrogation.

"Longview."

"You a family man, are you?"

"Yes, I'm married with two children"

"Oh good, we have a wonderful school here," Mabel interjected.

"That is very good, Miss Williams, but they are not old enough for school just yet. The oldest is three and the youngest is six months."

"Oh, I see."

"What kind of business are you in?" Harvey inquired.

"I'm a minister."

Mabel and Harvey looked at each other. Phillip couldn't read their expressions, whether they were of shock or if they were of disgust.

"Is something wrong?" Phillip asked the two city officials.

"Oh no," replied Harvey.

"No," agreed Mabel.

"It's just that you—" Harvey began.

"I'm what?" Phillip wanted to know.

"You look too young to be a preacher." Mayor Hanes volunteered.

"Really? I didn't realize there was an age requirement. I guess they forgot to tell me that in seminary."

"No, what we were saying is…" Mabel attempted to explain, "It's just that we a have a preacher here, Rev. Potter over at Wesley United Methodist Church, and he is getting along in years."

"I guess I always thought that the good Lord didn't call a man until he had some worldly experience behind him," was Harvey's lame attempt for an explanation.

"I see. I guess God being who He is and all can call whomever He wants whenever He wants. If He can make a donkey speak, I guess he can speak through the young as well as the old." Phillip, with an attempt at humor, replied to the mayor. "Now, Miss Williams, the reason why I'm here—about some property."

"But of course, what exactly are you looking for?"

"Well, I need a house with at least three, preferably four bedrooms, sitting on at least three acres of land."

A look of bewilderment came across Mabel's face. "Wow, that's a big bill. May I ask why so much land?"

"I intend in the future to build a church."

"Well," Mabel slightly hesitated, "I would have to go to the office and see what I have available. Let's see, today is Thursday. I have a city council meeting tomorrow. Why don't you just give me your phone number, and I will call you when I think I have found what you are looking for."

"About how long do you think that will be?" Phillip wanted to know.

"I would say, possibly by the middle of next week but no later than the beginning of the next."

"All right, sounds good." Phillip handed Miss Williams

one of his business cards. "I will be expecting your call, until then, good-bye, Miss Williams, mayor Hanes."

"Look forward to seeing you again," mayor Hanes replied.

Waiting until the door closed behind him, Harvey Hanes, with a look of dread, remarked to Mabel, "Just what we need—a young holy roller preacher coming in here to save the souls of Evansville."

"That won't be as easy as he may think." Mabel laughed. "Rev. Potter has been trying for forty years without success."

Staring out the window, watching Phillip's car pull away from the curb and fade down the street, Harvey remarked, "And he won't either, I am afraid. Don't you agree, Mabel?"

"I believe you are right, Harve. This place is beyond hope."

⚡

It would take almost two weeks before Phillip would receive a call from Mabel Williams. Ms. Williams told him that it had taken a lot of searching, but she believed she may have had found something that he may be interested in. Phillip and Sherri made another trip to Evansville to see the property. It wasn't at all what they had really wanted; it was on the west end of town. At one time, it had served as a small farm of some sort. It had approximately five acres and a one-story house with three bedrooms and one bath. The house was in need of a lot of repairs. Phillip had figured that out when Mabel had said it was a 'fixer-upper.' In reality it was more like a 'builder-over,' but the price was reasonable; the asking price was only $45,000 for the house and the land.

Sherri and Phillip discussed the options and decided that they could buy a doublewide mobile home and put it on the lot. Then they could do some work on the little house, converting it into a small church. This would give them time to save some money to build a church. After thirty days they closed on the property, and within three weeks, they had their new doublewide mobile home moved onto the property and so had begun their new life in Evansville.

VII

The worker made his way breathlessly into headquarters. Without waiting to be acknowledged, he burst into the main office.

"Boss, that stranger is still in town. I saw him this morning; he was out on the east end of town at that Mamie Webb's house."

"Mamie Webb's," the boss growled. "Where is Orthan?"

A small, frail little worker came into the office after being summoned by Mastema with a sheer look of fright on his face.

"Yes, boss," he mumbled.

Jesse, with glaring red eyes, looked at the little worker with pure disgust. "What is the meaning of this? I assumed I sent you over to Mamie Webb's house to do a job."

"I did, sir; I did exactly as I was instructed. Everything was going fine when I left."

"When you left? Did anyone tell you to leave?"

"No, sir, but I thought..."

"You don't nor can you think. That is *not* your job. I am the *only* one allowed to think! It is your job to follow orders. And because of your incompetence, we now have a *big* problem."

The little worker knew that he was in trouble—big trouble. He would more than likely be sent off to the utter ends of the world to be a resident force in some old empty building or dwelling. This was the worst thing that could happen; only the workers that had proven to be nonproductive were banished to such positions.

"The simple little job that you were assigned to do has failed. The Rollins girl and her kid are fine and well."

Total shock came over the nervous little worker. "That's impossible! With all due respect, sir, she was unconscious on the floor, bleeding profusely, and there was no one there to assist her. She had been in that position well over twenty minutes before I left."

"Twenty minutes?" Jesse asked with a little concern in his voice. Then anger began to rise up in him until the workers standing in the room believed he would literally explode.

"There is only one explanation to this. She had to call out for help before she passed out. This is more serious than I had imagined."

Turning to the worker/sentry that had originally brought him the news, Jesse drilled him for further information.

"What else did you see and hear at Mamie's house?"

"Cherish was holding the baby and rocking her to sleep, and Mamie was reading in *that* book."

Turning back to the little worker that was in charge of watching the activities of Mamie Webb, he asked, "Have you ever noticed her reading from the *Bible*?"

"On occasion, sir, and then she will stop reading and start talking to herself."

"You fool! She is not talking to herself; she is *praying*." All the workers gasped at the word "praying." They all knew what that meant—it would be the cause of their demise.

"Oh, this truly is a terrible thing. How many others in this town are praying? Summon all the crew together. We have an extreme emergency situation," Jesse shouted.

⚡

Michael, in an instant, arrived at the city hall, going unnoticed by anyone except the calico cat lying under the sheriff's desk. He positioned himself to be able to hear and see all activities without being discovered. One of Jesse's strongest bodyguards was standing behind Sheriff Wilson; another strong bodyguard was stationed to the left of Jack Sims, and a little feisty imp was stationed on the desk between the two as they discussed a matter of uttermost secrecy. Michael quietly prayed that the cat would not arouse the imp's attention to his presence in the room.

"Now, Jack," Sheriff Wilson was saying, "I know that things have not been good for you since you got back here, with business down and you expecting a new baby at anytime now, which is why I wanted to talk to you. I have a business proposal that I feel will be of great benefit to both of us. Something that will be a win-win situation for all parties involved. I have heard that you were going to start demanding payment from the people who your father had extended credit and had not paid. However, what if I told you I have a way of making you a substantial amount of money and the people in town would not have to worry about paying up their accounts? Actually, they could still come in and get credit, and it wouldn't hurt your business at all."

Jack had a slight feeling of apprehension, but in his present condition, he was willing to do almost anything to pull himself out of this lake of quicksand he had found himself in.

"What kind of proposal?"

"It is something that could make you and me more money than we could ever imagine, Jack. I didn't attend any big university to learn how to run a business, but I do know that if you give a person what they need, they will buy it. They may not necessarily buy the things they want, but they will buy the things they need. For example, nobody just wants toilet tissue, but they have to have it, so they buy it. You get my drift?"

"Yes, true. However, what is it that the people of Evansville need that I do not already have in my store but they can't seem to buy or at least pay for now?"

"Well, Jack my boy, I wasn't just thinking about the people here in Evansville. I was considering people coming from all over the southeast part of the state, Arkansas and Texas."

Jack's curiosity was beginning to peak. The little imp on the desk was feeling very proud as he ran his finger over the pencil holder on the sheriff's desk with a mocking smirk on his face.

"What is it Hank, that you believe I could stock on my shelves that would create that type of demand?"

"Hold on, I never said it was something that you would stock on the shelves. I said it was something that people need, and they would come from all over to get once they knew it was available to them."

"You're being a little evasive, aren't you, Hank?"

"It's not until I know that I can completely trust you that I want to go into all the details. Besides, it is not a good idea to give out too much information before it is an official deal, you know, in case someone would want to steal the idea."

"I really don't know about this, Hank. Until I know exactly what your idea and product are, I can't say either way." Jack had a strong feeling that this was another of Hank's ideas that would end up getting them both in serious trouble.

"Just think about what I said, Jack; think about being able to care for your family in a way that you really want to and becoming one of the most influential men, both financially and politically, in this area. Jack, also remember one hand scratches the other, if you know what I mean."

"Yeah, Hank, I know."

"Then just give it some thought. Then let me know if you really want to be healthy, wealthy, and wise. Then I will let you in on all the details."

"All right, I will."

"But, Jack, don't wait too long. This is a big project, and I need to know something no later than Monday morning. That gives you, let's say, three days to think it over."

Both men got up to leave the office, bodyguards and imp closely behind. After Jack had left the building, Hank Wilson turned to Mabel and said, "Mabel, I will be out of the office for a while. I need to go check on some things out on Lone Oak Road."

"All right, and by the way, Hank, your mother called while you were in with Jack."

"Okay, I'll stop by there while I'm out. She probably wants to tell me about her latest bout of arthritis."

The previous conversation deeply concerned Michael; he knew that Hank Wilson was being influenced by some evil motives and intentions. This was evident by the number of workers needed to be around him. Michael knew he had to keep a close watch on Hank and his activities. Michael had to get out to Lone Oak Road.

⚡

Crossing over the West River Bridge, the enemy forces were in full attendance. They were stationed in every tree, bush and behind every rock and limb. To the human inhabitants, their presence would not be detected unless one had a strong sense of discernment, and even then, there were times that they could go undetected.

With the number he was up against, Michael knew that he was in no condition to be detected; his energy was way down. His energy level had been dwindling for several hours now, and before long, he would be almost to a point of helplessness. As much as he wanted to, he knew it still was not time to call in the reinforcements. He still didn't have all the needed information nor had he found all the volunteers that would be needed for this battle. All he could do at this point was to seek out cover and avoid being spotted by the company forces that were all over this small town. Michael had discovered that there were at least thirty company workers for every resident in this town, and for some, there were as many as fifty.

Altogether, there had to be close to twenty thousand in this small rural town. Michael knew how much chaos even five of these workers could cause, but twenty thousand could not only devastate this town but could easily destroy the whole state. The sad part was that the people were totally oblivious of their presence and had no idea why the things were happening that were or why some of the things that were occurring was causing so much misery.

⚡

Hank was less than thrilled about going out to the Rollins place. Hank had always considered Nolan Rollins as a lowlife individual that had no ambition or gumption. Nolan talked loud and bad, and he let it be known that he had no fear of anything or anyone. Hank was also aware that he had to be very careful in his dealings with Nolan and his two boys. What they lacked in brains they made up for in brawn. More than one person had been on the receiving end of the Rollins' wrath, and some never lived to tell the story—or at least that was the rumor. At any rate, Hank didn't want to have firsthand knowledge of this assumption. Sometimes one has to put aside personal feelings in order to get what they want and make happen what they need to happen. Nolan Rollins and his boys were the best people he knew that could bring this plan into a reality.

Hank had been working with the Rollinses on this project now for a little over three months and up to the present moment, it was going well. As long as things remained as they were, all would be great. For the Rollinses, it wasn't about becoming rich and influential but more about having enough money to buy a new pickup truck, a few new rifles, and go out to the surrounding towns and carouse in the local nightspots.

Driving up to the Rollins' place, the first thing that he

saw as he crossed over the beat-up old cattle guard onto the Rollins property was a sign hanging on a cross that read, "This property protected by Smith & Wesson." The house was well isolated in a dense area of the woods; there were no trespassing notices posted all round the property. It could easily be missed unless one knew exactly where he was going. This was a situation that fitted the Rollinses well, because they could pretty much do as they pleased without anyone interfering.

The house was a dingy little run-down place they liked to refer to as the farm but was far from resembling a farm. The only livestock they had consisted of three old mangy dogs, a couple of cats, and a handful of chickens. During the summer months, Mrs. Rollins had a small vegetable garden on the north side of the house. That was the extent of their farming. Nolan Rollins had never held a job in his life. His boys had tried to put up a front of employment, but neither one ever held a job over two weeks at a time. They had a real problem with anyone telling them what to do.

The family survived on the money they made from their corn whiskey and the wild game they obtained in the woods that surrounded their house.

Nolan Rollins was sitting on the front porch of his house, watching as the sheriff's car pulled up. He never gave a thought to it being the law. Although they were not what some would consider good law-abiding folks, the sight of a police car stirred no emotions in him. Besides, he was pretty sure of the business Sheriff Wilson would be coming out here to conduct with him.

"Afternoon, Nolan," Hank addressed the man as he stepped out of the car.

"Hank," Nolan Rollins never addressed Hank as sheriff. That would be giving him a position of authority, and Nolan never considered anyone in authority over him.

"Just thought I would drive out and check on things. Plus there are a couple of things I need to talk to you about."

"Then start talking," Nolan replied in his usual hateful tone of voice.

To the unseeing eye, the activity around the Rollins place was in full swing as unseen figures were busy going to and fro around the property. Several of the little workers were inspecting the sheriff's car, while others sat on the hood and the trunk. Busy little workers were chattering among themselves as they peeped and peered around the house, climbed in and out of windows, and some were perched on the roof as lookouts. Two large bodyguards were posted at the entrance to the old barn on the back of the property, and one stood attentively behind Nolan Rollins on the porch. One bodyguard sat in the sheriff's vehicle as if he was an honored passenger.

"Are your boys here?" Hank asked.

"They're out at the barn," Nolan motioned with his head. "Why ya askin'?"

"Well, the office got a call last night from old Mrs. Whitaker. She reported seeing a new red Silverado parked out by the schoolyard, and there were "about three suspicious characters," as she put it, standing around the truck. They looked like they were exchanging something. So I was just going to say to keep the boys out of town for a while until everything is sewed up."

"Runnin' the town and keepin' the mouths shut is your job, Hank. I'm not gonna tell my boys they can't come into town just 'cause folks might talk." Nolan said as he spat a mouthful of tobacco juice over the porch railing, landing only inches from Hank's highly shined boot. "What else ya want to talk about?"

"Well, the other thing is," Hank continued as he stepped over to the left to avoid the disgusting spit, "I think I may have a plan to increase our sales. Do you think you and the boys will be able to keep up the production, let's say, if we were to begin selling maybe three to four cases a day?"

"That's a lot now, ya know, with the cost of supplies going up and all. I don't know if we can keep working as hard as we do for what ya payin' us."

"If you can keep up the production, I will make sure that you have everything you need. As a matter of fact, I have some connections that are willing to come in and supply you with your own labels and bottles for your corn. Next thing you know, you'll be right up there with Jack Daniels and Hiram Walker. All you have to do is make it, and they will bottle it and market it."

"But that means they will get all the credit for our work and our recipe, and we will be nothin.'"

"No, Nolan, they will put your name on the bottles. It will be called 'Rollins Royale,' so you will get the credit, plus make a profit. Just think; after all these years, your corn will be in every liquor store in the state, maybe even the nation." Hank had to think fast to persuade Nolan that this was for his benefit, if he expected him to go along with the plan.

"Why ya so concerned about us getting so much credit? What's in it for you, Hank?"

"Well, Nolan, you know I'm not trying to get a lot. I just

need a little for hooking you up with the right people." Hank had to handle this situation very carefully; he never wanted Nolan to figure out it was more to this arrangement. Some things needed to remain a secret for now.

"I got to get back to town now, Nolan. I'll be back in a few days, and we can work out the details." This was just the first step. Before long, he would have the whole county under his control. There were still some more angles that he had to work out. Then it was easy street.

VIII

Where could he possibly be? Mildred wondered to herself. She had phoned the sheriff's office four times; first time he was in a meeting. Then he was out, but Mabel said he would be by her house. *That was over an hour ago; just where could he be?* Hank knew she couldn't drive, but now she needed to get some things from the store. He was her only way of getting there. Besides, she didn't have any money, so he was going to have to buy them for her. *Since Nathaniel's little punk of a son came in and took over the store, no one can get anything on credit.*

This was the gratitude she got for raising Hank all by herself. After her husband had died, she had tried to maintain the old run-down boarding house that had belonged to her mother-in-law. She had tried to give him the things he needed *and wanted*. She had to sacrifice and do whatever she had to do for them to survive. Now he practically ignored her.

Mildred knew there was a way to get even with him or at least give him a guilt complex. She would tell him about her getting the dinner from Mamie but after taking only one or two bites she had become deathly ill. It had only been because she was hungry and didn't have anything to eat that she even remotely considered eating it. This would cut him to the bone. Just the thought of Mamie Webb always managed to stir up a reaction in Hank. Mildred was well aware of how Hank felt about Mamie. She wasn't sure if he was afraid of her and what he thought she could do or because of what he knew she could do. She had felt for years that there was more to Hank's disdain for Mamie than the mere thought that she was a witch; there was something deeper and more serious than even she knew.

⚡

Jesse was in a terrible mood; he was snapping at everybody he came in contact with. The rumor was going around that headquarters had gotten wind of the lone crusader that had come into town. It was also feared that some of the big power sources would be coming into town to expel this problem. If things went too wrong, Jesse could be banished from this place to another place of lesser importance. He would be demoted, and someone else would be selected to take his place. All the workers were worried. They all knew that they would never be selected for Jesse's position. They were not in the right class; it would have to be a prince or principality to be selected to run a territory. Though they feared Jesse, they feared even more who might be chosen to replace him.

Jesse was very worried. *How did headquarters get wind of this problem?* Somebody else had to have tipped them off; he surely hadn't. He was also concerned about what to say when the strong powers came up to confront him. He would just let them know that this was not as big a concern as they were notified. This was not something that he could not handle. After all, didn't he handle the situation on September 11, 2001? Didn't the project go as planned? Then they had no reason to worry. If he could control a project of that caliber, this little dinky town was nothing. Nevertheless, even assuring himself of these facts, he still had a sinking feeling in his stomach. He glanced at the spiritual clock on the wall; it was now well into the fourteenth generation. There were approximately only thirty-three years remaining in this generation. No wonder headquarters was so worried; there wasn't much time left.

⚡

The idea that something was terribly wrong in this town continued to eat at Phillip. Ever since he had moved to this town, there were too many unexplained things happening. It was as if something or someone wanted him gone. Of course, he would not be the one to accuse anyone of anything unless he had proof, but it was as if someone was intentionally sabotaging his property and belongings. Phillip and Sherri had worked very hard to convert the house that was originally on the property into a small church. They removed walls, added new carpet, painted, and decorated. They purchased two hundred sanctuary seats and a pulpit for a very reasonable price from a church in Mount Pleasant. Phillip had rented a U-Haul, went down and picked the items up, and brought them to the newly remodeled church. The next morning he went over to arrange the seats to get things ready for the first service he hoped would take place the very next Sunday, but entering the building, what he found was devastating.

He found the floor was soaked, and many of the new chairs were wet. This was very puzzling; there were no apparent leaks anywhere. The city water department came out, checked all the pipes and connections, and found no leak. He and Sherri had to work all day, trying to get the water out of the carpet and chairs before they were mildewed. Using a Wet-Vac to get up as much water as they could, they then placed commercial fans in the building to dry out the rest. This caused a setback in the official opening of the church.

One week later the telephone lines came up mysteriously cut and not having an extended repair plan with the telephone company. It cost him three hundred and fifty dollars to get the house rewired for telephone service. Reporting the incident to the sheriff's office, it was dismissed as maybe an opossum or raccoons that had gnawed through the wires and nothing was ever done or investigated.

Then Naomi had suddenly come down with a high-grade temperature and became lethargic and lifeless. They rushed her to the emergency room at the Hugo Hospital. However, by the time they got there, she had no temperature and was wide awake and playing. The emergency room physician empathically stated that children sometimes run high fevers for no reason and soon recover, but if it happened again, they should bring her back. Phillip and Sherri both got the feeling that the E.R. staff believed they had been lying about her fever.

Once they had gotten moved in and settled, they received a letter from their homeowners insurance that they could not insure their house because it was, by all means and purpose, a mobile home, and that made it a high risk for that part of the country.

It had been one thing after another, since they moved here. What Phillip had dreamt would be a successful ministry in a small area was turning quickly into a nightmare.

The first time they met Rev. James Potter, pastor of the Wesley United Methodist Church, he had received Phillip very coldly. Deciding that he should meet and talk to Rev. Potter—after all, they were both in the same business and maybe they could work together to give the people of Evansville a life-changing experience that would carry on through the years—Phillip made a visit to the man's home one evening. Phillip soon learned that Rev. Potter did not share nor did he even care about bringing revival to the people of Evansville. Rev. Potter authoritatively informed Phillip that the people here were, for the most part, conservative; they didn't go in much for that new fangled religion of the big cities. They went to church on Sunday if they had a mind to. They listened to the message and then went home and lived life as it had been lived in Evansville for the past eight decades. He let it be known quite plainly that he had no intentions of troubling the water; he actually said, "Son, sometimes it is best to just let sleeping dogs lie, because if you don't, they have a tendency to bite you where you sit."

Rev. Potter's non-caring attitude is not going to deter my work here, Phillip had decided. He had Sherri make up some flyers on the desktop publisher, and he went about distributing them through town. Some people looked at them with a strained attempt to show care. Others simply tossed them away while mumbling, "We already have a church." When the time came that he could officially open the doors of his church, he was totally devastated. There had only been one old lady who showed up. Phillip got the impression that she was only there out of curiosity, because halfway through his sermon, he had noticed she was nodding off.

Going home that afternoon, he was in a state of utter despair. Where had he gone wrong? Maybe he wasn't supposed to come here after all. He would not be able to support Sherri and the kids like this. His personal savings were dwindling fast after buying the land, making a big down payment on the house, buying the materials to remodel the old house, and buying the furniture for the church, not to mention all the other unforeseen expenses. He probably had enough money left to last maybe three months, but then what? Sherri wasn't saying anything, but he knew she had to have some concerns. He was not the husband that he should be; he had failed miserably.

Thinking back to his father's words when he told his parents that he was going into the ministry, he couldn't help but to believe it was true when he had said, "Unless you have a lot of rich folks willing to pay you a lot of money to tell them what they want to hear, you are going to starve to death," now he had come to this godforsaken place, sunk all his money into trying to establish something that was never going to come to pass. Bitterness began to move in. Phillip was beginning to have serious doubts about him and the ministry. Why had God allowed this to happen? He had worked hard trying to do the will of God.

He had prayed, continually studied hard, and given

unselfishly of himself and his money; now it looked like it was all for naught. What else could go wrong?

⚡

Reports coming from the workers concerning Phillip Fields gave Jesse a ray of hope. They reported that he was getting tired and run-down. He was depressed and worried. They also reported that he was not praying as much or as often as before. Plus, he hardly ever opened his Bible these days. It was looking very promising for the Company.

The Company had never had to worry about ole Rev. Potter. He only went through the motions. He never got the people's curiosity up. No one took what he said seriously; that was due in part to the fact that he never really said anything.

He would read the stories of the Bible and go into some sort of explanation on the meaning. He never called attention to any promises to claim or instructions to follow. There were no revelations in his sermons. Jesse always made sure that there were at least two or three workers assigned to be in every Sunday morning service at Wesley United Methodist Church—just in case someone *felt* some form of revelation from the message. It was one of the worker's jobs to dissuade them and convince them that it only sounded good. The things they had heard only happened thousands of years ago; none of those things could or would happen in their time.

The Company had managed for years to maintain an atmosphere of doubt and unbelief in Evansville. Sure, people went to church. For some it was out of some type of responsibility; for others, it was the only place they held a position of importance. They could actually run all the decisions of the church. They could decide where and when the money was going to be spent. Those who had no importance in the town were important in the church. This status of self-importance would lead to many quarrels and arguments among the church leadership, creating situations that fit perfectly into the plan of the Company.

The more confusion orchestrated within the church, the better. Sunday morning service was not a time of worshipping God but rather a power struggle to see who the most important person in the church was. There were presidents and chairmen of every organization, and each organization tried to outdo the other to show who was the most powerful. It truly was a perfect place to keep the town divided.

After service was the best part of the day for the Company. It was then that the telephone conversations started, members calling each other to talk about what had happened that day. They would discuss who believed they were better than everybody else and to remind each other of a certain member's shortcoming and faults. Yes, Wesley United Methodist Church was one of the best weapons that the Company had.

Then out of nowhere, this new preacher shows up! Jesse knew how dangerous his kind could be, but in the same token, Jesse also knew how easy it was to break his kind. This new preacher, straight out of seminary studies, with high hopes, ambitions, and goals. They came out of seminary with the ideals of changing the world. They are all fired up with the idealistic teaching of seminary professors. It was the Company's job to show them that what they had learned was idealistic but not realistic. This was an area in which Jesse had a lot of experience.

He had seen more than a few new ministers fall after coming out into the world to fight a battle with his boys without the proper weapons. Of course, they had all been instructed on the use of the weapons and the types of weapons in their seminary training. However, when the battle heated up and they had attacks coming from every direction, it never failed. They would get nervous and forget which weapon to use or not have the correct ammunition.

It was quite comical to see how these mighty young men and women of God soon gave up the fight or would succumb to Jesse's warriors and become an asset for his cause.

Jesse had learned that there were only a few of his workers that were usually needed to achieve his goal in bringing down ministers. Whether they were new seminary graduates or more seasoned in the ministry, the best workers to use on ministers were doubt, fear, lust, and greed. With these members of the Company at work, it was easy to bring the minister right into a position of usefulness for Jesse and the Company.

Jesse and his crew had managed to turn hundreds if not thousands of ministers around from being threats to his company into allies. The best part was they didn't even know that they were working for him and not for God. As long as they were deceived to believe that they were doing God's will, they could do more for the Company than the Company by itself.

With the ministers working on their side, there was really no need to use a lot of workers. This was something that was fairly easy to do in the United States, but in the third world countries, it was harder to turn the ministers of God into allies. It had always required more manpower of workers in those countries than in America. That was why the Evansville operation was so important. When the operation was in full swing and the groundwork had been laid, nothing could come in or hamper progress. It was a project that would carry a global prospective.

With the super powers from corporate headquarters expected to be arriving any day, Jesse had to be able to assure them that everything was under total control. The report he had received concerning Phillip was the best thing he could have heard. With this new revelator being contained, there would be no reason for the higher-ups to worry. Things were still going to turn out the way they had planned. He would draw their attention away from this little nobody preacher and turn it to Hank Wilson, their strongest ally. He was diligently working hard at the plan that the Company had planted in his mind, trying to bring it into reality. The materialization of this plan was one that Jesse and his crew were working for day and night. Jesse had to admit to himself that it was one of the best plans since the one with the fruit. Once the plan was launched, there was nothing that would stop it, and the whole world would soon come under their total and complete control.

IX

Mamie had a strong sense that something was going terribly wrong. She wasn't sure exactly what it was, but she had that distinct feeling of impending danger. Mamie had heard that there was a new minister in town, but she had not met him. Although she had seen him a few times, she did not feel that it had been the right time to approach him. She wasn't sure what his beliefs were or how she would be accepted. Even so, now the time was quickly approaching that she was going to have to go and introduce herself to this young man. She had heard that his ministry was not going very well; no one in the town was supporting his endeavors, but that was not a surprise. Maybe once she had a chance to speak with him, all that would change. She could then talk to the others, and they could make a choice on what to do.

After Hope turned three years old, Cherish had begun looking for them somewhere to live. She had found a little house that Ms. Williams had for rent, the old Patterson place.

Ms. Williams had said that there were a few minor repairs that needed to be done and that she would see about getting them done if she could find Isaiah. Isaiah was the local odd jobber who made extra money to supplement his miner's pension by doing the things in town. He mowed lawns, did minor repairs, and such. The house was in dire need of repair, but Cherish guessed that it would have to do for some time anyway. The house being only three doors away from Mamie made it easy for her to baby-sit while she was at work. Cherish had gotten a job at the Hugo Hospital as a nursing assistant. She found it a truly rewarding job. It was now her goal to eventually go to nursing school and become a registered nurse. She knew it would be a permanent, well-paying job. She would never have to worry about making a living again.

She didn't have a car as yet, so she rode to work with Shelly Davenport. Shelly was one of only about a hundred more or less young women in Evansville. Shelly had a husband, Dan, and four children. It was an arrangement that was working out very well for Cherish, she had arranged it so that her schedule was the same as Shelly's. She paid Shelly twenty dollars a week for the ride. This still left her enough money to pay her four hundred dollars a month rent, keep up the utilities, and buy some of the requirements for the house. She was even putting back a little for the future. Things did appear to be looking up. Cherish could actually see a future down the road. She would be away from the stigma of being a Rollins, and who knew? Maybe she would find the perfect man, get married, and have a couple more children. If she would get married, she would no longer have the Rollins name, and all ties would be broken.

⚡

Hank Wilson was excited about his new business venture; the one thing that worried him about this was if the Rollinses were going to be capable of supplying the amount of moonshine that was going to be required for an operation of this size.

The boys in Dallas were prepared to bring over the ingredients for its production. It was then up to the Rollins to meet the demand with the supply. Hank knew that they were not the brightest light on the Christmas tree. Although they carried themselves to be Evansville's equivalents to the terminator, they didn't have the brains of a cockroach. It would be easy to get them to use the materials that he would supply; after all, they were lazy. Anything that would keep them from any form of true work would be right up their alley.

In order to make this project truly successful, he had to make sure that Jackson Sims would cooperate. With that in mind, he knew it was time to visit Jack and make sure that he was going to do what Hank needed him to do. If he showed any sign of hesitation, he would have to pull his trump card. Hank always knew that one day his information would pay off.

Jack was busy putting the shipment of cigarettes in the display case as Hank came strolling in. "Morning Jack," Hank said with a tone of intimidation in his voice.

"Hey there, Hank, what can I do you for?"

"Oh, just give me a pack of Dentyne." Hank was leaning on the counter, looking around the store. "How's business been?"

"It could be better," Jack replied, not wanting to get to the subject of their last meeting but knowing that it was the only reason for Hank's visit to the store.

"So, Jack, you think about what we talked about?"

"Hank, I would like nothing better than to see this place become a booming business...but I'm not sure about your proposition." Jack was attempting to sound as authoritative as he possibly could. He didn't want Hank to feel that he was scared or to give Hank any ammunition for threats.

"What do you seem to be having a problem with, Jack? Is it the fear of making a lot of money and you not knowing what to do with it? On the other hand, are you afraid that you aren't a good businessman? With your big fancy degree, it couldn't be a fear of not being a good businessman, so it must be the fear of money." Hank had not to hint of humor in his tone.

Jack trying to make light of the situation said, "Of course not. I would have no problem with what to do with the money. Actually, I may have a problem with the means of the money."

"Oh, now you going to try and get all moralized, are you? Let me just remind you that I know you, Jack, and having high morals is not your strong suit." These were the words that Jack had been afraid of. Ever since he had been called to the sheriff's office for a meeting, he had a feeling that Hank was going to try to capitalize on past events. Even though things that had happened in his life were well over twenty years ago, Jack understood that men like Hank would use whatever it took to get them where they wanted to be.

Jack and Hank had been friends all through school; they had run around together. They would sneak out to the Rollins place at night and purchase moonshine. It was not a rare occasion that they would get into trouble with the law, but old Sheriff Whitaker would always just warn them and send them on their way. This was one such incident that Hank was making an unspoken reference to an incident that if the truth were truly known, it could have dire circumstances for Jack. He was beginning to feel the pressure that Hank was exerting on him. If he refused to go along with whatever this scheme of Hank's may be, he was sure that he would have some terrible consequences to pay.

"Jack, you know I have always felt that friendship was something that a person should take serious. That is why I have always been there for you, no matter what."

Hank was looking at Jack with a look of utter evil. Jack very easily read between the lines of this last statement. This was not something that Jack was going to get out of, so he might as well agree now and make the best of the situation. After all, Hank was not making him do something that only Hank would benefit from; he had said they both would make money. What the heck? If he could make money, whose business was it?

"You know, Hank," Jack started, "I do need something to boost sales here. Do you really think that your product will do that?"

"Oh, Jackie boy, I don't think; believe me, I know it will."

"All right then, let me know what, when, and where, and we will be on the road to riches."

"That's what I'm talking about. Believe me, Jack; this is bigger than anything we have ever done and a lot more profitable. All those days we would dream about being rich and famous is about to pay off. You are sure I can trust you on this? After all, it is a big operation, and the least little thing that would go wrong and we both would be facing big trouble. I'm sure you understand that. Therefore, it will be up to you to keep this project secret."

"No problem, Hank." Jack was already dreading this; he knew that Hank had a secret that he had never revealed, and now it was payback time.

⚡

Rachael, overhearing the conversation, was deeply troubled. There was a feeling that swept over her, a feeling that she needed to take some type of action, but she wasn't sure what or how. She was afraid for herself and her family. Lucas was only three years old; she couldn't support herself and him on what she was making as a part-time paralegal if something bad happened to Jack. The money from the insurance was almost depleted, and the store was barely hanging on. It made maybe four hundred dollars in a good month.

That was due in most part to the price of gasoline, not from the store itself. They were in a terrible condition that appeared only to be getting worse. Now she had overheard Hank and Jack talking about a new product that would boost sales, a product that would pull the store and them out of financial ruin. It wasn't the idea of a new product; it was the way they were discussing it that caused Rachael major concern. Something about this did not feel right. *Please do not allow anything bad to happen,* she secretly prayed. She wasn't sure to whom that request had been made, but at any rate, it couldn't hurt to ask for a little supernatural help.

Astaroth stood silently behind the crates stacked in the storeroom, watching the events unfolding in the store. He heard Rachael's strained attempt at prayer, and of course she was right, it didn't hurt to ask for supernatural help, and it was his mission to make sure that nothing wrong happen. It was too important an endeavor to allow any interference to take place.

Astaroth was a strong leader for the Company; as a matter of fact, he was a *great* duke. He had been sent to Evansville along with Belial and a few other strong powers to investigate the situation. The king was highly disturbed with the message he had received from Mastema about the sighting of Michael. The king knew that if they had sent Michael that they were planning an all-out war. The king wasn't sure whether Jesse could handle this battle or not; the last time Jesse came up against Michael and his crew, there had been a major devastation to the Company and its kingdom. He did not want that to happen again. He truly believed that the location of this operation would go unnoticed, but there was a leak somewhere, a leak that had to be stopped immediately. Astaroth had seen and heard enough in this place. It was now time for him to report in.

Belial was sitting behind the large desk that had been up to the present moment reserved for Jesse. Jesse was now sitting on a makeshift chair slightly behind and to the left of Belial.

"Now, Jesse, it has come to our attention that there is a situation here which is not being handled appropriately,"

Belial said in a putrid-smelling voice. Belial was the leader of the Company. He emitted a fetid odor that was undeniable, and anyone that came in contact with him could not help but become suddenly nauseous. It was for this reason that Belial was not allowed out in the field if it was a covert operation.

Visibly shaken, Jesse's voice came in a weak, whispering tone. "I can't imagine, sir, who would have told you that. There is nothing going on that I can't handle."

"Well, what about the presence of Michael?"

"Oh, that. You don't have anything to worry about there, sir. I have already initiated the emergency procedures required for that type of thing. The rapid response team has been activated, and all things are going as planned."

"If that were the case, Jesse, Michael would not be here. He is never dispatched to a place unless the Power knows that a situation takes the higher host to handle. This is *not* a good thing."

Jesse could feel his authority slipping out of his grasp. He had to do something fast to rectify this very threatening situation.

"I want to know," Belial continued, "where is this leak coming from? How did the Power know about us here? Once that source is identified, it has to be handled appropriately."

As Belial was speaking, Astaroth entered the conference room. "What did you find out, Astaroth?" Belial quickly asked.

"Well, it seems that Hank Wilson is truly doing his part to bring this project about. He was in the store talking with Jack. Jack is now being convinced that it is to his best interest to cooperate with Hank."

"That's good news—," Belial said before he was interrupted by Jesse's weak voice.

"See? That was what I was trying to tell you, boss—"

The statement was cut short by a vicious rebuke from Belial. "Silence. I didn't say you could speak!" Jesse shrunk deep into the crate in which he had adopted as a chair.

"There is only one thing, sir, that I saw that could turn into a slight problem," Astaroth continued with his report.

"And what might that be?"

"While I was there, Rachael, Jack's wife, was listening to Hank and Jack's conversation from the back room. She whispered a prayer not to let anything go wrong or happen. She really didn't know who she was praying to; in fact she actually said she needed some supernatural help. It was just good that I was there to intercept that request."

This was something that really could cause a big problem. What if she actually started to pray or learned to use the code word that summons the Powers? They had to make sure that she never got a revelation of that powerful code; it was all right for her to whisper a prayer as long as it was one that his boys could intercept. It was when she learned the code that they would be in trouble. Belial sent Mastema to gather Rachael's historical information. He needed to know if there was anything in her past that he needed to know about. Had she been raised in a religious family? Had she ever attended church, and did she have any clue about what the Bible said?

Looking straight into Jesse's eyes, Belial said, "As of immediately, I am in total control. You will begin to work in the field. Astaroth, Azazel, Foras, Malphas, and I will handle the operation on the management level. You get out there and watch over the day-to-day, minute-to-minute operation."

"Yes, sir," Jesse sadly replied as he got up to go out of the office.

"And, Jesse," Belial, in his position of authority, called out.

"Yes, sir?"

"Find the leak and find it fast, or you will find yourself walking the halls and rotunda of the Oklahoma State Penitentiary."

"Yes, sir, I will, sir." Jesse replied as he disappeared out of Belial's sight.

Jesse was angry and for good reason. Who had snitched to the king about that interfering little weakling Michael? Furthermore, why did the king send all of the mighty powers of the Company to Evansville? With that many superpowers, this would truly be a major event of the supernatural type. Leaving the office to go into the field, Jesse ran into Mastema standing outside the door. "How did it go in there, boss?" Mastema asked.

Jesse just growled at him that he was no longer the boss. If he wanted to see the boss, he would have to go in and see Belial.

This was a great stride for Mastema; with Jesse out of the way and him being able to prove himself to the high powers, he would probably get a promotion and a territory of his own.

X

Things were going very well for Hank Wilson; he could envision himself in a few years not wearing a sheriff's uniform, but rather dressed in the latest men's fashion from Armani and Ralph Lauren. His contacts from Dallas were ready to start transporting the materials to the Rollinses so they could get production in full swing.

The last time he had visited with Nolan and the boys, they had already constructed three new stills that could hold fifty gallons each. It would take about two weeks to turn out one hundred and fifty gallons of the new and improved "corn," or as it was dubbed, Rollins' Royale. It had taken him some time to convince Nolan that this new commercially prepared mash would only help make production faster. This new mash had all the ingredients already mixed together in the right proportions. All they had to do was cook it to about one hundred and seventy-five degrees and let the fermentation process do the rest. He had suggested that with the first batch they should taste a little to see if it was up to their qualifications, and if not, they could add their own ingredients to make it better.

If the Rollins could turn out one hundred and fifty gallons every two weeks, that would be approximately three hundred gallons a month. At that rate, they could have Rollins Royale in every liquor store, nightclub, tavern, and bar in the two-state radius within the next three months. Hank had wanted this all his life. He had invested untold amounts of money into get-rich-quick schemes. Then like magic, this proposal happened to fall into his lap.

It all started about six months ago. Hank had stopped the car on State highway 281 for speeding. He soon realized this was not an ordinary traffic stop; the occupants were obliviously men of importance. They were all dressed in three-piece suits and looked to be very influential businessmen. After not giving them a citation, only a warning, the person who was obviously the boss had given him a business card. This man told him if he ever wanted to make more money than he could ever make as sheriff, to give him a call.

It had taken him about a month to actually call Shesapeake Enterprises the first time. It was during a time that nothing was working out for him. He was behind in his car payment. The rent on his apartment was due, but the landlady was going to work with him because he was the sheriff. The subject of his rent had gone before the city council; they had decided to pay his rent, but his other bills were strictly on him. Hank had almost $20,000 in credit card debt. He could feel himself sinking fast. Out of desperation, he called the number on the business card and got Manuel

Lopez's. After reminding Mr. Lopez who he was, Hank was then invited to come down to Dallas and discuss a business proposition. He was totally impressed with the operations of Shesapeake Enterprises. They owned a variety of businesses dedicated to entertainment. They had several nightclubs across Oklahoma, Texas, and Arkansas, as well as a record publishing company. They also had a division dedicated to the automotive industry. They owned and operated several paint and body shops and a chain of automotive parts stores. They were also the major sponsors of many local and corporate car shows. Hank was totally taken with the full scope of this man and his operation. He wanted nothing more than to become a partner in this very lucrative enterprise. During his first meeting with Manuel Lopez, Hank was questioned as to what or who it was that he could bring to the Company as an asset. Not knowing exactly what type of asset they really wanted from him, he was a little confused.

It wasn't until his third meeting that he was finally let in on a few of the business' secrets, and then it all began to make sense, and it was a plan that he instantly believed would work.

"Look, Hank," Manuel had stated, "you are the perfect person in the perfect place for this. Look at us; being the businessmen that we are, we would never be involved in anything but the most respectable of ventures. And you being the sheriff, you would never do anything that was not legit."

"I think I can see what you are saying," Hank thoughtfully stated. "I am the sheriff, and my area is one of seclusion and low visibility. I haven't been known for anything except being an upright citizen—that is, since I've been an adult anyway."

Everything had been arranged, and Hank had kept up his end of the bargain. The Rollinses were in on the major end of the production, and Jack had agreed to enlarge his store to include a liquor store. All the pieces were starting to come together. It was now just a matter of time before the operation would be in full swing and the cash would begin to start rolling in.

Hank had already contrived a way of explaining his newfound wealth. He was going to report that he had taken his part of his grandmother's inheritance and invested in a small, unknown company and now that company was paying off big dividends. In a way, that was exactly what he was doing. He was investing in a company, and it was going to pay off big. He didn't want to include too many people in on this, but he knew that he needed other people to help pull it off. The Rollinses he knew wouldn't be a problem; they weren't that smart. But Jack, on the other hand, may be another issue; he was smart and could figure things out pretty quick. Hank would have to make sure that Jack would not start wanting in on the big action.

But of course, he pretty much had Jack where he wanted him. Jack never wanted anybody to know the truth about a secret that Hank had kept all this time. A secret that Hank knew one day would be of great benefit to himself.

⚡

Phillip was still struggling with his life in Evansville, and it was beginning to become a burden. Even if he wanted to, he couldn't move his family now; he had invested all his money time and effort into this place. Phillip could not just leave.

He knew that the house would not sell in this town, and the church was truly not an asset that anyone here wanted. Besides which, he didn't have the resources to relocate. This had been a very trying year; he was almost to the point of giving it all up. He had studied and researched Evansville from every angle. There had to be a clue to the town's stagnated condition. The only thing he had found that may have a bearing on this place was a twenty-year-old story. The story was about the tragic and brutal death of a young girl in which a young black man had been convicted and executed.

Phillip could not understand why that story kept going through his mind. There was no mystery here. The suspect had been apprehended and convicted. Nevertheless, the story kept haunting him. He was even having nightmares about the murder. He could actually see the young lady, hear her screams, and see the torment on her face. *I must be losing my mind*, he thought. The town truly was really beginning to get to him. When he would ask about the murder to people in town, they all just seemed to dismiss it as a terrible thing but that was all. It didn't appear that anyone really cared.

"Hey, honey," Sherri addressed Phillip, "what you thinking about?"

"Oh, nothing really," Phillip lied.

"Must be something. You have been so distant lately; it is as if you were carrying the weight of the world on your shoulders."

"Oh, Sherri, I don't know what to do. It seems like every which way I turn I am running into a brick wall. Nothing is going right. I just can't understand this."

"Maybe it isn't for you to understand just yet, Phillip,"

Sherri comforted him. "After all, if God brings you to it, he will surely bring you through it."

Phillip had repeated those same words again and again on countless occasions, but he was having a lot of doubts whether he truly believed them himself. He was even beginning to wonder if it was really true. Did God actually take an interest in man? Furthermore, why was he allowing all of this to happen to him? It wasn't fair he had turned against his parents, family, and friends to follow what he felt God wanted him to do. Now he couldn't even pay the student loans he had taken out to attend seminary, let alone support his family. Maybe what he had been taught was actually all a fantasy. Maybe life did just evolve from a higher life form. Maybe God did only help those who helped themselves. One had to go out and make things happen for themselves; then God would step in and allow them to get ahead. Phillip had put all of his trust in God, but at this point, he was beginning to question his own faith and motives.

Sherri understood where Phillip was mentally. She had also had to fight the doubt and discouragement that was rising in her. The one thing that greatly helped was her conversation with her father. Robert Johnson had been in the ministry for well over thirty years. As he would tell you, he had seen the good, the bad, and the ugly. Sherri had asked her father to come down this weekend after church on Sunday, and maybe he could give Phillip a little encouragement. She had not informed Phillip of her invitation to her father; she felt it better if he just showed up.

"Phillip, I'm sure that everything is going to work out. You have to remember, all things work together for good to those who love the Lord and are called according to his purpose," Sherri reiterated.

"I truly hope so," Phillip said.

"Now that is not a statement of faith. You are supposed to say 'I *know* it will.'"

"I know you are right, Sherri. It's just I can't seem to get over this feeling; maybe I am not doing the right thing. I must be a terrible minister. How could I have spent four years in seminary, a youth minister for two years, and an associate pastor three? Then as soon as I get out on my own, I crumble? Maybe God never intended for me to go out on my own. Maybe I was supposed to just serve under the leadership of your father or someone else."

"Now you know that is not true. God said to go out and make disciples. He never said to stay in a church and listen."

"But maybe I moved out ahead of God. Maybe I am not in his timing. Maybe I am trying to make things happen that He never intended to happen."

"Haven't you been taught and also preached that God speaks to your heart, not your head?"

"Yes, that is true,"

"Then where did you get the call to come to Evansville? In your heart or in your head?"

"I thought I had it in my heart, but now I'm not sure."

"All right then, would Satan tell you to go to a small rural town and convert the people?"

"What do you mean?"

"What I'm saying is that Satan would never send you to a place to tear down his domain. He would much rather you have stayed in Longview at True Light than to come here and uncover his wiles."

"Maybe you are right." It seemed that Phillip perked up, just for a moment. "But if God sent me here to uncover the enemy's camp, then why am I not finding the camp or even knowing where to look? Jesus asked Peter to feed his sheep, but how can you feed others if you can't feed yourself? How can you clothe others if you have no clothes?"

Sherri knew it was going to be very difficult to convince Phillip that he was in the right place doing the right thing when he was only looking at the circumstances. It was going to take a divine revelation for him to understand. *Dear Lord, please open his eyes that he may see*, she silently prayed. "I'm going to go to the store and get a few things. Do you want me to pick you up anything while I'm out?"

"No, I'm good. Are you taking the kids with you?"

"Naomi is asleep in her room, and Phil is playing in the den. Do you need me to take them?"

"No, I just needed to know so that I wouldn't walk off and not realize they were here."

"I'll be back in a few minutes."

"Take your time. We'll be here when you get back."

Going over to the desk, Phillip once again picked up the old newspaper from July 1989. Why was this so pressing on him? What was it he was supposed to see or learn?

Michael stood silently in the corner of the office, his energy radiating throughout the room.

For the first time in a long time, Phillip had a deep unction to pray. Falling to the floor in the office, Phillip began to pray an earnest, heartfelt prayer to God. Michael, swiftly ascending through the ceiling, headed toward the eastern edge of town.

For what seemed only a few minutes, Phillip came out of the office to find Sherri busy cooking dinner. Surprised, he questioned, "I thought you were going to the store."

"I did," she replied, "but when I got back, you were in the office in devotion, so I just came on in and started dinner."

"Did I actually pray that long?"

"I don't know when you started, but I went to the store, came home, and started cooking. I have been home at least thirty minutes now."

Phillip realized he must have been in prayer for the better part of an hour; he hadn't been that deep in prayer since before he left Longview and came to Evansville. It was truly remarkable to him. After his prayer session, he could actually feel a weight had been lifted. Was this for real, or was it only psychosomatic? Was it really the peace of God, or was it a form of self-hypnosis? Phillip was so confused.

⚡

Michael was beginning to feel a strong force around him. The hordes of hell were closing in. He knew that now was the time to call headquarters for reinforcements.

"I thought I had better check in," Michael reported to headquarters. "I know that Belial is here because I got a distinct odor coming from the old warehouse building at the edge of town. I'm not sure how many are here, but I know that he never travels alone."

"Yes, we are well aware of their presence in Evansville. Your crew will be there in a matter of minutes," the dispatch informed Michael. "You will find them at the New Life Fellowship Church on Modoc Street."

"Does Phillip know that he has help here?"

"Not really. He is still in a state of discouragement. But with the way things are heating up, I am sure that the Power will start his overt operation very, very soon."

"Good, it is time to begin this battle now," Michael confidently confirmed.

"Michael, be very careful. Phillip still doesn't know what to believe about us and our mission."

"I understand, and I will. Today is a good day. I have a lot more energy than I have had in weeks. The energizing power was released in full force."

"That is why we knew it was time to send out the crew. The power level is increasing and will continue to increase as time goes on. But there will be those dry times when the energy will be drained. At those times, you all just be patient. This is not going to be an easy war because the king of darkness and his boys are playing for high stakes here."

With that affirmation, the conversation ended. Michael had to get to the New Life Fellowship to brief his crew on the state of affairs in Evansville. To fill them in on the people and the roles they played in the major scheme of things. This was going to be a hard and timely war, and Michael was sure that some of the battles in this war they were sure to lose, but the supreme victory would without a doubt be theirs.

Michael knew all too well the superpowers of the Company, as they liked to be called. They had crossed paths too many times, but the one that he most dreaded coming in contact with was Belial; he knew that Belial had a personal vendetta against Michael. He would pull out all the stops to get to him. This could be very tedious. He and his crew were going to have to be very careful in all their maneuvers. As he had already reported to headquarters, there were at least twenty thousand workers in this small community; it was heavily saturated with evil. The evil had been there for so long they actually felt an ownership. It wasn't until this latest scheme to take over the whole world that it became a true concern. They could always be put in their places very easily. That was before Jesse moved in and started the town in an all new directions. Until he got to the soul and mind of certain people in town and turned them to their wicked devices. Now they had gone way too far; it was time to shut down their operation and cast them out, return the town back to its original state, willingly help the people fulfill the destiny that was originally planned for their lives. The clarion call had gone out, the sound had been heard, and the war was about to begin.

XI

It was a normal Monday in Evansville. The city hall was in its usual state of inactivity. Mabel was surfing the Internet, researching Realtors.com, looking for comparable home prices in a seventy-mile radius of Evansville. There was not any huge demand for houses in the area. Nor was there any available decent property to be had. However, it never hurt to look. Who knows? Someday she may even leave this place for bigger and better things. Harvey Hanes was sitting in his little office pretending to be working on a revision to the city charter, something that had not changed in over thirty years. There really wasn't a lot for him to do these days; crimes were almost nonexistent, so his services as judge were not really needed. He focused on the workings of the city council to keep him busy. It was already ten o'clock in the morning, but Hank Wilson had not made it into the office as of yet. Hank was not a very good sheriff by any means, but he was always on time, so this was a little unusual.

Mamie was busy going about her usual Monday routine. She had washed her white clothes and was in the process of hanging them out on the clothesline, when she heard the sound of trucks going down the dirt road toward West River Bridge. Looking at her watch, it read ten o'clock. *Something is surely outta kilter,* Mamie considered to herself. It was Monday morning, and she took note that for the last three months, there had been large trucks going across West River Bridge out toward the Rollins place. They usually came in at night, always on Saturday night. Mamie had lived in this house for over forty years, and she had never seen or heard more than two cars a week going over that bridge. She knew in her heart that something was taking place, and whatever it was, it was not good.

Hank Wilson was sitting on the hood of the police cruiser as the first truck came off the bridge. Waving at the driver, he went to the driver-side door, got in, and followed behind the second truck.

"Yep," he stated out loud, "this is such a wonderful operation. This is the best thing that has ever happened in my life."

The trucks slowly made their way down the bumpy dirt road; large ruts had been worn in the road due to the size and weight of the trucks and their frequent trips across them. Hank made a mental note to put in a work order to the county commissioners regarding the road condition.

Hank wanted to make sure they would get a road crew out there to grade the road before Saturday night. He definitely did not want anything to hinder the major production that was taking place out at Nolan Rollins' place.

To date the Rollinses had produced and shipped over a thousand gallon of Rollins' Royale; this would actually amount to over four thousand gallons of finished product. When the corn got to the distillery, it was cut from the original one hundred proof to approximately eighty proof. This produced four times the original amount. Hank's partners in Dallas were well pleased with the production that was coming out of Evansville. With the added ingredient that even Sheriff Wilson was unaware of, it was the biggest case that they had ever undertaken. Manuel knew the time had come to increase the supply of the main ingredient needed to make this liquid gold as soon as possible.

"Mario, hey, yeah, it's me." Manuel made a quick call to his largest supplier. "I had a talk with our connection over in Evansville, and I want to get a hookup on a larger amount of our product. Do you think you can handle that?"

"Yeah, man, give me a few days to talk to some of my people, and I will get back with you, but remember we haven't had this—"

"Yeah, yeah, I know. You think I'm stupid?"

"All right, just making sure. Later."

This was easier than Manuel could have even imagined. He couldn't have planned it better if he had tried.

Who would have believed the night that he was stopped by that backwoods sheriff that something this ingenious would just fall into his lap? Manuel was beginning to believe that crime really does pay, especially when he had a cop doing his dirty work.

If anything ever went wrong, there was no way that Manuel and his boys could be accused of anything at all. This was the best gig he had ever had.

⚡

Sitting on the bridge with ice-cold eyes, Jesse was carefully surveying the scenery for any sign of intruders. Hank Wilson had arrived right on time. Jesse was confident that his boys were well stationed on the road around the house and barn. With everything being secure at the bridge, he now needed to go down to the house and check out some things. He had gotten the report that Marge Rollins had been behaving somewhat funny lately. Actually, Nolan had to correct her just yesterday. She had taken it up on herself to question him about his activities out at the barn. She had even told him that she really didn't trust those people from Dallas and that she also had her doubts about Hank Wilson. She had insisted that Nolan and the boys break any ties they had with these people and just let their life return to normal. Normal—Jesse assumed she didn't even know the meaning of normal. If the life they lived before was normal, what was abnormal? Jesse knew that if Marge started to get really worried about what was happening; there was a possibility that she may turn traitor. That idea sent fear through his whole body. It would not be good if she turned to the other side; actually, it could be disastrous for them.

It was Jesse's job to make sure that Marge stayed in her place. It would take some persuading. She had to get it in her mind that she had nothing to lose but everything to gain by remaining loyal.

Marge was extremely worried about the activity going on at her home. There were strange people coming in delivering huge bags of premixed mash. They would then take out large barrels of liquor. Furthermore, there were the strange men that showed up last week. They had worn three-piece suits with dark shades. They appeared to be looking things over as if they owned the whole place. Even Nolan had a problem with those people. He had told them that this was his place and his "corn." If they came in here trying to tell him what to do, he would just shut down the whole business.

When he had said that, Marge had heard the larger man, who looked to be Mexican or something like that, say, "That would not be good for you or your family. And remember, Rollins, if we find out that you and your boys are holding out on us, or you are trying to get to us, it will be real bad." This was the first time that Marge could ever remember seeing a look of what appeared to be fear cross Nolan's face. She also believed that was why Nolan had slapped her around when she had tried to talk to him about what was happening.

Marge was not unaccustomed to being hit by Nolan, but this time it was more as if he had to hit her because he couldn't hit the man who had threatened him. It was something really wrong here; she could feel in her inner being that Nolan and the boys were getting themselves into something that was not going to be easy to get out of. Nolan had been making moonshine their whole married life, but now there were people that were watching their every move. They were keeping track of how much was being produced.

If there wasn't as much as they felt it should be, they started demanding that the next batch better measure up. Marge was worried and scared.

She knew those where not the kind of people that Nolan—or anyone—could cross and get away with. These were not the people down at Lenny's Alibi or over at the Spot in Hugo; these were big-time people with big-time stakes.

Not only was she afraid for her family, she was really scared for herself. She knew firsthand what Nolan was capable of if things were not going his way. She would become the object of his anger. Lately, Nolan and the boys were all acting different. They were staying out at the barn sometimes all night and well into the next day. They were not even coming to the house to eat. Not only were they staying in the barn for extended periods of time, they seemed to be working much harder than she ever remembered them working in their lives. What was going on?

⚡

The New Life Fellowship was extremely small in comparison to most church buildings; after all, it was a converted house. Once the walls of the living room had been removed, there was a small sanctuary that would seat approximately seventy-five people. A pair of wooden swinging doors had been installed to separate the sanctuary from the vestibule. One bedroom had been converted into an office; a wall was removed from a second bedroom that had originally adjoined the kitchen, and it had been converted into a fellowship hall.

It was in the fellowship hall that Michael found his backup warriors. The warriors took up the whole area.

Their sizes were enormous. In attendance, Michael found Uriel, Gabriel, Carmuel, Raphael, and Ariel. These were the mightiest warriors from the Realm. They were of the highest level. They each had a host of other soldiers that could defeat the mightiest armies of darkness.

Each of these mighty warriors had a specific duty to perform. Uriel stood guard at the gates of the city with a sword of flame, Gabriel brought revelation to the prophet, Raphael brought healing to the wounded, Carmuel showed the shortcomings in all things, big and small, Ariel guarded the water sources, and Michael was the leader of the Army.

"I am glad you all are here," Michael greeted the others.

"We have been anxiously awaiting orders to come," Gabriel replied. "What exactly is going on in this place?"

"The Company has succeeded in claiming this town over the years. Then Jesse was assigned here to bring in and put a new weapon into place."

"Do they actually think they have something new?" Carmuel asked.

"Actually, if their scheme succeeds, it could be very devastating to the people of this town as well as the state as a whole. If they are allowed to continue with the work, they are doing at the rate of speed they are performing. It could spread across the whole earth and cause more devastation than this planet has known since the great flood," Michael explained.

The soldiers sat quietly and listened as Michael laid out the whole plot. This was a very serious matter; now it was evident why they had all been summoned to Evansville. This operation was going to take the mightiest of the mighty to conquer these evildoers.

One of the first things they had to do was make sure that Phillip and Mamie met. These were the two people that would be instrumental in ending this reign of terror that was overtaking this whole community.

"You all look much rested and energized," Michael observed.

"That is because there is a high level of energy in this building. Take a look inside the sanctuary, Michael," Uriel urged.

Inside the sanctuary, Michael made out the figure of someone sitting on the front seat with their head in their hands. It was Phillip, and he was praying. That was the source of energy.

"Who are some of the Company that we will be coming up against?" Gabriel inquired.

"There is Belial, Astaroth, Azazel, Foras, and Malphas."

"Wow that is a strong force. This project really must be of uttermost importance. Sending those guys in is saying that they will go to any length to make sure it succeeds."

"Now you see this is not going to be an easy war. We all know how down and dirty these guys can be. They will stop at nothing and try anything to get an advantage. So we are going to have to be on our guard at all times. They will go after the strongest allies we have and do whatever they can to get them off focus. They will throw any hindrances in their paths that they can. With stakes as high as these, they will not stop at anything or anybody. Nobody in this town is safe."

"When do we begin, Michael?"

"As soon as we possibly can. Do you all have your hosts in place and prepared for action?"

"We surely do," Raphael gladly replied. "We are ready for everything and anything."

"I have a platoon at all four gates of the city," Uriel volunteered.

"I have the West River covered," Ariel added.

"I have platoons at the One Stop grocery store, Wesley United Church, and the Old Wilson boarding house," Carmuel stated.

"I have Phillip Fields,' Mamie Webb's, and Cherish Rollins' houses guarded," Gabriel interjected.

"And I have a platoon intermingled with all the others in all the target areas," Raphael finished.

"Good," Michael congratulated the warriors. "It seems that everything is coming together. Do all the soldiers know where we are headquartered?"

"Yes," Gabriel said. "That was the first thing we did when we got here. We first went to Wesley but soon found out that it was in the total grasp of the enemy. As a matter of fact, I knew that Belial was here. I caught that distinct odor that only he could emit. It is all around the Wesley United Church."

"Well, the time has come. It is time for the battle to commence," Michael announced.

XII

Phillip found himself spending more and more time at the church as of late. For some reason he found a sense of peace and comfort inside the church building, peace that he had felt was long since lost. It was when he left the borders of the church that the feeling of dread and uncertainty would sweep down and envelope him like a dark cold blanket.

It was while he was inside the church that Phillip would get an urgent need to pray. This feeling was completely overwhelming. He would stay at the church for hours, praying and listening to praise music. Today he decided to sit in his small office and study.

Not since the church had been completed had Phillip used the office for meditation and study. But now it seemed only right that he should use it for what it was originally intended.

Here he could research some of the principals of the Bible, delve deep into biblical history, and receive direct revelation from the Word of God. Phillip knew there was something within the pages of his Bible that would illuminate what was going on with his life. He wanted God to reveal to him what it was that he was suppose to do and how he was to do it.

For reasons Phillip could not explain, he was feeling his faith returning and increasing. He knew it was time that he had to repent for his prior doubt and unbelief. Opening the Bible, he found himself in the book of Daniel, the tenth chapter. As he was reading through the chapter, the verses ten through thirteen appeared to jump off the page at him. Trying to get a clear understanding of what the passage meant, he read and reread the verses. Gabriel had a look of satisfaction on his face as Phillip read the predestined passage of Scripture. Gabriel knew that the meaning would soon become evident to him. Leaving his most trusted platoon leader to oversee Phillip and his family, Gabriel had someone else to visit. He started out toward the east end of town.

⚡

Gabriel could hear the commotion coming from the woods behind Mamie's house. There were loud shrieks, low groans, and muffled cries. No human person heard or saw anything; no one could. It was out of the scope of the human realm. Suddenly a dark, slimy creature with wings similar to those of a bat, an oblong head that came to a point at the top, and close-fitting, oblong ears came limping out of the woods, spurting blasphemies. Right behind him was the glitter of a long sword followed by an exploding figure like the sun itself. With one swing of the sword, the ugly little creature lay on its back, looking up at the impressive figure over him.

"What is your name?" the heavenly creature asked the slimy little demon.

The little demon defiantly refused to answer; the sword pierced his right ear. A thick green liquid spewed out of the wound.

"What is your name?" he demanded, holding the sword above the boney chest of the creature.

"Doubt," the creature replied.

"Why are you here?"

"I have to make sure that Mamie continues to have doubts."

Gabriel, walking over to the little creature and in one continuous motion, snatched up the pitiful little critter and flung him into the atmosphere. As he flew through the air, all that could be seen was a dark puff of smoke as the creature disappeared.

"How many of that kind have you encountered?" Gabriel asked the warrior.

"That is the sixth that I have had, but the platoon has been fighting them all night. We have managed to defeat fear, discouragement, loneliness, frustration, depression, and now doubt."

"Good, I knew there would be a whole army around here. Mamie is one of the biggest threats the enemy has. It is not a surprise that they have been assigned in large numbers to her."

"Some of the squad is looking for illness and disease; they were spotted hiding under the house, but when we went after them, they had managed to escape. But we are on their tracks."

"They must be found and defeated," Gabriel reiterated. "Those two are some of the worst. They have so many devices and cohorts to use, so many areas of attack, that if they get a chance to get in, they can really be a problem. Although it would not be a problem that we cannot overcome, but it would be an inconvenience."

"We will get them. They have been rearing their nasty heads for centuries. Then they try to run and hide. But we always manage to find them and cast them out. They won't stay hidden for long. They are too stupid for that."

"With the majority of the weaker workers defeated, it is now time to put our first plan of defense into motion," Gabriel stated as he swiftly entered into Mamie's house.

Hope was sitting in the floor playing with a set of little plastic blocks, the kind that can be snapped together to make a long chain. Hope always became very excited when her little chubby fingers managed to get two of the blocks to stay together. Mamie loved watching her play; she couldn't help but feel a sense of pride knowing that she had been instrumental in bringing her into this world. What if she had hesitated in coming home that night? This little angel of God could possibly not be here. *Praise the Lord! He is always right on time*, she thought.

The feeling that she should go and meet the new preacher was getting stronger and stronger. This was a feeling that no matter how hard she tried to dismiss kept creeping into her mind. She had long ago learned that when she had a feeling this strong, she must act on it.

"Well," Mamie said to Hope as she started to get the little girl cleaned up, "no better time than the present. I guess we best go and meet the good Reverend Fields." Hope gaily jumped up and down as Mamie got her little sweater; she understood that when she put on her sweater it meant it was time to go bye-bye.

Belial was in a state of rage. Workers had been coming into the office all day, wounded and scared. They had related horror story after horror story of how these well-equipped soldiers had waged an all-out attack on their forces. They had explained how everything would be going as planned; then out of nowhere, these shining white warriors with flaming swords would suddenly be there, slashing and cutting through the forces until none was left standing. Then after the attack, these warriors would take over the workers assigned positions and stand at attention.

Belial was furious; he was going to have to rethink his strategy. There must be some of the mightiest warriors from the Power here. If not, they would not be having the victories that they were. He would call a meeting of all the leaders and soldiers in his command and put together a plan of war that would be very hard to beat. He was quite familiar with these warriors, and he was very well versed in their techniques. This was not a battle that he intended to lose. He was prepared to do whatever it took and to use whoever he had to use in order to make this project success.

"Astaroth," Belial called out, "gather up every worker, imp, and warrior. Have them here at three o'clock in the morning. And, Azazel, start working on an offense that will bring those despicable creatures to their knees, and while they are there, they can practice their prayers," he chuckled.

The majors stood, waiting for further instructions. "Well, get going. Time is of the essence," Belial growled.

Under the bridge, Ariel's platoon was watching all the activity that was going on across the river on Lone Oak Road. Little imps and bodyguards were patrolling the road. There were Company workers sitting in the trees, on rocks, and behind bushes. The little harassing spirits were so comfortable and sure of themselves, some were cleaning their talons while others played around the trees.

Clearing the bridge had been a tedious task. The warriors had to make sure that they eliminated the patrolling spirits on the bridge without being noticed by those stationed up and down the road and in the woods. The warriors had distracted the spirits one by one. As the spirit would go to investigate the noise or movement, the warrior would silently disable them and banish them to another area. Once these forces had been eliminated, Ariel's warriors took cover under the bridge in the dark water of the West River. Imps had a problem with being in water; the thought of washing off the putrid slime from their bodies sent a wave of fear through them. Without the slime, they could not slither into tight forbidden areas.

Michael and his forces were stationed high up on the mountain behind the Rollins farm under the cover of the dense undergrowth and inside the numerous caves that could be found on the hillside. Belial had not positioned any of his soldiers in this area. He apparently had not considered it of any importance; he was too preoccupied with the activities of the farm to worry about the forest behind the place.

From this position, Michael could survey the entire area of the Rollins farm; he could see the house, the barn, the yard, and the road leading up to the house. For now, he and his warriors would just wait and watch until he received the orders from the commander in chief to initiate the attack. Michael knew that this was the center of the evil operation. He still did not know what it was that was taking place, but he knew whatever it was, it was of the uttermost evil.

Hank Wilson was making nightly rounds through Evansville. This was not something that he enjoyed and usually not something that he did, but that little hayseed of a deputy had decided to call in sick, so now he was stuck patrolling one section of town.

This might be a good thing, Hank thought to himself. He could drive out to Lone Oak Road and investigate the Rollinses just to see if they were actually working or if they were just sitting around. Hank drove across the bridge and down the dirt road a ways. Pulling over into a small clearing, he decided to walk down to the edge of the woods where he could see the Rollins place. From this position, using his night binoculars, he had a perfect view of the barn. He would then know exactly what was going on. Getting out of the cruiser, by instinct he felt the .45 revolver on his right side.

The night seemed extremely dark; the woods quiet except for the occasional sound of a frog coming from the pond. The sound of a lone owl sent a sudden start through Hank. He instantly grabbed for his service revolver then remembered it was nothing but an old owl.

Taking a position behind a cluster of small bushes, Hank lifted the binoculars to his eyes. There was a light on in the barn; he could see Sam and Brent inside, but Nolan was not at the barn. Watching them closely, he could see that they were drinking from pint jars. It was something about their behavior that didn't set just right. They had been drinking corn whiskey all their lives, and he knew from experience that drinking corn would not have them acting that way. Unless they had been sitting there drinking all day. If that was the case, how much of his profit had they consumed? Did they have a secret still that they were hiding from him and his partners? Were they actually producing a lot more than they were letting them know about? These were questions to which he needed to know the answer. Hank was going to have to make a trip out here tomorrow and get some things straight with Nolan about his boys' activities, activities that could cost him a lot of money.

⚡

Jack was sitting at the dining room table, thinking about his business; things were definitely beginning to look up. Ever since he had included the liquor store, he was making a sizable profit. He was getting all the liquor at a very cheap price except for the Rollins Royale; it was expensive even for him to buy. He could put a two hundred percent markup on all the other brands, but he was limited to a hundred percent on Rollins. Last month alone, he had a clear profit of $6,000. This was more than the One Stop had *ever* made in a one-month time. Even when he was a kid and his father ran the store, he could remember if the store made a $600 profit; his father felt it was a good month, but $6,000—that was phenomenal. It was still a mystery to him why the Rollins'

Royale was selling so well. Of course, he had all the major brands of alcohol in the store, but it was the Rollins brand that was the top seller. At first, he felt that the people were buying it because it was made locally, but everyone was buying more and more of the stuff. It was so popular that Jack had decided he might need to get a bottle and see what the big rush was. He had drunk the Rollins moonshine as a teenager because that was the only place an underage person could buy alcohol. But when he became legal, he wanted the bonded brand of alcohol, Hennessey and Crown. But he really needed to taste this stuff and see what it was that the people were finding so irresistible.

XIII

Mamie never thought that the old Jackson house could be made into something this magnificent. Just walking into the vestibule, Mamie could feel a strong power of heavenly presence. There was a feeling of comfort and peace.

"Well, Lord," Mamie said, "this must be the place." Walking through the swinging doors, she could see the sanctuary nicely furnished and decorated in a simple but welcoming style. The pulpit was not the new fancy type but was impressive and stood in a place of dominance.

Just standing there with Hope at her side, Mamie was basking in the calm and peaceful surroundings, when she heard a strong voice coming from what seemed far away.

"Hello, may I help you?"

Looking toward the front of the sanctuary, Mamie could make out the figure of a person standing on a chair hanging some type of framed art.

"Are you Rev. Fields?"

"I am. What can I do for you?" Phillip was a little surprised. Someone had actually come to the church looking for him. He made his way down off the chair to see exactly who this person may be. Getting closer he could see it was an elderly black lady with a small white child. He instantly began to wonder if maybe she was bringing the child to him for some assistance. Maybe she wanted him to take the child in or find her a home. He didn't want to appear skeptical, but he was in no position to take in a child nor did he know of any agencies to contact about a child if this was what the old lady was seeking.

Extending his hand to the woman, he said, "I'm Pastor Fields. How may I help you?"

"Maybe it is not just you helping me; maybe we can help each other."

"I don't understand, Miss ... ?"

"Oh, my name is Mamie Webb, and I have been debating whether to come here and talk to you. Then it was like something was telling me that I had to come here and see you."

Looking at the woman, Phillip realized that she was the woman that everyone in town referred to as a witch and thought was crazy. *Great, this is just what he needed—a senile, deranged old woman.* Phillip had not had any real experience with dealing with the mentally ill, but he was sure that it was not going to be an easy task.

"What do you need to talk to me about, Mrs. Webb?" Phillip said in the most compassionate voice he could muster up.

Mamie was looking straight into Phillip's eyes, making him feel a little uncomfortable. He had the feeling that he was about to be attacked. He was all alone in the church with this woman. What if she had violent tendencies, or what if she totally freaked out on him? What would he do? Trying to lighten the mood, he quickly turned his attention to the little brown-haired girl that has hanging on to the old woman's hand.

"And who is this?"

"This here is Hope; I tend to her while her mama is working."

"Oh, I see." That was a relief; at least she wasn't bringing the little girl to him for any purpose of refuge.

"You said something told you to come and talk with me? I don't understand." *She is probably schizophrenic*, Phillip reasoned. *Somebody that heard voices talking to them.*

"Yeah, you know when something just keeps telling you that you need to do something but you just keep putting it off."

Phillip did understand that scenario because he had been getting strong urges to do some things that he just couldn't pull himself to do.

"Yes. Let's go into the office and have a seat. Then we can talk." Phillip lightly touched the old lady's arm to lead her toward the door marked "Pastor's Study."

He was thinking as they made their way to the office, *Webb... Where have I heard that name?* The thought kept bothering him. He was sure that he knew that name from somewhere. He didn't personally know anyone named Webb. So why was it so familiar?

Sitting in the first chair she came to, Mamie was determined to come right to the point. She was not one for formalities or one that beat around the bush. This was something that needed immediate attention. She had wasted far too much time already; it was now or never. She had that feeling of assurance, that she was in the right place, doing the right thing, and whether Rev. Fields knew it or not, he was the right person.

"Now, Rev. Fields, like I said, we can help each other."

Phillip listened as the old lady began her story, a sad story of heartache and misery. Mamie had moved to Evansville in 1945 when she was only nineteen years old. She, her husband, and three kids at that time, had moved from Van Buren, Arkansas. Her husband, Elijah, had gotten a job with the Evans Mining Company. This was going to be their way of making it. It was during this time that the South was still very segregated. The black families had to live in a small area of land adjacent to the mines. The white citizens lived across the river. There had been an old run-down building that the state of Oklahoma had declared to be used as a school for the little colored children. They sent a lady who had graduated with a teaching certificate from Langston University there to teach. It was a one-room school, and all the kids of school age attended that school, they were all taught in the same room by the same teacher who made an unsuccessful attempt to divide them into grades according to age.

The river, which in actuality was only a creek, separated the white folks from the black folks. The river then became known as the West River because the river was west of the colored community. At that time, there were approximately sixty to sixty-five families of blacks living in what was known as the Lone Oak Community. All the husbands and sons that were old enough worked in the mines. It was the black men that were required to do the hardest work and go into the most dangerous areas of the mines.

Mamie and her family had lived comfortably in Evansville

for almost fifteen years; her family had grown from three children to include eight children. Then one day in 1960 there was an accident at the number nine. Twenty-two men were trapped in the mine, and no one was able to get them out. Three of those men were her husband, Elijah, and two of her sons, Matthew and William. The mining company said they would make things right for her and the other women that had lost their husband, but that was a long time coming. Some of the women packed up and moved back to their hometowns. There were a few, like Mamie, who stayed in Evansville and tried to make the best of the situation. Leaving her with six children to raise alone, Mamie had to start doing whatever she could to make a living. Times truly were hard in those days; black folks were treated very badly.

Mamie hired herself out as a cook in one of the local cafés to help with the bills and the kids. It was in 1965 that the Evansville mines closed down altogether. Some said it was due to the decrease in the need for coal, but Mamie knew that it was because the mining inspectors had said the mines were not safe. After the accident at the number nine, it was going to cost more money than old Mister Evans wanted to spend to get them up to specifications.

With the mines closing down, it was as if the whole town shut down. Sure, there were people still living there, mainly because they didn't have anywhere else to go. With the mines gone and the economy dwindling to nothing, the City Café had to lay her off. They were not making enough money to afford a full-time cook. The remaining citizens of the town started to just throw off all restraints, and things just seemed to fall to hell. Robberies increased; domestic violence took on an all-new meaning, as did child abuse.

Mamie's oldest three children, Marilyn, Peggy, and Joann, had all left Evansville to make new lives in other parts of the state. In 1971, Joann had been killed in a car wreck. Peggy came down with ovarian cancer in 1993 and died. She had no idea where Marilyn was at this time or even if she was still alive. The three younger children, Joshua, Wilma, and Roscoe, had stayed in Evansville, but after the big tragedy happened, she was left there all by herself. She felt, as she said in her own words, "like Naomi in the book of Ruth."

Phillip looked over and smiled at Hope as she busied herself in the corner of the office with the collection of toys left by his own children. After listening to Mamie's account of her life in Evansville, Phillip was still a little confused as to why she needed to talk to him. Maybe she had no one else to talk to about these things and by him being new and not having any ties to Evansville, she felt comfortable. He would just listen and try to encourage her as much as he could.

It was in 1961, the story continued, that one night a group of men had came riding through the Lone Oak Community, burning crosses in the yards of the colored folks. It was that night that they went in and drug a young black man by the name of Curtis Meadows out of his house. They had lynched him in his own front yard while his wife and kids stood watching in the door. They had said he had made some kind of disrespectful comment to ole lady Sims at the store. Of course nobody knew exactly who these men were and nobody was about to say anything.

So the colored folks just cut him down after they had left, had a quiet little funeral, and buried him on his property.

That was the beginning of keeping the black folks in their places. The colored people were scared, and the white folks were doing any and everything imaginable. It was after the Rollins had moved over across the river and started making the moonshine that things went from bad to worse. Old Sheriff Whitaker had tried to keep things under control, but the local white kids were going out to the Rollins, buying moonshine and then going into town, vandalizing property. The rumor was they were also molesting young women but then blaming the offenses on the black boys. It was nothing for those young hoodlums to make their way into Lone Oak Community and assault a young black girl.

Mamie explained that was why there were so many biracial children in Evansville. Things began to change a little in the late 1960s early 1970s with the black folks in the south marching and demanding the right to vote and equality. The people of Evansville had made a feigned attempt at accepting the black folk. Mamie had moved out of her old house in Lone Oak in 1973 and bought the old Jenkins place. This was an arrangement that suited people just fine. She was far enough away from the *good* white folks, but she was still technically living within the town itself. Nobody could say her civil rights were refused.

Although there was for all outward appearance an acceptance of the blacks in Evansville, there was still a deep-seated prejudice in the hearts of the people.

Then on a hot night in 1989, the beginning to the end happened. "It was as if the forces of evil actually had returned with a vengeance and took over this town and the people, Mamie said. "It was almost to the point of no return; greed, hatred, and misery were in full force."

Phillip had listened intently to Mamie's story; he couldn't help but remember the story he had read about in the newspaper of a murder in 1989. That's it! The name Webb—that was the name of the man that was executed for the murder! Could this be Mamie's son? He didn't want to ask that question right now, but he was sure that he would get the whole story as time went on.

"Mrs. Webb, you said that we could help each other. After listening to you tell your story, I must admit I am a bit confused. I am too aware of the hardships you, your family, and people have had to endure not only here in Evansville, but across the nation as a whole. But how can we be of help to each other now?"

"Don't you understand? We are not wrestling against flesh and blood here. You are here in this place for a reason; you are on a mission. You weren't sent here to have a big fancy church and make a lot of money. Matter of fact, you probably won't make enough money to make ends meet. You was sent here to do a work."

To Phillip it was as if Mamie had been reading his mind and thoughts. How did she know that he had those aspirations when he came here? How did she know that he wasn't going to be able to make ends meet? Just who was this woman? "What are you saying, Mrs. Webb?"

"I'm saying that the devil is taking over this place, and it is not God's will to allow him to do so. We used to have another church here in Evansville, The Community Center of Hope.

The preacher was Rev. Moore. He was truly an anointed man of God—that is, in the beginning. But he moved on to bigger and better things, or so he said. He told us one day that the Lord had released him from this place and was moving him to Missouri." Mamie hesitated for a moment then she continued, "We had a fair-sized congregation, about seventy people or so. After he left, the congregation just kind of scattered. Some tried attending Wesley but found it was not a place to be if you wanted to hear the Word. Now most of us just stays home and prays and reads the Bible."

Was Phillip hearing this woman right? There were actually people out there that wanted to hear the Word of God?

"A small group of us get together about once a month and have intercessory prayer. We had been praying that God would send to us a pastor. Someone that could come in and help us fight this warfare that we are in. When we heard about you, we wasn't sure if you were that person or not, so I am here now to find out if you is truly the person that God has sent or if you are just a counterfeit."

Phillip had a strange feeling coming over him. Just this morning he had been led to read Daniel chapter ten verses ten through thirteen. Now here sits a woman in his office, telling him there is a congregation out there waiting on a pastor and that the devil and his evil forces are in full swing in this town. Now she is wondering if he is a counterfeit.

"You know the devil is a deceiver, and he will plant people in places and make you believe that they are who you want and need, but then you finds out they are really working for him. Like Rev. Moore, he wasn't the man God had for this place. It was obvious when things started heating up; he skipped out."

"Mrs. Webb, I came here not because I looked on the map and saw Evansville, Oklahoma and thought I want to go there. No, quite the contrary, I was prompted and led here. And you are right; I had thought about growing a large ministry and doing all the things that I saw other ministers doing. But once I got here, everything started going wrong, and to tell you the truth, I couldn't leave now even if I wanted to."

A big grin came across Mamie's face, a grin one gets when a great victory is obtained. A grin that said everything is going to be all right now.

"I believes that you truly are the one, Rev. Fields. If you weren't, the devil wouldn't be working on you so hard. What time is church in the morning?"

"It starts at eleven o'clock, but I must tell you it has only been my wife, kids, and I here. One time a little lady came, but she hasn't been back. She actually nodded off during my message." Phillip laughed uneasily.

"You don't worry about that. You just be here in the morning."

"Okay," Phillip replied. For once, he was beginning to see a ray of hope. Maybe he was supposed to be here; maybe he actually *had* heard God.

XIV

Rachael was increasingly more worried about Jack. Over the last few months, they were really doing well; all the bills were being paid on time. They had money left over to do some of the things they *really* wanted to do. Business was going so well that Jack had actually hired a young woman to work in the store. This gave him more time to do things with the family. He had taken Lucas and her to Dallas, shopping, and bought her, Lucas, and himself new clothes.

He had even purchased her a new vehicle, a Cadillac Escalade. From all outward appearances, they were doing great. Still Rachael worried. It wasn't the business or how well it was doing that was bothering Rachael; it was that Jack had taken to drinking more and more. She had found four empty bottles of Rollins Royale hidden under the kitchen sink. She knew they had been there less than a week, because she kept all of her cleaning supplies under the sink, and the bottles had not been there last Friday when she did her general cleaning.

Rachael had also noticed a change in Jack's attitude. It was as if he really didn't seem to care much about anything or anybody. He would go off all by himself and be gone for hours. He also seemed to have a newfound energy level that was almost frightening. He would go and go, and most times, he would not sleep at all. He would be up for days at a time. When she had tried to talk to him about his lack of rest, he had told her that he just had so much on his mind that he couldn't sleep but that he would be all right.

Rachael thought that maybe he had something physically wrong with him. She could remember that her mother had a thyroid problem, and she had not slept and was always going in high gear. Maybe Jack had something like that.

Rachael had started to dust the furniture in the house when she came over to the table lamp that sat in front of the west window. She noticed there were six cars sitting in front of the store. There was always a constant stream of traffic in and out of the store lately. And most of those coming and going were there to buy alcohol from the liquor store. Of course, there were a few that actually brought other things—some groceries and gas—but the majority of the sales came from the liquor store. Rachael had also noticed that it was usually some of the same people every day. In the last week or so, however, there were also out of state cars pulling in. This was just too strange.

⚡

Hank knew it was time to confront Nolan and his boys about what he had seen that night out at the farm. He had intentionally waited a few days because he didn't want them to know he had actually been spying on them.

But now he had to because Manny and the boys would be coming in tomorrow, and he didn't want anything being screwed up.

Nolan Rollins was sitting on the porch, rocking back and forth; Marge was sitting on the other end of the porch, peeling potatoes as Hank got out of the car. Marge kept her head down as though she didn't even see him. It didn't take a rocket scientist to figure out the reason for this behavior. The left side of Marge's face had a bruise from the hairline to the jaw. Nolan had once again taken out his frustration on Marge. It would be the proper thing in normal circumstances to question the marks on her face, but Hank could not risk making Nolan angry—not now.

Nolan was watching Hank under a suspicious eye. He wasn't sure whether Hank was going to say anything to him about Marge's face or not.

"How's it going, Nolan?"

"Fine. How about you?"

"Just fine. I came out here today to remind you that Manny will be here tomorrow with your money, and I hope everything is going okay."

"What ya mean, going okay?"

"Oh, you know, production up where it is supposed to be, nothing missing." Hank wasn't going to let Nolan know that he had seen the boys partaking of the sauce, but he was going to say enough to give him a warning.

"There will be plenty, but if you think I'm going to make all my corn and not have a little, then you got another think coming. That would be like a man having a cattle farm and having no meat to eat."

"Oh, no, of course not. I don't expect you not to keep out a few bottles for your own personal use, Nolan. But in the same token, I wouldn't expect that you would be holding out a large quantity. After all, Manny is supplying all the premixed ingredients for you so all you are really doing is producing the product using his materials."

"Whose stills you think is making this stuff? If Manny knew how to make moonshine, he wouldn't need me and the boys now, would he? So he best be satisfied with what he gets." Nolan was in a state of total relaxation; he was leaned back in his chair as if he didn't have a care in the world.

"Are the boys out at the barn?" Hank inquired.

"Nope, they went over into Hugo. They had some things they wanted to do. Should be back tonight or maybe tomorrow."

"Oh, I see. I sure hope they are back. I don't want anything to go wrong tomorrow."

Hank decided he was getting nowhere fast with Nolan; there was something not right with him. Turning to leave, he acknowledged Marge, "Evening, Mrs. Rollins."

"Evening, Sheriff," Marge said in a slight whisper, still not raising her head.

Hank backed up, turned around, and drove back down the lane to leave the Rollins place. *This doesn't sound good*, he thought to himself. He wasn't sure what Manny would do if he came here tomorrow and the boys were not here and Nolan was in a state of total indifference and the product was not ready. There may be hell to pay.

Watching him leave, Jesse was leaning over the rail of the porch, feeling quite smug. Things were going just great.

Mastema was riding in the front passenger seat of Hank's cruiser, arm resting in the window. He waved to Jesse as they drove off. Mastema carried on a conversation that only Hank could hear: "Nolan is trying to cheat you, man. Manny is going to think that it is you. You better get this thing in check as soon as possible. What you need to do is go over to Hugo tonight, find those good-for-nothing Rollins boys, and get their butts in gear." Hank agreeing with what he was hearing decided that was just the right thing to do.

⚡

Marge was in a total state of despair; she was in state of total fear. She was too scared to even look Nolan in the eye. He was worse these days than he had ever been before. It didn't take anything for him to go off on her. Just night before last, he had sat with a rifle on her, daring her to move. He now had it in his mind that she was stepping out on him. That she was having an affair and of all people with Isaiah Brown, the black man that did odd jobs around town.

Isaiah had come by one day, wanting to know if Marge needed him to do anything for her. Maybe cut down some weeds or something like that. As he was leaving, Nolan saw him, and right then and there, he decided he was there to mess around with his wife. When Marge had tried to explain the reason he was there, Nolan declared that she was defending him, so they must be carrying on an affair.

Isaiah lived in a little shack with his mother, Lillie, about two quarters of a mile north of the Rollins' over in the colored section of Lone Oak. The colored folks hardly ever came close to the Rollins place because of Nolan's open hostility toward them. Instead, they would go around the bend about a mile to get to the West River Bridge and into town.

Going this way, they would bypass the Rollins' farm. Marge had a feeling there was going to be trouble. With Nolan drinking more of that moonshine, he was making—and the boys too—it was a total mess around her house. They all were staying up all night mostly drinking. She would cook, but they wouldn't eat. But if she didn't cook, Nolan would get angry and slap her around. For Marge everything was getting worse and worse; she never once imagined that things could get any worse than they were, but she was wrong. They were many times worse than they had ever been. She was so thankful that Cherish had gotten out of there. Although she missed her terribly, she was glad for her.

Marge was aware of the fact that Cherish had stayed with Mamie until the baby was born, and now she had a job over in Hugo and was living in the Old Patterson house. By no means was Nolan ever going to allow her to go to see her. Marge had never even laid eyes on her granddaughter but had heard she was a living doll; she longed to be able to see her.

Secretly she was making plans to go over into town and see her grandchild. Maybe one of those nights when Nolan and the boys were out at the barn all night, she would get a chance to sneak out to go and see Cherish and the baby.

⚡

Mamie was very sure that Rev. Fields was the man that God had sent to Evansville. This would be the best news the others would get this year. *Praise God!* There was a change coming. Although it had been years of trials and tribulations, it was now all about to turn around. Mamie had to keep encouraging the others over the years; she reminded them that gratification delayed did not mean gratification denied.

Sitting in her favorite chair, Mamie began to make the phone calls that everyone was waiting to hear.

"Bertha."

"Yeah?"

"This is Mamie. I went over to that new church today and talked with the new preacher. Girl, I believe that he truly is the one that we been waiting for."

"For real? You think so?"

"Yup, he is young, but he seems to be sincere. And let me tell you, since he been here, everything done come against him so hard he don't know which way to turn."

"Sounds like he the one," Bertha agreed. "If he weren't, the ole devil wouldn't be messing with him. He don't mess with that old Rev. Potter like that. He just let him do whatever he wants."

"Okay then, Bertha. I told him we will be at church in the morning. It starts at eleven o'clock."

"Girl, I hope I can find me something to wear. It's been so long since I actually went to church."

"You'll find something, I'm sure. Talk with ya later, and, Bertha, you call Dorothy, Esther, and Eunice."

"All right then, I will. Bye."

"Bye." Within seconds of the first call, Mamie was on the phone again. "Hello, Miss Whitaker, this is Mamie, and I got some good news…"

Mamie had started the ball rolling; Gabriel was well pleased. It was now time to pay a visit to the good Rev. Potter. Gabriel remembered a time when Rev. Potter had truly been on the side of the Lord. He hoped it might be that way again—soon.

⚡

It had started back about twenty-some years prior. Rev. Potter had been working very hard at bringing around revival into the small town of Evansville. He and Nathaniel Sims, the chairman of the deacon board, had put a plan into place to have a revival meeting. They were going to rent a huge tent and have an old-fashioned tent meeting. Two weeks before the meeting was to take place, Rev. Potter received a call from Norman, Oklahoma. His son, Jonathan, had been in an awful accident, and he needed to get there as soon as he could. It was the most devastating thing he could imagine. Jonathan was his and his wife's only child, a child that he had prayed for over fifteen years. When she found out she was expecting, it was the most joyous time of their lives. They praised God and rejoiced the whole term of the pregnancy. Jim Potter knew that God really did answer prayer, and he was determined to get the whole world saved. Jonathan had grown up to be a happy child with a very bright future.

Because of Jonathan's high academic achievements, he was given a full academic scholarship to the University of Oklahoma. Now to get the call that there was an accident, their hearts appeared to stand still. They drove the three and a half hours to Oklahoma City, to the University Hospital, where they were informed Jonathan had been taken. By the time they arrived, it was too late. "It was just a freak accident," the police officer was saying to the Potters. "Jonathan was sitting in the coffee shop across the street from campus, and this lady had parked her car and gotten out. Some way or another it jumped gear and went through the plate glass window and struck Jonathan as he sat there studying." After that dreadful day, Rev. Potter lost all interest in the work of God. He actually blamed God for Jonathan's death.

How could God allow that to happen? Why his son, the son he had prayed over fifteen years for? How could he get up and tell people how good God was when he didn't really believe it himself? Where was God when that car just mysteriously jumped gear? He determined that he would not make any special effort to reach the "lost." If he couldn't win the people by having normal routine church services, then that must mean that there were no souls to win. He would just continue to preach to the members that he currently had. Didn't the Bible say that sheep beget sheep? The shepherd didn't produce sheep; sheep produce sheep. It was the members' job to recruit new members, not his; and if none came, then so be it.

From that point on, Rev. Potter merely went through the motions; he didn't take his calling or the work of God serious anymore. Now it had just become a job. Besides that, he was now seventy-two years old. He didn't see the need in worrying himself about something that would never change. As long as the things that were going on were not affecting him, he would not be the one to have any effect on them.

XV

Azazel and Astaroth stood off at a distance under the cover of darkness, watching as Gabriel came out of the New Life Fellowship. They knew they could not go on the property; Gabriel's warriors had the place surrounded, standing guard over the house and the church. The spirits of discouragement, doubt, fear, and empathy had all came back to the office and reported how the Power's warriors came in, attacked their forces, and overran their positions.

Now it was in their hands; there was no way they could regain their advantage on that territory. They would have to wait until they could get one of the protected targets away from under the protection of the warriors and move in on them as an individual.

Right now, however, they had another job to do; they had to confront Gabriel. He was all alone and heading toward one of their most protected fortresses. *What was he thinking? Has he lost his mind?* They chuckled.

Gabriel was well aware of the two dark figures that were following him to Rev. Potter's house. They always thought they could sneak up on one of the warriors unaware. But their presence was something that always stood out.

Rev. Potter's house was close to the exit ramp off highway 281, close to the edge of town. What the two sons of darkness did not know was Uriel had a platoon stationed just out of sight at the entrance of the off-ramp coming into Evansville. Gabriel would lead these two valiant warriors, as they believed themselves to be, right into Ariel's and his platoons' hands.

Earlier that morning, Belial's meeting had, for all intents and purposes, appeared to be productive for the Company. Mastema had brought in the report on Rachael Sims that Belial had asked for. Apparently, as a child she had attended church with her grandmother on her mother's side. But after her mother had died at the age of forty-nine from a complication of Graves' disease, she and her grandmother had pretty much given up on God and religion. She had not set foot in a church other than to attend a funeral in over eight years, and as far as her ever praying, there were none recorded anywhere. Belial felt that she was pretty safe.

After that many years, she would have no clue on what to do if she had to, and if she did decide to say a prayer, one of his boys could always intercept it. All it took was for a person to halfheartedly pray for the prayer to be intercepted by one of the workers. Then the person will soon lose faith and will disregard prayer as a mighty weapon. If humans only understood that if they would just stand firm on faith, anything they wanted they could get. But if he and his crew could interfere and cause doubt and unbelief, answers could be delayed and often cancelled—not by his crew, but by the person themselves. It never failed; if a prayer is not answered in the time limit that the person has set, they will doubt the existence and faithfulness of God and cancel out their own request.

"We do have a serious situation here," Belial had told all the workers of darkness during the meeting. "It seems as though there is now a full crew of the Power in town. It is very hard to fight them when they are fully armed. So it is our job to weaken their defenses and deplete their ammunition."

"How do we do that, boss?" Mastema questioned. It was important that he understand exactly what needed to be done. If he could show the bosses that he was a capable warrior, then he could possibly replace Jesse as the territorial leader when this little battle was over. Jesse had allowed things to get bad. He, in turn, had to be instrumental in turning things around.

"The secret to their strength and power is prayer!" Just speaking the word "prayer" made Belial sick. If they had any chance of defeating these mighty warriors, the crew had to know what they were up against and put plans into action that would stop the Power's mighty warriors from obtaining the power required to defeat them.

"Prayer?" Mastema questioned again. "If they are praying, then they get power?"

"Not them praying, you idiot. The prayers of people."

Belial's sharp rebuke cut deep into Mastema. He felt instant anger; he would find a way to get even with Belial for his insulting him in front of everybody. He was not going to allow him to degrade him like that and get away with it.

"If these people start to get worried and begin to pray, their prayers bring power and energy to the angels, making them an unbeatable foe. That is why we have to make sure that the people do not pray," Astaroth explained.

"How do we stop the people from praying? They could be praying in their heads and we wouldn't know it," Azazel wanted to know. Azazel's job was to make sure that all the workers were where they were supposed to be, doing what they were assigned to do.

"We don't know if they are praying in their heads," Belial replied, scratching the side of his head with a look of bewilderment on his face. "We have got to devise a plan to make sure that they do not pray secretly, openly, alone, or with others."

"It multiplies their power one hundred times if two or three people pray together," Astaroth informed the group.

"How long does this power last?" the question was raised from the floor.

"It depends on how strong the prayer was. If it was just a short, quick prayer, it will energize a minimal number of warriors. They would get a burst of energy that will last only a short time. But if it is a strong, heartfelt prayer, it could energize several dozen of warriors and last for hours. But if a group of people are praying at the same time, it could energize hundreds of warriors and last for days," Belial reluctantly admitted to the group.

"We have to make sure that the people *do not pray!* If the warriors have no power, they cannot stop or hinder what we are doing. All they can do is stand around and watch. Without prayer, they are rendered helpless."

Approaching Rev. Potter's house, Gabriel began to feel his power beginning to fade out. *This is not good,* he thought. He knew that he would have to postpone this encounter for now. If he continued in his present state, it could be a terrible loss. He had just enough power left to ascend back to the church in a state of formlessness and go undetected.

"Where did he go?" Azazel blurted out.

"I don't know, but he can't be far. He was just here a second ago," Astaroth replied. "Come on, we will find him."

The power of the mighty forces was dwindling quickly. Michael and the other leaders knew that something had to be done. It was not a surprise to Michael that the power of prayer was weak in the town. It was the way it had been the whole time. There would be a quick spurt of energy, and then it was gone. It may not return for hours or sometimes days later. All they could do now was to wait. They did not have the means of convincing the people, or volunteers as they were known, to pray. That was a personal choice, a decision that had to be made by the individual.

A cold, dreary feeling could be felt throughout the town, an eeriness that the warriors knew all too well; there were major demonic activities taking place. The town was being held hostage unaware by forces of evil. Evil that would, if not stopped, succeed in catapulting a catastrophic plan onto the whole of the earth, a plan that had been devised from the beginning that would destroy man and dishonor God.

Hugo was a small community, but compared to Evansville, it could still be classified as a city. With a population of 6,000 residents, it was three times the size of Evansville.

Now where would those no-account Rollins boys be? Hank thought to himself as he drove through the business district of Hugo. *Wherever it was, you could bet it was a sleazy little place for low lives. Did these idiots know how important it was to have the product ready when Manny got there tomorrow?*

He should have known when he first started with them that they were not dependable. They had never worked in their lives. They had just sat around and waited on the handouts from the state to survive. But Hank had actually believed if they were making money doing what they did everyday; it wouldn't be hard to get them to do it on a larger scale.

After driving around for over thirty minutes, Hank finally saw a sign, The Silver Dollar. This place didn't really look too bad; it had a nice exterior. He would try there anyway. Just maybe the boys had stepped up their places to hang out. He parked his car and started to the entrance where a man stood, ready to receive and inspect his identification to make sure he was legal.

The room was dimly lit; it was so dark, it was hard to actually identify anyone in this place. Taking a seat at the bar, Hank ordered a Bud Light. He surveyed the room for any sign of the Rollins. After about ten minutes, he heard the unmistakable voice of Brent Rollins yelping like a cowboy on a bucking horse. He made his way toward the area where the sound had come from.

Samuel and Brent Rollins were seated in a far back booth with two women that were there only for the money that the two boys were throwing around.

The four people sitting there were totally intoxicated with strong intentions of consuming much more. One could tell that the evening was far from over for the Rollins and their two accomplices.

"Hey there, Brent, Samuel," Hank announced as he walked to the booth.

"What's up, Hank?" Brent Rollins yelled out, obviously drunk. "This here is Hank Wilson. He is our business partner."

Hank showed an expression of disgust at that statement. *What have these fools said to people? How much information had they revealed and to whom?* Hank wondered. He had to get them out of there and now.

"That's one of the reasons I'm here. You boys know we have a big day tomorrow. Our marketing manager will be here in the morning to inspect our manufacturing and production."

"Oh, sit down, Hank. Have a little fun. We can't have all work and no play," Samuel said. "That makes Sam a very unhappy boy."

"No, I really need to get back to Evansville. I have some things to do before morning. And I suggest that you boys head that way pretty soon yourselves."

"Oh," the young blond, who was sitting so close to Samuel Rollins that she was practically in his lap, said with a feigned pout on her face. "Is my little oopsey poopsey gonna leave? I thought we were going to go to my place and the four of us was gonna have some fun."

Showing the woman that he was in control and that no

one was going to tell him what to do, Samuel stood up face-to-face with Hank and sneered.

"Look, you can't tell us when and where we better be. We will be back in Evansville when we get good and ready and not before. You got that, Hank? Now either you sit here and enjoy yourself with us or you get going, but you don't tell us what to do."

Hank knew it was no use attempting to talk to these boys. First of all, they were drunk; second, they didn't take to anyone telling them what to do. Hank knew from firsthand observation how when they got riled how mean and ornery they could become. It was best if he just left.

⚡

Driving back to Evansville, Hank had mixed feelings of anger and of fear; he was angry because of the lack of concern shown by the Rollins clan and afraid of what Manny would say when he got there tomorrow and the stuff was not ready for shipment.

Although he had never had a serious confrontation with Manny, Hank could sense that this was not somebody you would want to cross. It was something about the way he carried himself that let you know "Do not mess with me if you know what is good for you." A feeling of regret was trying to creep into Hank's emotions. He was actually beginning to wonder if this was truly such a good thing after all.

Manny had told Hank at the onset of their partnership that he had discovered a new ingredient to add to the moonshine. He had explained to Hank how everybody was on the energy kick bandwagon. There were all types of energy drinks out there on the market, and people were buying them by the truckloads. Manny had said that the new ingredient was a form of high-power nutrient that would help boost energy. When it was added to the moonshine, people would feel so good that they would want to continue to purchase the Rollins Royale because of the boost it gave them.

So far, this had actually proven to be true; people were buying the stuff like crazy. Of course, he had never divulged this secret to the Rollins, because he didn't want them to start getting greedy and wanting a bigger cut of the profit. He just told them that the bottlers had come up with some premixed mash that would make it easier on them. Right now, the Rollins Royale was selling for thirty dollars a fifth, and it was not unusual for people to buy three and four fifths a day, every day. This was a very profitable enterprise for Hank, the Rollins, and Jack Sims, and of course Manny.

XVI

It was getting very close to time to go into the office; Hank had just finished his usual breakfast of Grape Nuts and toast. This was going to be a busy day; he had to go over the weekly reports and get them filed in the court clerk's office. He had to check and see if there were any outstanding warrants that needed to be served as well as meet with the council. He was trying to get more funds loosed up for the jail. Then he had to be out at the Rollins place at two o'clock to meet Manny. He didn't know how he was going to manage to get all of those things done and make it to the Rollins' on time. He was still concerned whether the Rollins boys made it in last night. From the impression that he had gotten from them, it did not appear that they had any intention of leaving Hugo that night. This could have dire circumstances for them as well as himself. Manny was a businessman, a professional, and he did not like things run haphazard. Before going into the office, Hank thought it a good idea to stop by the One

Stop and have a chat with Jack just to make sure everything was going good on his end.

"Good morning, Sheriff," Michelle, the new clerk that Jack had hired, said as Hank came into the One Stop.

"Good morning, Michelle. How is everything going?"

"Just fine, Sheriff. Can I get something for you? A cup of coffee maybe?"

"A cup of coffee would be fine—light and sweet. Say, Michelle, is Jack here yet?" Hank asked after looking around without seeing him.

"No, I believe he may have a touch of something, maybe that bug that is going around, because he hasn't been in here for a few days. Mrs. Sims has been coming in. She said he hasn't been feeling well."

"Oh, I hope it isn't something serious," Hank tried to sound concerned. *Oh, that is just great,* Hank thought. *Now he is sick or something. That's all I need. Manny coming in today, the Rollins boys off laying up in Hugo, and now Jack's got some kind of mysterious illness*! Hank paid Michelle for the coffee and started toward the door.

"Have a good day, Sheriff," Michelle called to him.

"You too. See ya."

Leaving the One Stop, Hank made his way to the city hall. Mabel was busy typing as if there was no tomorrow. Harvey was standing beside her with some papers that he needed typed right then. His deputy, Carey Mathers, was sitting at the desk next to his office door in deep concentration as he was filling out what appeared to be a police report. This was more activity than Hank had witnessed in this office in a long time. Matter of fact, he couldn't remember a time that he actually had seen this much activity.

"Well, good morning, everybody," Hank said, announcing his presence.

"Oh, there you are," Harve replied. "We've been wondering where you were."

"Wondering about me?" Hank looked at his watch and then reconfirmed its accuracy with the clock on the wall. "It's just nine. I'm not late."

"It's not that you're late, but we were looking for you most of the night," Mabel piped in.

"I went over to Hugo last night. I had some business to attend to. Why?"

"All hell broke loose here last night," Carey said. "But Randy and I handled it. Matter of fact, Randy is out now getting more statements."

"What kind of hell?" Hank wanted to know.

"Well, let's see," Mabel, grabbing papers off her desk, began to read. "At eleven o'clock, Lenny Mason of Lenny's Alibi called 911 because Terry Stevens went berserk and tore up the place, but not before he stabbed Wilma Rogers with a broken bottle. She is in the hospital over in Hugo, and he is locked up downstairs. Then," she continued, "Mrs. Whitaker phoned in about fifteen minutes later and said that there was somebody trying to get in her front door. Randy went over there and found Lewis Walker stumbling around her house. He had gotten to the back, had a brick in his hand, and was just getting ready to throw it into the kitchen window when Randy told him to drop the brick. He turned to throw it at Randy. In turn, Randy pulled his service revolver and shot him in the hand, but that still didn't stop him. He started to run, and Randy had to give chase and tackle him. He also ended up going to the hospital. They sewed him up, and he is downstairs. Then to make matters worse, after we had those two incidences under control, we got a call from the state police. There had been a car wreck right off the highway. Mitchell Warren and Sammy Jones were both killed. They had appeared to be drinking and driving. It truly was a night from hell."

"Terry Stevens, Lewis Walker... What on earth got into them?"

"Don't know, Sheriff, but whatever it was, it wasn't nice," Carey answered. "And Mrs. Whitaker, she is scared to death. You know, her being old and all."

"Yes, I can imagine she is. But I cannot believe that Lewis and Terry would be acting like that." Thinking about what he had just heard, Hank was wondering what could have caused Lewis and Terry to behave in that way. It was totally out of character for both of them.

"I will go over and talk with Mrs. Whitaker and Lenny myself. Call me if you need me."

There was so much going on that day, it was going to be hard for him to break away and meet Manny at the Rollins; he would give him a call and explain things to him and let him know he would not be able to be there and hoped that he would understand.

Azazel was very proud of what was happening. Now this would get people to talking and worrying. They would be so caught up in what was going on in town that they would forget all about praying. Phase one of operation shutdown was going as planned; now it was time to move on to part two.

⚡

The activities of the night before had spread through the town at rapid speed. Everyone already knew what had taken place at Lenny's, Mrs. Whitaker's, and the wreck on the highway. People were calling around, expressing shock and disbelief about the occurrences. No one could believe that Lewis Walker and Terry Stevens could have acted in such a manner, and wasn't it a shame about Mitchell and Sammy? What on earth were their families going to do now?

Older ladies were scared to death. If that could happen to Mrs. Whitaker, it could happen to any of them. Of course, they caught the perpetrator, but if those men could act that way, then anybody could.

There had not been excitement of this nature since they found that girl murdered over by the West River almost twenty years ago. What could happen next?

⚡

Rachael was washing the breakfast dishes. Although she was trying to maintain, she had so much on her mind that she felt as though she was going to lose it at any minute. There was something terribly wrong. Jack had started to get frightfully paranoid; he imagined that there were people out to get him, that there was a conspiracy of some kind. Big people in high places were scoping out their house. He believed that they were under constant surveillance. He was refusing to go outside. He was not eating because he said somebody was putting poison in all of his food. Last night had been a nightmare. He heard the sirens going around the town, and he knew they were coming after him. He ran and hid in the basement.

It was so bad that Rachael was afraid to sleep. She didn't know whether he would start hallucinating and try to hurt her and Lucas. She had taken all of the guns and hid them up in the attic. She knew that was a safe place, because he had barricaded the attic door in case the enemy tried to sneak in that way. She didn't know what to do. She had thought about sneaking out and going back home to Dallas, but she decided that Jack was sick and she needed to be there with him. She was determined to make an appointment and get him in to see a doctor, but she didn't know how she could manage to do that. He would never volunteer to seek medical help. But she had to do something; she couldn't live like this. The tears were flowing down her face as she stood in front of the sink. She was afraid, tired, and bewildered.

"Rachael, is that door locked?" Jack busted into the kitchen and questioned.

"Yes, Jack, it's locked."

Jack was going from window to door, shaking and checking to make sure they were locked. Rachael knew she had to keep up some type of outward appearance at normalcy so she calmly stated, "Jack, I will be gone for a while today. I need to go and check on the things at the store. I need to take an inventory and place orders."

"Place orders, place orders. What are you ordering, Rachael? What is it that you want?"

"I don't want anything, Jack. If we don't order things for the store, we won't have anything to sell and the store will go broke."

"Is that what they are telling you? Is that what they are making you believe? They just want to turn you against me too. There is nothing broke."

"No, Jack, it's not broke, but we have to make sure that it doesn't get that way. We have to keep the store well-stocked or *we* will be broke." She was trying with everything in her to reason with Jack to get him to at least understand from a financial standpoint. Money was the one thing that Jack held in the highest esteem, and if she could get him to understand that he was not going to have any if she didn't go to the store, maybe he would calm down.

Jack had turned his attention to something else. While she was speaking, he was looking under the sink, in the breadbox, and the cabinets, searching and searching.

"Jack?" Rachel called to him. "Will you be all right while I'm at the store? Do you need me to bring you home anything?"

Ignoring her, Jack continued to fanatically search. "Where is my bottle of Royale? Damn it, where is my bottle?"

"I guess you must have drunk it, Jack. But I'll bring you another one from the store, all right?"

"Yeah, you do that. Bring me two. And I want them now. Do you hear me? *Now!*"

Rachael quickly grabbed Lucas by the hand and started out the door. Jack was drinking more and more. Most people that drank that much eventually would pass out. Jack seemed to just keep going and going, never sleeping or eating. He just wandered throughout the house, going from one subject to the next. What was she going to do? Who could she talk to? Where could she go for help?

As she came through the back door of the store, Rachael saw Sheriff Wilson leaving the store. She wondered if he knew anything. But how could he? Jack had not been out of the house for days. Nobody knew what kind of shape he was in, and she had too much pride to air her dirty laundry in public, especially this public. She would get help, but it would be far away from here, and when Jack got better, nobody in this stupid little town would be any the wiser.

"Good morning, Michelle," Rachael greeted the clerk in as happy a tone as she could muster up.

"Good morning, Mrs. Sims. How are you today?"

"I'm good. Thanks."

Michelle prided herself on knowing all the latest happenings in town, and any opportunity she had to share, she didn't hesitate.

"Guess you heard about last night?"

"No," Rachael said as she pretended to study the inventory list and make notes. "What about last night?"

This was all the opening needed; Michelle began to relate all the happenings of the night before as Rachael stood and listened intently. Rachael knew all the people involved from their dealings with her in the store. She was in a true state of shock. Just listening to Michelle talk about Terry Stevens at Lenny's bar, about Mrs. Whitaker and Lewis Walker, she couldn't help but think about Jack and his bazaar behavior of late. She wondered if either of these men showed any signs before they went on their little rampages. She expressed deep sympathy for the wives and families of the two men that had died in the wreck. Michelle had said that they both were young—only in their early to mid-thirties.

That explained all the sirens last night, Rachael reasoned. It was the sirens that had Jack pacing the floor like a caged lion. He had envisioned them coming after him, and as they got close to the house, Jack was so scared he had taken refuge in the basement. But Rachael knew now that they were going over to Mrs. Whitaker's. Maybe when she got home, she could tell Jack about what happened and then reassure him that no one was after him. This may help him to come back into a state of reality.

⚡

Cherish did not know about any of the events of the previous night until she arrived at work. While she had been caring for Wilma Rogers, she had learned the gory details of the events that had occurred at Lenny's Alibi. Lenny's had always been a little rowdy, but Cherish could never remember a time that there was any real trouble there. And just to think that Terry Stevens had gone nuts and tore the place up. Wilma was a waitress at Lenny's; Cherish listened intensely as she related the events of the night before. She said that Terry had gotten really mad when Lenny refused to sell him another drink. He had been sitting in a back booth talking to himself most of the evening. Then he had gotten up and started going from table to table, trying to get people to buy him another drink. When they ignored him or flatly said no, he had gotten very obnoxious and vulgar. He had even propositioned a woman that was there with what he could do for her if she would buy him a drink.

"Are you sure you are talking about Terry Stevens?" Cherish asked in a disbelieving tone of voice.

"Yes, believe me it was Terry Stevens!" Wilma replied.

She was reliving the night as if it were a scene in a movie as she continued. Lenny had gotten fed up with the way Terry was acting; he went and told him it was time for him to leave, and if he refused, he was going to call the cops.

That was when, pausing slightly as if it the image was too horrible to remember Wilma continued, that he really got stupid. He knocked over two tables, picked up an empty glass, threw it, and broke the glass clock over by the pool table. He then broke a longneck beer bottle, got up on a table, was swinging the broken bottle, yelling something about "Can't nobody stop me. I'm the king."

Cherish sat motionless next to Wilma's bed watching the obvious pain and sheer terror on her face as she continued her story.

Wilma remembered she had tried to go around the table to get to the bar, when Terry jumped off the table grabbed her around the neck and told everybody to freeze. He said if anybody moved, he'd cut her. She had never been so scared she felt so helpless. She didn't know what to do. Lenny then made a move like he was going to tackle Terry. That is when Terry stabbed Wilma in the stomach. Things happened so fast after that, it was hard for Wilma to say what happened next. The best she could remember was that some guys managed to get behind Terry and hit him with a pool stick.

When he fell, they pinned him to the floor. Thelma, the other waitress, had already called the sheriff. She then called for an ambulance to get Wilma to the hospital. Wilma told

Cherish that she had never been so afraid in her life. She just knew she was going to die and there would be no body to take care of her two kids. She said all she could do was pray, "God, don't let me die."

Wilma had to have emergency surgery after arriving at the hospital; the bottle had cut deep into the abdominal cavity, just missing the pancreas, and she was bleeding internally.

After about two hours, the surgeon said she would be fine, but there would be a nasty scar. He felt she would be able to go home in a day or two *if* there were no complications.

Listening to Wilma's story, Cherish really couldn't understand what was going on with Terry. She had known Terry most of her life, as he was two years older than she was, and he always appeared to be an okay person. People used to think he was gay because he never seemed to show any interest in girls; he was typically a very quite and shy person. It just wasn't making much sense to Cherish. She decided to put those thoughts aside for now and focus on the rest of her patients.

Cherish was anxious for her shift to end at three and begin her weekend off. She had to get home, pick up Hope from Mamie's, and then prepare for Sunday. She would get Mamie to take them over into Hugo and pick out a Sunday dress for herself and one for Hope. This was going to be a whole new experience for her. There really had not been any reason before to get a fancy dress for Hope. It was only since she had been around Mamie that she had learned so much about the Bible, but she had never attended a church service before, and she was a little apprehensive about what to expect at church.

XVII

Michael, Uriel, Gabriel, and Ariel were sitting in the back of the sanctuary, going over what had taken place in the last few days. Gabriel related his experience on the night before last as he was en route to the Rev. Potter's house. Things were coming to the boiling point. The Company had stepped up their defenses, and it was becoming evident that they were worried. The Powers knew that when they became nervous, they made many mistakes. But also when they got nervous, they could cause major havoc.

The incidents at Lenny's, Mrs. Whitaker's, and the highway were, they knew, just the beginning of the things and events. They would start to implement more schemes that could prove dangerous and lengthy.

"We have to be very careful right now," Michael was speaking. "The Company will do whatever they can to stop our volunteers and devoted followers from praying. We have already learned that the prayers in this place are inconsistent, to say the least. There is a time that prayers are frequent and strong; then they dwindle down to barely anything."

"We have our warriors in good number around the Rev. Fields and Mamie. We know that they are on our side. There are some others, but we know that Mamie and Rev. Fields are the strongest, the leaders of this army. We have to keep them protected at all cost. It is through them that this battle will be won or lost," Uriel stated.

"True, in all actuality, Mamie was the one person that started this war. It was she that has been praying and praying for years. It was because of her relentless praying that the Rev. Fields was commissioned here. Of course, he has no idea that is why, but before it is all over, he will come to realize that Mamie is the strongest ally that he has in this place." Michael shared with the group, "It is of the uttermost importance that we keep her lifted up and well protected."

"Knowing Belial and his crew, they will stop at nothing to defeat us and destroy the people of this town. If they ever get smart enough to figure out that Mamie is as big a danger to their kingdom as she is, there is no telling what they will attempt to do to her," Ariel remarked.

"Raphael, have your warriors be especially mindful of the spirits of illness and disease. That will be the first line of attack they will send out against Mamie. They know she is getting along in years, and they will think that any little ailment will render her defenseless," Michael instructed.

"How is our energy level?" Michael wanted to know.

"I have gained back a lot of mine," Gabriel informed his leader, "but one can never know here. I believe that once things begin to heat up, the more prayers will continue to flow, giving us the needed edge that we will need to go forth. I am not really worried too much right now. It is when the full-fledged war begins that I will be worried."

"Do you think, Michael, that this is going to lead to the final battle, the one that will be fought to bind Satan and his evil forces into the abyss?" Ariel asked.

"I don't know. I know that the trumpet has not sounded yet. That will be the sound that will bring about our ultimate victory. At that time, every warrior in heaven will descend upon the earth and wage war with the forces of darkness. I will get the privilege of casting that old dragon into the lake of fire. That shall be a glorious day."

"It's the evil one's desire to take over the world with this scheme; it very well could be the beginning of the tribulation," Gabriel spoke up and said.

"Yes, that is his desire. Every scheme he has started from the beginning had the ultimate goal of taking over the world. But they have all been foiled, rendered null and void over the centuries. We will just have to wait and see where this one is leading. When the Divine Master gives us the signal, we will know what to do. For now let us just get ready to fight this battle as we always have and leave the rest to the Father," Michael directed.

⚡

Today was a good day, Mamie was thinking to herself. She had a strong feeling of satisfaction rising within her. She felt that everything was going to be all right, no matter what happened. She had the assurance that God was in total control of everything. She was busy cleaning her house, singing an old hymn she had known most of her life. It was this song that gave her the biggest peace she could have even when things were at their darkest, a song that had helped carry her through when her husband and sons had been killed in the mine, when her two daughters died, and that terrible ordeal with her youngest son. It was this song that kept faith alive within her—"The Lord Will Make a Way Somehow." Mamie's routine was interrupted by the ringing of the telephone.

"Hello," she answered.

"Hi, Mamie, this is Bertha."

"Oh, hi, Bertha. How are you?"

"I'm fine. I was calling you about what is happening in this place. Did you hear about everything that happened last night?"

"No, what happened?"

Bertha began to relate the events that had unfolded on the previous night. Mamie was totally taken aback by all the information. The whole thing was terrible, but the part about Mrs. Whitaker was very disturbing. Mrs. Whitaker was a very strong prayer warrior, and the news let her know that the forces of evil had put her under attack. Mamie was in deep thought as Bertha was continuing with her conversation.

"I don't know what is happening here, three tragic events in one night. That is totally unreal. We really need to get on our job and get some focused prayer going up in this place. The devil is running rampant in this town," she was saying.

"You are so right, Bertha. This is only the beginning. It will get worse and worse unless we stand up and take our positions of authority. We need to storm the gates of heaven and ask God to intervene on our behalf. Did you let everybody know about church Sunday?"

"Sure did. I have phoned everybody that you told me to. Plus, I called Mildred Wilson and Helen Robertson and told them. I know they used to go to church with Rev. Moore for a while. I don't know if they will come or not, but at least I told them."

"That is great, if we can get enough interested people to work on the side of the Lord, then we will be able to turn this place around. With enough prayers of petition going up, the Lord will right all of the wrongs that ever have been and are now being committed in Evansville. There is something very evil taking over here and it has got to be stopped."

⚡

Manny was wrapping up some loose ends in Dallas before he headed over to Evansville. It was about an hour and a half drive. He was going to have to leave at least by twelve thirty in order to be there by two. He had gotten a call this morning from that Barney Fife, Sheriff Hank Wilson, saying there were some things that he had to attend to and he would not be able to be at the meeting today. He had sounded a little evasive, like something was not quite kosher. It caused Manny a little concern, but he was sure that it was not something he and his boys wouldn't be able to handle. He was not going to allow a group of inbred country hicks to jeopardize the operation. He had too much at stake to allow that to happen. It was the biggest thing he had ever undertaken, and he was determined that it was going to succeed, no matter what it took or who got hurt in the process.

Nolan Rollins was doing what he did best—nothing. The boys had not gotten in yet, but he was not going to go out there and do all the work by himself. He was going to wait. He wasn't afraid of that small-time thug out of Dallas. He wasn't going to come in here and tell him what he had to do. Nolan didn't care what he and his company were providing him. The mash wouldn't do any good if they didn't know how to make the corn. Nolan had to admit that the stuff was pretty good; he wasn't sure what the mash had in it, but it made the corn taste really good. The boys had said that it was the talk of the town. Everybody was bragging on it, and it was even in some bars around. *If this Manny got too high and mighty,* Nolan thought to himself, *he would just stop messing with him and make his own stuff. That way he wouldn't have to give a cut to anyone including that lowlife Hank Wilson.*

"Marge," Nolan yelled, "get out here."

Marge reluctantly stopped making the bed and went out on the porch to see what Nolan wanted.

"What ya need, Nolan?" she asked as she went to the porch.

"Why ain't you already cleaned out that mash bin?" Nolan asked with a tone of authority.

"I was goin' to as soon as I get through makin' the bed."

Nolan never liked it when Marge would come back at him with a strong will. She was supposed to do what he said, when he said, and how he said. *What gave her the idea that she could sass him? Hadn't she learned by now?*

"You get out there and get that done now, woman," Nolan

demanded. "Manny will be here today, and I don't want him to think that we're nasty."

"Okay, I'll go now," she meekly replied as she stepped off the porch and started toward the barn.

The smell of alcohol was strong in the barn, a smell that Marge hated. Just smelling the alcohol brought memories to her mind, memories of abuse and mistreatment. Cleaning out the mash bin and filling it was hard work; the bags of premix weighed over sixty pounds each. Straining to lift the bags caused a sharp pain to shoot across her back. The pain was so sharp that she lost her breath. Tears began to well up in her eyes; she just couldn't keep living like this. She had to get away and soon. There was desperation in her that she had never felt before.

With an unknown strength, Marge managed to lift the heavy bag of mash and get it emptied into the bin to begin the process of fermentation. It was almost as if somebody was helping her to lift the bag. She knew it was extremely heavy, but she lifted it without effort, even with the shooting pain across her back.

⚡

The barn was clean of spirits that morning. Some were off following after Brent and Samuel. Some were laying around in the yard. Others were chattering around the chair in which Nolan was sitting. Jesse was preoccupied with his own fate. So it wasn't hard for Michael to get into the barn without being noticed. Even if he had been seen, he and his warriors had enough power to defeat the little imps at the Rollins. But now was not the time to be discovered in this area. There still were plans to be implemented before that could happen. If Belial found out he and his crew were there, a major battle would break out before the cleanup plan was put into place. Michael had to use extreme caution.

Michael took a look around the old barn. Four stills were in full operation. He knew the dangers that had always been involved with the making and distributing of illegal whiskey. But there was something different about this operation—something more sinister, something more ominous than the people knew. This was a deadly mixture, a mixture that would prove disastrous for all those who drank it. He and his crew would have to make sure that this stuff did not get into the hands of unsuspecting people.

⚡

Getting out of the car, Manny took special care not to step in any chicken droppings. He made that mistake the last time he was there, something that he found totally disgusting. He had literally thrown away a pair of three hundred dollar shoes because of it.

Looking around the property, Manny surveyed the barn, the yard, and the house. Nolan Rollins was sitting on the porch, rocking, a large plug of tobacco in his cheek.

"Rollins," Manny greeted.

"Manny," was Nolan's reply as he spat tobacco juice over the railings to his left, unlike when he spit at Hank Wilson's feet. Nolan thought better of that with Manny. He was feeling quite smug today; after all, he was in control here. It was his property, his still, and his corn. If Manny had a problem with the way he was running his place, then Mr. Lopez could just go and find somebody else to do his bidding. Nolan was not the person that was going to take a lot of orders from anybody and especially not this Al Capone wannabe.

"Is everything going okay?" Manny asked Rollins in a condescending voice.

"Just fine," Nolan answered.

"The boys working in the barn, are they?"

"Nope, they ain't here right now."

"Oh, is that right?" Manny asked, looking over at Jason, his bodyguard and sidekick. "And just where might they be this warm fine day?"

"They went over into Hugo. They had something to tend to."

"Oh, I see. Then the stuff must be ready to ship. I know they would not have left and it wasn't ready."

"Yup, there is some ready for shipping. Let's go out to the barn, and I'll show you."

Nolan leisurely got up and started to the barn. About halfway he turned to Manny, "You best have that guy that does the driving to pull up here to the barn so we can load it in the trunk."

Anger began to swell up in Manny when he heard those words.

"What do you mean so we can load it in the trunk?"

"Well, you want to take it, don't ya? Oh, and by the way, I decided that the price is going up. I think that with us doing all the work and all, we need to charge more—let's say nine hundred dollars a barrel."

Manny and Jason both broke out into a loud laughter.

"You decided?" Manny mocked. "Did you hear that, Jason? Mr. Rollins decided that they need to charge more."

Inside the barn all Manny saw was two barrels sitting on the ground next to the still. Manny turned to Nolan with anger seething from his entire being.

"Look, Rollins, I told you once before; you don't cross me. You don't decide anything. I do all the deciding around here. Where is the merchandise? I came here expecting a truckload of whiskey, and you have the audacity to show me two measly barrels! Jason!"

Acting on Manny's command, Jason grabbed Nolan by his neck, pushed him up against the wall, and began to hit him repeatedly in the stomach. After hitting him several times, he turned him a loose. Nolan, falling to the floor, holding his neck, and gasping for breath, was powerless to fight back as a booted foot came toward his face, sending him backward onto the ground. Wiping the blood onto his sleeve that was coming from the right corner of his mouth, Nolan staggered to his feet. Manny, holding a hand to Jason as a sign of stopping, informed Nolan, "Now, Mr. Rollins, I will tell you again; I want my stuff, and I want it on time. If at any time I feel that you or your boys are trying to get to me, there will be more of this. Do you understand?"

"Yes," was all that Nolan could say. He had excruciating pain in his abdomen and head. His mouth was burning from the cut to his lip, and there was a throbbing pain in his right eye.

"Good, I will be back here Sunday *at* four o'clock, and I expect to find a truckload of whiskey ready to be shipped. Do you hear me? And about your boys...you better inform them not to try to be heroes or they could come up missing, *never* to be found again."

Manny and Jason left the barn and walked back to the waiting car. Jason took a handkerchief that he has taken from Nolan's overall pocket, wiped his hands, and threw it on the ground.

The little imps were gaily chattering around and around the barn. This was exactly the kind of situations they enjoyed; this was their kind of action. The imp of retaliation quickly started talking to Nolan. "Who does that Manny think he is? Doesn't he know that this incident won't be taken lightly? If he keeps messing with you and your boys, doesn't he know that he will find himself dead and buried in a place that no one will ever find his body? Oh no, this is not going to happen. Not here, not now, not with the Rollins."

Nolan went toward the house, nursing his wounds. He was in a mood for sure. Marge was peeking out of the window, watching the events that took place. Although she was unable to see inside the barn, she knew whatever happened in there was not good. She also knew that when Nolan got to the house, she could possibly be in for trouble.

She tried to make herself busy, hoping that Nolan would be so preoccupied with his own problems that he would not take notice of her. She would make sure she was in a different part of the house where she would be safe.

The longer she could avoid him, the more time he would have to cool off and forget about her. As she watched him coming closer to the house, she could see that his lip had blood on it and the right side of his face was red and swollen.

"Oh my goodness," she gasped. This was not good at all. He was really going to be angry now. Just because he was helpless with Manny and his goon, he wouldn't be helpless with her. She would be the one that was *totally* helpless. She looked around the room, trying to find some type of weapon to use in self-defense. She could tell that it was going to be a bad situation. She was subject to get hurt worse than she had ever been hurt before. He would take out all of his anger and frustration on her—his anger at himself and his anger at Manny. He would be frustrated because he felt defenseless with Manny, and now he had to make himself *feel* like a man again.

XVIII

Now that the children had eaten breakfast, it was time for Sherri to begin getting them ready for church. She was so happy this morning. She had not seen Phillip this excited in a long time. She couldn't do anything but thank God that things were beginning to turn around in his ministry and in their lives. She knew that everything was working out in God's timing. Her father's visit a few weeks ago had seemed to help encourage Phillip somewhat. It wasn't until his visit with Mamie a couple of days before that he had really started to show a difference in attitude. However, in the back of her mind, she was a little worried. *What if Mamie truly was mental and everything she had told him was just a figment of her imagination?* Instantly she dismissed that thought because if it was God's will, nothing could stop it.

Standing in front of the mirror, Phillip was making sure that his tie was tied properly and going over his sermon in his mind. He had a feeling of apprehension. He had not been this nervous since he had left seminary. He had spent hours the night before studying and asking God what he was to talk about today. He had finally settled on the topic of faith. Faith was always a good topic; the Bible said without faith, it is impossible to please God. Satisfied with his reflection, Phillip gathered up his Bible and notes and headed to the church. He would go straight to the office and do some last-minute preparation before service time. This was going to be a true test of his ability and calling.

He figured there would not be that many people there today, but at least there would be more than just Sherri, the kids, and himself. If there were two or three, that would be good. Two or three could go out and tell two or three more, and before he knew, there would be a decent size congregation. At any rate, the number of people that were or were not there he would leave up to the Lord. It was his job to bring hope faith and inspiration to the people from the Word of God; it was God's job to send them.

Sitting behind his desk, Phillip's concentration was suddenly broken with the sound of singing. It was some of the most beautiful singing he had heard. *Sherri must have gotten a new praise and worship CD,* he thought. But listening, he could tell that something was different. There was no music with this CD.

The singing was acappella, and these were live voices coming from the sanctuary. Deciding now was the time to make his appearance; he got up with notes and Bible in hand and entered the sanctuary. What he saw took him aback.

Sitting in the sanctuary were thirty-five people. He had believed that Mamie would call a couple of her friends and there would be three, maybe four black people there. What he found was a congregation made up of both black and white, male and female, young and old. Tears of joy began to well up in his eyes; Sherri and the kids were sitting on the front row, and she met him with a smile of sheer delight.

Phillip began his message by first thanking the people for being there then offering a prayer for guidance. He then began his message on faith. The more he tried to preach about faith, the more he struggled and the more the Scripture from Daniel kept coming up in his mind. Before he knew it, he was preaching on the power of prayer and a battle between the prince of Persia and the archangel, Michael.

Mamie was extremely pleased, listening to this young man exhort on the power of prayer and the forces of evil. *Yes, Lord, he is the one*, she thought to herself. Now that it was confirmed to her, she knew there were some things that he needed to know about Evansville and the people in it, and then they could come up with a plan of action.

At the close of the service, Phillip, taking Sherri's hand, went to the front door to greet each and every person that had blessed them with their presence. All of the people either stopped and offered encouraging words or just smiled at the Fields as they went out. Mamie and Cherish were the last to exit the building. Hope was happily jumping around and smiling; she appeared to be so happy and carefree.

Phillip could but only think about the teachings of Christ which said unless you receive the kingdom as a little child... Phillip introduced Sherri and the children to Mamie; she, in turn, introduced Cherish and Hope.

"Pastor, that was a powerful message," Mamie said. "It truly was a word in season."

"Thank you very much, Mamie. Coming from you, that is a true blessing," Phillip replied. "But all I want to know is how did you get all of these people to show up today?"

"Pastor, I told you there were a few of us that were just waiting for a pastor. We had prayed that the Lord would send one to us. God does answer prayer."

"Yes, he does," Sherri agreed, smiling up at Phillip.

"Will there be Wednesday night service, a prayer meeting, or Bible study?" Mamie inquired.

Bible study, Phillip thought. That was not something that he had thought about before. Why should he? There had not been anyone that was interested before.

"That would be good, but I didn't announce it this morning. How will everybody know?"

Cherish laughed. "That won't be a problem, Pastor," she said and gestured toward Mamie.

"I believe you're right." Phillip laughed. "Let's say seven o'clock then."

"Sounds good. We will see you then."

"Phillip," Sherri said as they were walking to the house, "what do you think about today? Isn't wonderful how God brought these people together and led them to your service?"

"Yes, it is, and it is very amazing how we have been here almost a year and are just now reaching people that seem to have a true hunger for the Word of God and are willing to do the will of God."

⚡

Watching the activity of the church from the top of a large elm tree across the street, they were in a state of confusion. "Where do you think all of those people came from?" Astaroth asked Azazel.

"Beats me. I never knew there were that many people in this town that thought anything about church."

"And did you see them when they came out? They all seemed to be happy and carefree.

It is now time to put an end to all of this stuff. Let's go and report in and let the boss know what we have found out."

⚡

Mrs. Whitaker felt better emotionally than she had in months. After her scare the two nights before, she really needed that message. It was so good to have a pastor that truly taught the Word of God, a preacher that took his calling serious and wanted to make a difference in people's lives. She was so thankful to Mamie for calling her. She now had a new inspiration; she could feel her desire to pray returning. She had a renewed hope.

Going into the kitchen to make herself dinner, singing as she opened the cabinet, she had decided to have salmon croquettes. The can of salmon was pushed far back on the shelf; she would have to get her little step stool to reach it. Taking her time, she carefully stepped up on the stool, steadied herself, and reached for the can of salmon. At that moment, the stool started to slip, and then it was totally out from under her. Mrs. Whitaker fell, hitting her head on the corner of the microwave table as she went down.

Unseen and unheard, the little imp joyfully celebrated as

he scrambled out of the house and down the street, his mission accomplished.

⚡

As Mamie pulled up to the curb to let Cherish and Hope out, her nine-year-old Chevy sputtered as if it was going to stop. "It's time I got a tune up or at least the oil changed in ole Betsy." She laughed. She told Cherish that dinner would be ready in about an hour; that would give them time to change clothes and have a little downtime. Cherish had expressed her total delight at attending church that morning. Although it was her first time, she was really impressed; she also had a new outlook on some things.

"Mamie," she asked, "do you believe that there really are unseen forces? Demons on the earth?"

"Of course I do, chile. How else can ya explain all the bad things that is happening here and in the world? There got to be something behind it all." Mamie was very serious when she talked about the powers of darkness and their activities. "You go on now and get out of your clothes, and we will talk about it at dinner."

Entering the house, Cherish could feel that something was not quite right. There was just a feeling of something wrong. *You are just a little spooked by what you heard at church today,* she reasoned to herself. She was hoping that she would not get all paranoid and start spotting demons under every rock as the pastor had put it. Cherish had never thought that there could be evil forces in the world that were actually influencing the thoughts and actions of people. *But,* she thought, *if there is a God that you can't see, there possibly could be demons that you can't see.* This topic was weighing heavily on her mind as she changed Hope into her play clothes and she changed into a comfortable pair of slacks and a shirt. *Could that be,* she thought, *why her father had done the things he had done to her mother, her brothers, and her? Could he have possibly been influenced by demons or the devil?*

She really wanted to learn more about this subject, and she hoped that Mamie would be able to tell her. Mamie was really smart when it came to things in the Bible and all.

Making sure she had everything she needed, she decided she had better get Hope's favorite cup to take with them to Mamie's; it was Hope's version of a security blanket. That cup had been transported between Mamie's and her house more times than she could count. In the kitchen, she once again got a chill, as if she had been suddenly startled. There was nothing or no one in the kitchen to startle her, but still the feeling wouldn't go away. Checking the windows and door, Cherish noticed that the door was slightly ajar. Fear shot through her. Somebody had been in her house. What if they were still there? She instantly remembered the story about Lewis Walker at Mrs. Whitaker's house. Should she call the police, or should she just get Hope and go to Mamie's and then call the police? She didn't know what to do.

All right, she thought, *just calm down. Get yourself together.* Hope was sitting on the living room floor, playing quietly. Cherish cautiously went into the bathroom, making considerable noise. If they were in there, they would know she was coming in. Maybe that would scare them. There was no one in the bathroom. There was no one in the bedroom in the closet or under the bed. Feeling relieved, Cherish began to try to remember if she had accidentally left the door open before she left for church this morning. Did she go out the door? Thinking back, she remembered that it was last night when she had set the garbage out on the back porch. She must have not locked the door, and the wind could have blown it open. That was the only logical explanation. She was going to have to be more careful from now on.

Cherish returned to the kitchen to get the cup. Reaching into the cabinet for the cup, she noticed that a plate and a coffee cup were missing.

She then looked in the refrigerator and found the bowl of spaghetti she had cooked the night before was gone. This was no coincidence. She knew she had not removed the spaghetti; there had been someone in her house. Now she really was scared. She quickly locked the back door, grabbed Hope, and ran from the house on her way to Mamie's.

⚡

Rachael sat at the counter, looking out of the window. The sun was shining brightly outside. Activity at the store was a little slow that morning, but it was still early; plus, it was Sunday. She knew things would pick up during the afternoon hours. Jack had actually gone to sleep last night, allowing Rachael to get a little rest. But he was up bright and early this morning, rambling through the house, talking to himself, and paranoid again. When she left, he had calmed down and was sitting on the sofa, staring at the television. She couldn't tell if he was actually watching television or if he was just staring at the screen. She got herself and Lucas dressed to go to the store because today was Michelle's day off. She would never leave

Lucas at home with Jack anymore, not even for a few minutes. She never knew what he might do. There had to be something that could be done to help Jack. She had made an initial attempt by contacting a Dr. Baker in Dallas for an appointment. Thursday at one thirty, she had been told. She could only hope that he would go willingly to the appointment and that the doctor would be able to diagnosis his problem, and he would be able to get some help.

Thinking back, Rachael tried to remember just when all of this had started. Jack had *never* been this way before, and from all the information she could gather, there was no mental illness in the family. His mother had Alzheimer's disease, but she had researched the signs and symptoms of Alzheimer's and learned that it began to manifest in the middle adult years, around fifty. Jack was only thirty-three, so she had eliminated that as a possible cause for his bazaar behavior. Whatever it was, he needed help and he needed it fast.

So far, Rachael had managed to keep his condition a secret from the town, but she didn't know how long that would last. It seemed that no matter how hard you tried, things just sort of got out in this place. Before long, everybody in town knew everybody else's business. Hank Wilson had come into the store late on Friday and asked for Jack; she had told him that he was at home in bed. She guessed he had a bad case of the flu that was going around. But she assured Hank that she would let Jack know he asked about him. This could only go on for so long, and Rachael knew that time was not on her side.

Looking over at Lucas, she had a deep concern that if Jack's condition was actually mental in nature, he could have passed that gene on to their son. Would he one day display the same signs and symptoms of his father? This was another reason it was so important to get Jack to a doctor; she had to know the answer to that and many other questions.

⚡

Helen Robertson was the town's equivalent to the National Enquirer; if there was anything that needed to be known, she was the one that would know. If there was anything that didn't need to be known, she was the one that would know that also. She was glad that she had gone to church today. She had wanted to go there before today, but she didn't want to be the only person that was going there. She wasn't going to have the folks talking about her. For all she knew, it might have been some kind of cult. So she was real glad when Bertha had called and said that several people were going to go to New Life Church on Sunday, giving her the opportunity to go. That way she didn't look like she was being nosy and just checking things out.

Helen felt a certain amount of pride in the fact that she had been the first person that met Phillip when he had come to town looking for a place to live. She had told him where to find Mabel, so she guessed she could say if it had not of been for her, he wouldn't still be there.

Mabel had told her that he was a preacher, and he was coming there to start a church. But it was Mabel's opinion that it wasn't a good idea. Mabel went to Wesley, and church folks always seemed to have some type of competitive spirit about them. It was as if they thought that if another church cropped up, then their church would just collapse.

Helen wasn't that way; she was always open to new things. Going to church was going to church, regardless of where it was. She didn't go to Wesley because Rev. Potter was old and antiquated. She wanted to hear somebody young with fresh ideas and new concepts. It probably didn't matter that much, but at least the presentation would be different. With the church being new and just now being established, she could get in on the ground floor. She could possibly be elected to some position; then she would be in the know of everything that was going on.

⚡

Mastema was sitting leisurely on the arm of the sofa. Now it was time to get the ball rolling. He began to tell Helen things that needed to be done in the new church. "The preacher is young. He has never had a church of his own before. He said that himself today. He is not familiar with the people in town. He doesn't know what they like and what they don't like. If you could get on the board of directors of the church, then you could help direct the operation of the church in the right direction. Hasn't God given you special talents of administration? It wasn't by accident that you spent twenty years working as an administrative assistant for the director of the state department of agriculture."

By planting these thoughts into her mind, Mastema had accomplished his mission. If Helen got on the board of directors, it would be very easy to infiltrate the ranks. She could be easily influenced and persuaded to do the bidding of his company. Before long, the church would be in such shambles that this little upstart of a preacher would be packing his bags and leaving between suns.

"Don't be overanxious about getting on the board, but act more like it wouldn't matter if you were selected or not. But be sure to act very surprised and humble when you are nominated," Mastema warned in her mind.

Going to the phone, Helen thought she would call Mabel and tell her about the new church. She was sure that Mabel would have something negative to say. But she wanted her to know that there was a large crowd there today and that the new preacher was very good. "That will really get her goat," Helen chuckled to herself.

"Hello," Mabel answered the phone.

"Hi Mabel, just thought I would call and see how you are doing."

"I'm good, a little tired right now. I have been working on my kitchen sink. It is all backed up, so I've been messing with it all morning."

"Oh, hate to hear that. So you didn't go to church today?"

"No, I had more important things I needed to do, so I just stayed home and tried to get some things done around the house."

"Well, I went to church today."

"Really? I bet Rev. Potter almost fell out of the pulpit to see you walk in." Mabel laughed.

"No, I didn't go to Wesley."

"Where did you go?"

"I went to Rev. Fields' church, New Life Christian Fellowship."

"Oh, I see," Mabel said with a slight tone of disgust in her voice.

Ha! Helen thought, *got her.* "Yes, and service was very good. I really enjoyed it. He is a very good speaker. There were about *fifty* people there; it was good."

"That is really nice, Helen. Look, I would love to talk with you more, but I really have got to get my sink unstopped, but I'll give you a call back when I get finished. Are you going to be home later?"

"I don't plan to go anywhere, so I should be," Helen answered.

"Okay then, talk to you later."

"Bye now," Helen said.

"Bye."

Hanging up the phone, Mabel shook her head. *How can people be so stupid?* she thought. *That church is not on the up-and-up. I'm sure it is probably some type of cult. That preacher comes waltzing in here, opening a church. After he has drained them dry, he will be gone.* Mabel had seen that type before, she reminded herself. She hoped it wouldn't be another Jim Jones and his Guyana incident.

XIX

Mamie had fixed her traditional Sunday soul food dinner: fried chicken, candied yams, collard greens, cornbread, and peach cobbler. The table was set and would be ready by the time Cherish and Hope arrived. While preparing the meal, Mamie couldn't stop thinking about the church service. She felt better today than she had in a long time.

She had a sense of hope and encouragement. For so long she had felt that God had totally forgotten about her and the town of Evansville. She could really understand how the children of Israel had felt while they were being held captive in Egypt. But everything was going to turn around now. The Lord had heard and answered her prayers. Humming along as she prepared for Cherish and Hope, her thoughts turned to Mrs. Whitaker. She would have to give her a call later today to check on her and to tell her how much she appreciated her going to service today. Mamie also needed to let her know about Bible study on Wednesday night.

Suddenly a knock at the door interrupted her thoughts. Cherish and Hope arrived sooner than Mamie had anticipated. The cornbread was not quite brown, and the collard greens needed about another twenty minutes or so to cook.

"Come on in," Mamie called from the kitchen. "I'm in here. Dinner ain't ready yet, but it will only be a few more minutes. Just make yourself comfortable."

Cherish headed straight to the kitchen, breathless as she rushed in and sat at the table. Mamie, noticing the look of sheer fright on her face, stopped washing dishes. Wiping her hands on the tail of her apron, she came over to Cherish with a motherly approach.

"What on this earth is wrong, chile? You look like you done seen a ghost or something."

"Mamie," Cherish began, "after you dropped us off, we walked into the house, and I got this strange feeling. You know the kind of feeling you get when something just ain't right?" Cherish started to explain, pausing in order to regain her composure and to catch her breath.

"Go on, chile," Mamie prodded. Mamie realized she needed something to drink; whatever had happened had obviously frightened her pretty badly. Handing her a glass of ice water, Mamie once again insisted that Cherish continue and tell her what had happened.

After taking a drink of the water, Cherish continued. "Anyway, I could just feel something was wrong or out of whack. But I thought that I was just thinking about what the preacher had said and I was just over reacting. So I got Hope dressed, and I changed my clothes." Mamie wanted her to get to the point, but she had learned over the last couple of years that Cherish was a person that went into great detail in telling any story. Mamie would just have to wait while Cherish continued her detailed account of the events before she got to the important stuff.

"But the feeling was still there, so I went into the kitchen and found the back door was ajar. I immediately thought that somebody had gotten in the house while I was at church."

"Was somebody in the house?" Mamie questioned, hoping this would bring Cherish to the point.

"No, I looked in the bedroom and the bathroom, and there was nobody there." She paused to get another drink of water.

"So if nobody was there, why are you so scared?"

"Well, because I remembered that I had put the trash out on the porch last night, and I thought I must have not locked the door back and the wind had blown it open."

"Oh, so the idea that you had slept all night in the house with the door unlocked is what scared you. That is a scary thought."

"Not only that, but I knew I had to bring Hope's cup with us because you know how she is about her cup, so I went to get it out of the cabinet, and that's when I saw a plate and a coffee cup was missing."

Mamie was really not following this story. First, she thought somebody was in the house, but then she decided it was because she had left the door unlocked. Now she is talking about a plate and cup missing.

"So, I looked in the refrigerator, and the spaghetti that I had cooked yesterday was gone," Cherish was finishing. "So I just grabbed Hope, and we ran over here."

"What you are telling me is that somebody really was in your house? And they stole a plate, cup, and spaghetti?"

"Yeah, I don't know if they were in there last night or today."

"Maybe you should call the sheriff's office and report it," Mamie encouraged Cherish.

"If somebody was in your house, they may not be able to find anything, but they can start watching your house at night, and if anybody is messing around, then the police can catch them."

Cherish knew that Mamie would know the right thing to do. Receiving the confirmation from Mamie, she placed a call to the Evansville sheriff's department and related her story, again in detail, to the dispatcher. They assured her they would send someone right over to take her statement and survey the area for any possible clues.

Mamie removed her apron, turned the fire out from under the collard greens, and took the cornbread out of the oven. She would take Cherish and Hope back to their house to wait on the sheriff's deputy to arrive.

⚡

Nolan Rollins was getting worried about his boys; today was Sunday, and they still had not come back from Hugo. Manny had made the point that he would be back today and there had better be a shipment ready. With the boys missing in action, this meant that Nolan would have to get the shipment ready by himself. He had worked all through the night Friday, Saturday, and all day Sunday. Up until that moment, he had about twenty barrels. Of course, he had to retrieve the ten barrels that he and the boys had hid out at the old mineshaft. Now was not the time to try to keep back a little for himself. Just where were those good-for-nothing boys of his? They said they were going over to Hugo to the Silver Dollar to have a little fun. That was Thursday, and he had not seen hide nor hair from them since. Of course, there was no way he could go and look for them because somebody had to run the operation and keep strangers away.

Lifting the barrels was hard work, especially with his back hurting and his face swollen from Jason's tactics of persuasion on Friday. He needed some help.

"Marge," Nolan yelled from the barn. "Marge, get out here. I need you to help me get these barrels in here so they can pick them up."

There was no answer. Now he was wondering where she could be. He couldn't stop now to go looking for her. She was probably in the house with her eyes glued to that television set. In his opinion, that was the worst thing he could have brought. Every since that thing had been here, that was all she wanted to do. Nolan was sure that she was around somewhere. She never left the place unless he gave her permission. She never even went for a walk without letting him know where she was going. He would have to deal with her later, but right now, he had to get the stuff into the barn; it was two forty-five, and Manny said he would be back here at four o'clock. Nolan had to work fast and hard to have all the corn barreled, corked, and ready for pickup.

⚡

A lone cockroach was scrambling across the floor; the cracks in the concrete floor had been there for so long there was a green mossy substance growing in therm. The bunks were concrete with a thin vinyl-covered mattress to lie on. The meals consisted of scrambled eggs, one sausage link, and a piece of dry toast, a cup of coffee or, for those who didn't like coffee, a four-ounce cup of orange juice for breakfast. Some sort of sandwich and milk for lunch and pinto beans, white bread, and milk for supper. In the corner sat the only commode, enclosed with a makeshift curtain of blankets. The cell, also known as the bullpen, was originally designed to hold twelve prisoners, but today there were a total of fifteen. That meant that three of those calling the place home for the time being were without a bed and had to lie on the cold, concrete floor with only a jailhouse-issued blanket. Samuel and Brent Rollins had been in the establishment now going on three days and were fortunate enough to have a bed due to their status of seniority.

They had been arrested Thursday night, not long after Hank Wilson had left the Silver Dollar. Apparently, one of the girls that had so willingly agreed to partake in a little extracurricular activity with the Rollins boys actually had a boyfriend. As they were preparing to leave the club and go to one of the girls' house, a truckload of cowboys pulled up. A man about six foot two, one hundred eighty-five pounds, wearing a white hat and oversized belt buckle, got out almost before the truck stopped rolling, demanding to know just what was going on here. One of the women, his apparent girlfriend, started unsuccessfully trying to explain away her current situation. She had thought he was over in Oklahoma City at the finals rodeo and wouldn't be back until late Sunday night. That had changed after he had lost the bull riding contest; he and his friends decided to come back home. Immediately, without asking the Rollins boys any questions, a fight broke out. Brent Rollins got a broken nose, and Samuel sustained a laceration to his face. It wasn't until Brent pulled the knife and cut the man across the cheek that the owner of the Silver Dollar called the cops and they were thrown in jail.

Due to the lateness of the hour, they were not allowed until Friday morning to make a phone call. Samuel had tried to call home, but the phone just rang and rang without an answer. Brent waited until later in the afternoon to call. That time there was only a busy signal, so they had no way to make contact. On Monday afternoon, they were to go to their arrangement. At that time, bail would be set along with a court-appointed attorney to represent them. It was nothing they could do now but sit here and wait. Hopefully, once they were appointed an attorney, he would get in touch with their father and he would come and make bail for them. Both of the Rollins boys knew that there would be hell to pay when they did get home. Manny had probably come on Friday; everything wasn't ready, and now they knew that their father was really angry. To make matters worse, he was going to have to pay money to get them out of jail. Maybe it wasn't such a bad idea for them to be in jail after all.

⚡

Belial was pacing the floor, back and forth, back and forth. His Highness had made contact today. There was a strong chance that he would be coming up to Evansville to check out the situation for himself. He had made it quite plan that he was not pleased with the way things were going. He had said that the one main person that needed to be subdued was still walking around and doing what it was that they did best, and that was not good.

Going over recent events, Belial could not understand what the big concern was. Hadn't everything they had attempted to do been a success? Wasn't the groundwork being laid for the destruction of the new church and preacher? Was the secret weapon that would take over this planet already in the making? It wouldn't be very long until it was launched across the world. So what was the problem here? His Highness was always worried about his position on this planet; he knew that the future didn't look promising, but he wanted to make sure that he had accomplished what he had set out to do from the beginning.

Well, Belial thought to himself, *I guess I better call a meeting and see if everything is going on schedule.*

He, better than anyone else, knew what it was like to be on the receiving end of His Highness' wrath. He had the power to banish them into realms unknown. It was not a matter of *if* he would, but *when* he would. Although Belial knew that he was one of the most trusted of all the princes of darkness, he also understood that this project was of the uttermost importance. This could be one of the final battles waged before the big climax would take place. A lot was riding on the outcome of this operation. While Belial was thinking over what to do next, his concentration was interrupted.

"Excuse me, boss." It was Mastema.

"Yes, what is it?" Belial was not ready for any bad news; he could only hope whatever this measly little creature wanted was good.

"I don't know if this is good or bad, but I thought I better let you know that the Rollins boys are locked up in the Choctaw County Jail as we speak."

"Locked up?" Belial shouted. "Just how did that happen?"

"It seems they went over to Hugo on Thursday, and they ended up in a fight with some cowboys, and next thing you know, they are locked up," Mastema explained.

"Who is the idiot that is supposed to be in charge that has allowed this to happen?"

"I believe that is Jesse's territory, sir." For Mastema, sharing this tidbit of information was the most pleasurable thing he had done since he informed headquarters about the presence of Michael.

Belial was seething with anger. This is just what he needed. If His Highness found out that two of the main players in his game of destruction were locked up, it would mean that the production could be delayed; this would not be pleasing to him at all.

A delay in production could give their enemy an advantage, an advantage that could be very costly to Belial and his crew of workers. Something had to be done, and it had to be done quickly before His Highness arrived.

"Bring that idiot, Jesse, to me at once!" Belial commanded Mastema. "I want him here right now!"

"Yes, sir," Mastema replied as he vanished from Belial's sight.

Belial was furious. With fist balled tightly, he beat the desk repeatedly. "Astaroth, Azazel, in here right now!"

Carmuel was pleased with the results of his crew's actions on Thursday night. If they could get the major players fighting among themselves, the battle would be half won. It wasn't hard to get the Rollins boys out of the picture for a while. All the warriors had to do was leave them to their own devices. It was only a matter of placing the right people in the right place at the right time. Then they could just sit back and watch the action.

Although this was a small victory, Carmuel knew it was just a matter of time before Belial was informed of Samuel and Brent's condition. Then there would be an all-out battle to get them released. What Carmuel didn't know was which means Belial would use to accomplish it. Now it was a matter of extreme importance to station some of his strongest warriors at all strategic locations to find out what his next move would be and when.

⚡

Cherish and Mamie had met with the sheriff's deputy, and he had gone around checking for any sign of forced entry into her house. There were no apparent signs of any forcible entry. Actually, it was hard to really be sure that there really had been somebody in the house. All he had to go on was Cherish's word that there was a plate, cup, and bowl of spaghetti missing.

To reassure her that everything was going to be all right, he promised that he would patrol her house every night that he was on duty. He would also make a report of the incident, and whoever was on duty on his off days would also patrol.

After the deputy had left, Mamie, Cherish, and Hope

got in the car to return to Mamie's for dinner. She hoped that it was not ruined, but she knew that Cherish and Hope's wellbeing was more important than the meal. Mamie had begun to think of Cherish as her very own daughter. She could have hoped and imagined that her own daughters would have turned out like Cherish. Of course, Cherish had a hard time, and there were sure to be more to come, but she had managed to overcome so many obstacles and make a start at a decent life.

As they were getting ready to pull away from the curb, Mamie decided that it would be good to have some ice cream with that peach cobbler. She turned down Front Street to head to the One Stop. This would take them right by Mrs. Whitaker's house. As they approached the house, Mamie got a strong desire to stop and check on her. Once again, that well-known voice was saying, "You need to go in and tell her about Bible study Wednesday. You know she usually goes to bed early. Since you are right here, it won't take but a minute. Then you won't have to worry about calling her later."

"Cherish, since we are right here, I'm going to stop by and let Mrs. Whitaker know about Bible study on Wednesday. Then we can go get the ice cream, go home, and eat dinner. Is that all right?"

"Sure," Cherish answered.

Why was Mamie all of a sudden so determined to tell Mrs. Whitaker about Bible study? It was still three days away. She could call her tomorrow, Cherish thought but was not going to say to Mamie. She had learned that when Mamie made up her mind to do something, there was no stopping her. This was something Cherish had come to admire about Mamie. She was not one to do a lot of talking; she took action.

Mrs. Whitaker's house was a large eight-room dwelling that was built in the early fifties. The front porch was made of concrete and went the entire length of the house. Two brick columns held up the roof of the porch. In the front yard was a large elm tree with a lover's bench that encircled the trunk. Old Sheriff Whitaker had put that bench there when their children where young. He would laugh and say that "someday they can sit there and court, and Mama and I can watch them from inside the house."

The front door was open; Mamie knocked on the screen door while calling out for Mrs. Whitaker. There was no answer. Mamie thought maybe she was in the back and couldn't hear. After all, she, like Mamie, was getting on in years, and as time goes on, hearing ain't what it used to be. Knocking again without an answer, Mamie tried the screen and found it to be unlocked; she entered into the living room, calling out for Mrs. Whitaker. Moving through the living room through the glass French doors that separated the living room and dining room, she made her way toward the back of the house and the kitchen. As she got right to the kitchen door, she could see Mrs. Whitaker lying lifeless on the floor.

"Oh my God," Mamie gasped, running as swiftly as she could for a woman her age. Making it to the front door almost completely breathless, she called to Cherish. "Come here quick. Mrs. Whitaker is hurt."

Rushing to the house, pulling Hope along as she went, Cherish entered the house. Mamie was shaking Mrs. Whitaker, trying to get her awake. The stepstool was lying across her legs and Cherish believed she understood what had happened. Working at the hospital, Cherish had learned basic life support techniques, and the first thing was not to move an accident victim for fear of neck injury. She gently removed Mrs. Whitaker's head out of Mamie's hand and laid it softly on the floor. She immediately felt for a pulse and checked for respirations; there was a faint pulse and breathing was very swallow.

"Mamie, you go and call 911. I will stay here in case she stops breathing," Cherish instructed. Her nurses' aide experience was proving very helpful in this situation.

"Mommy, why is Miss *Whiztaker* taking a nap on the floor?" Hope asked in her childish innocence

"Miss Whitaker fell down, honey; you know like you did when you tried to get the Peanut Butter off the cabinet?" Hope nodded like she now had total understanding of the situation. "Now you go in and sit on the sofa while mommy helps Mrs. Whitaker."

"911. What's your emergency?" The dispatcher asked.

"This is Mamie Webb, and I am at Mrs. Diana Whitaker's house, 804 East Front Street, Evansville. She has had an accident and is unconscious on the floor."

"Is she responding?"

"No."

"Is she breathing?"

"Yes, just barely."

"We have an ambulance on the way. Just stay right there."

A tall, strong warrior, wearing the armor of a Roman gladiator, stood in the corner of the kitchen; to his side he held a long, glimmering sword. Silently, he stood as still as a statue, watching as the paramedics arrived and rushed into the kitchen. After an initial assessment of the patient, they placed an intravenous catheter into Mrs. Whitaker's left forearm; an infusion of Normal Saline solution was started. She was then placed on the gurney, transferred to the ambulance, and rushed to Hugo Hospital.

Sheriff Wilson, hearing the call on his police radio, came immediately to the scene. He wanted to know exactly what had happened, who had been there, when it happened, and how it happened. It seemed a little odd to him that Mrs. Whitaker had made a report on Thursday night about a prowler and now today she had had a mysterious accident. It was a little suspect to him also, that Mamie Webb and that Rollins girl just happened to be in the neighborhood when this took place. He may not be able to prove it, but he was sure they had something to do with all of this. Something was telling him that he better do a little digging into this, some old-fashioned police investigation. He had waited a long time to get something on that ole witch, Mamie, something that could get her committed to the state hospital in Vinita.

Once the ambulance left, the warrior breezed out of the house through the side. As he flew out of the building, he came face-to-face with Mastema.

XX

"Just what do you think you are doing?" Belial was shouting into Jesse's face.

"Do you not realize that because of your incompetence, you have put yourself and all of the other workers, including my future, in jeopardy?"

Jesse could only sit there in fear, shaking. Belial was in his face, so close Jesse could actually feel the hot, wet moisture coming out of his mouth. He was sure that he was about to be eliminated, that he would be turned into a small puff of smoke. That when he reemerged, he would be on another planet so far away that the astrologers had not even discovered it yet.

"What I want to know," Belial was asking, "is just where were you when those two nitwits decided to get into a fight twenty miles away? Was it or was it not your job to keep an eye on them and make sure that nothing happened that would hinder our operation? *Wasn't it?*"

A weak Yes, sir, was all that Jesse could muster up in response to this interrogation.

"Well, Mister Goof Off, for your information, I got word today that His Highness is planning to make a trip up here sometime real soon! If he gets here and finds out how stupid and irresponsible you are, there is no telling what could happen to you. It is all because of your incompetence that it became necessary for us to come here in the first place."

Jesse could do nothing but sit there and listen to one insult after another being thrown at him. He really had no defense. He had no explanation for what had happened. Actually, he wasn't even sure himself how the Rollins had ended up in jail. When he had left them, they were in the bar drinking with some women, and it had already been orchestrated that they would go home with these women. They would decide to have a drink from their own supply in their truck, and the Company would have a couple of more recruits for the cause.

"Because you did not do your job that means that the product will not be ready for distribution as planned. This in turn causes a major setback in the operation. Now it could take maybe a week or more to catch up. Do you know what *that* could mean Mister Nitwit?"

"No, sir."

"That means you are giving our enemies a chance to put *more* monkey wrenches in our operation. *That is what that means.*" Belial was making a point at convincing Jesse that everything that was going wrong, he was directly responsible for. This was also Belial's way of making himself look good when His Highness showed up. He would simply use Jesse as the scapegoat.

"I would have believed that you would know better, Jesse. After all, you have been the leader of this operation now for decades. You, more than anyone else, should understand the importance of staying on top of any assignment. But there is only one way you can redeem yourself and that is you better make it possible for those boys to get out of jail and back here to work as soon as you possibly can."

"Yes, sir. I will, sir," Jesse piped up. At least the boss was giving him another chance. Jesse knew this might be his last, so he had to make it good.

"And, Jesse," Belial added, "it would behoove you to get started immediately, if you know what I mean."

"I will, sir. Right away," Jesse replied as he vanished from the office.

Where do I start? Jesse wondered. Just what means could he use to get those dim-witted fools out of jail? He didn't possess the power to open up the cell and set them free. Nor did he know of a way to blow up the jail. When it came to supernatural ability, he was very limited. He always needed a person to work his spells through. He had to find the perfect person that would be receptive to his influence. Then it hit him—of course! That would be the perfect person. Jesse was extremely proud of himself as he set off to Hugo to check on the boys and arrange for their release.

If things went right, and there was no reason why they shouldn't, the Rollins boys would be out of jail in a matter of hours and back at home, just in time for Manny and his boys to get there to load up the goods.

⚡

Michael, Uriel, Ariel, and Gabriel gathered together in the fellowship hall of the church, going over the plans for the next attack. Although there were prayers going forth from several people and the warriors and their platoons were receiving adequate amounts of energy for the jobs at hand. It was evident that the time was fast approaching that it was going to take much stronger, more heartfelt intercession to keep the warriors powered up for the big battle.

Lying out on the table was a map showing the location of all the enemy forces and their cohorts. The enemy had a substantial array of human cohorts and workers on their side. It was going to be Michael and his forces' job to turn these people around into subjects that could be used for their own benefit. This was not going to be easy. These people had functioned under the yoke of darkness for so long they honestly believed that everything was the way it was supposed to be. They no longer cared about what was happening in the world around them; they had become immune to evil and its affect on the world and the people.

The people under the yoke of the Company actually had no problem with some of the evils they encountered every day. Abortion was a choice. Drug addiction was just an illness. Greed was only a problem when it wasn't them being greedy. Poverty was because of the government. Inflation was something they just learned to live with. Murder, rape, and pornography were just the way of the world. Most people had been deceived to believe that it was due to possible mental disorders that people committed hideous crimes. Nobody recognized that all of those things were directly influenced by the god of this world and his army of evil workers.

The state of affairs in the very small community was representative of what the world had become as a whole. The saddest part of the whole thing to the warriors was that over ninety percent of those that were working for and under the influence of the sons of darkness were professing to be God-fearing. They were good churchgoing people—some on a regular basis, others infrequently, but nonetheless, they called themselves Christians.

"The Company is stepping up their defenses," Michael was telling his captains.

. "We have to get all the warriors together and let them know what we need to do at this point."

"Where can we all meet that we'll not jeopardize our position? The church is not large enough, so it will have to be an open area that is out of the enemy territory," Uriel commented.

"We can meet at the caves behind the Rollins' place. That is where my platoon is stationed, and as of yet, none of Belial's imps have wandered up there. Get everyone there in an about twenty minutes. Belial is getting nervous, so we have to stay on our guard. He can get very dangerous when he is cornered, and right now he is feeling the pressure," Michael concluded.

⚡

Mastema shot into the sky over Mrs. Whitaker's house, zigzagging back and forth, as he shot hideous balls of fire at Carmuel. He shot this way and that as he continued to zigzag through the air. Carmuel, the sun reflecting off his sword with a blinding light, slashed at Mastema as he drove head first toward Carmuel. Carmuel's sword made a fiery arch through the air. Meeting it with his own sword, the demon was sent spinning through the air from the blow. Straightening himself with his powerful wings, he turned once again to confront his attacker.

With blow after blow of the mighty sword of his assailant, Mastema soon realized he was no match for this mighty warrior. This warrior was much more powerful, much more disciplined than he could ever be. It would take someone with a lot more power than he to defeat a foe of this magnitude. Turning to flee, the edge of the mighty sword of his attacker caught him and flipped him high into the air, sending him flying into the elm tree in the center of Mrs. Whitaker's yard. Twisted and tied up like a rag doll in the leaves, Mastema hung there, a tangled mess.

Leaving the scene, Carmuel headed to the church. Arriving just as the other warriors were finishing their meeting, he swooped into the room.

"Good afternoon, Carmuel," Michael greeted the strong warrior.

"Good afternoon," he replied. "The Company has begun to attack the prayer warriors. I just came from Diana Whitaker's house. One of the little hindering spirits pulled a step stool out from under her, causing her to fall backward and hit her head. I led Mamie to the house just in time, and now they have taken her to the hospital. Of course, she will be all right, but it will be a few days before she will come around enough to pray."

"Is there anyone with her?"

"Yes, I sent Ruth, a guardian, to stand over her at the hospital. Cherish works at the hospital, so I know there will be a prayer covering over her until she regains consciousness." Carmuel was a little tired and weak from his encounter with Mastema.

"Carmuel, you look a little weak. What else happened?" Gabriel inquired.

"As I was leaving Diana's, I came face-to-face with one of Belial's under-princes. He, wanting to be a hero, engaged me in a battle. I sent him sprawling into a tree and came straight here. I probably do need to rest right now."

"True," Michael agreed. "You stay here; we are going up to the caves with all the warriors and lay out our strategy for this battle."

Leaving Carmuel in the fellowship hall, the other warriors ascended through the ceiling and were gone.

⚡

Sitting unseen on top of the filing cabinet, Jesse intensely listened as the sheriff of Choctaw County discussed the overcrowding in the jail with the undersheriff.

"Sheriff Martin," the undersheriff was saying, "if we don't get some of these people out of here, we won't be able to take in anybody else. Not only are the cells overcrowded, making it uncomfortable, it is just a breeding ground for something bad to happen."

"I agree totally, but right now what can we do to ease the situation?"

This was the question that Jesse was waiting on; now was his time to step in. Jumping off the file cabinet and into the ear of the undersheriff, he put his scheme into action. Sitting on the arm of the undersheriff's chair, he planted what he considered the perfect plan into his mind.

All of a sudden, the undersheriff in what he believed to be a stroke of genius made a suggestion to the sheriff that he felt would be the perfect solution to their problem.

"Well, let's see, you know those boys from over at Evansville that got into it with the Armstrong kid on Thursday night?"

"Yeah, what about them?" The Sheriff asked.

"If you could talk to Willie and remind him of his prior run in with this office, I am sure that you can get him to drop any charges against them. We could then turn them loose and make it plain that they are not to be here in Hugo again or they will get some serious jail time."

Thinking over this proposal, Sheriff Martin sat back in his chair, twirling his pencil between his fingers. *Could this be an option?* he thought.

"Okay, let's say we talk to him and he agrees. Will that truly help our situation here?" he asked.

"At least it would be a start."

Jesse, thinking about that prospect, gained an outstanding thought; what if several inmates were released on those terms? These would be people that may prove to be valuable to them in the long run. Now he instilled this idea to the undersheriff.

"Actually, there are several guys back there that could be given a similar deal that would free up even more space," the undersheriff continued.

"I guess that could work," the sheriff thoughtfully considered. "We don't actually have any capital cases back there. We could talk with the district attorney and get those terms negotiated."

Talk with the DA? Oh, that would never do; it would take

way to long, Jesse thought. He had to get the Rollins out now, not sometime tomorrow. Moving over to the sheriff, Jesse began to instill the thoughts in his head about the Rollinses. "Where are the Rollins guys locked up? In what section?" Sheriff Martin asked.

"I believe they are in the large bull pen."

"Gladys," Sheriff Martin spoke into the intercom on his desk, "how many inmates are currently being held in the bull pen?"

"Just a minute," she replied. After a few seconds, the sound of her voice came back over the intercom, "Sheriff, it looks like right now there are fifteen in the pen."

"Thank you," Sheriff Martin replied and shut off the intercom. "Fifteen; that is three more than is officially legal," he remarked to the undersheriff. "Let's see what we can do to get that number down. Has Willie officially pressed charges with the DA?"

"I'm not sure if he has or not; Gladys would have that information on file." He got up to go into the outer office and check with the secretary to see if the charges had been posted.

Reclining back against the wall with his hands behind his head, Jesse sat comfortably on the floor, waiting as the undersheriff talked with Gladys. He was contemplating whether Sheriff Martin could become an ally. It had not been hard to bring Hank Wilson in; it shouldn't be hard to recruit Sheriff Martin. But that would be something to be done at a later date. Right now, it was all about getting the Rollinses out of jail. There was also the problem with those heavenly hosts to deal with. But he would definitely make a note to come back here and work on this sheriff.

"Willie hadn't pressed charges as of Friday, Sheriff. Guess

he was just waiting until Monday. I believe he got a cut out of the fight, so he probably wanted to go in to the DA all stitched up and bandaged for a more dramatic effect."

"Good, let's go pay Mr. Armstrong a visit," Sheriff Martin declared as he was reaching into his drawer to retrieve his service revolver. It was then that Jesse saw the one thing he never expected to see lying at the front of the drawer: a Bible.

With part one of his plan put into operation, Jesse departed to the house where Willie Armstrong and his girlfriend shared residence. Entering into the house, Jesse could hear the loud exchange of an argument in progress; *this is even better,* Jesse thought. If he could just keep them arguing and fighting until Sheriff Martin arrived, it would strengthen the sheriff's proposal and then the Rollinses would be free in no time.

⚡

Cherish and Mamie returned to Mamie's house to eat dinner after seeing Mrs. Whitaker safely transported to the hospital. The idea of ice cream had been completely erased from their minds. What had started out as a beautiful and exciting day had began to turn into a nightmare. It was so unreal to Cherish. In just a matter of hours after leaving church, it seemed that whatever bad could happen did happen.

"Mamie, if you had not decided to stop at Mrs. Whitaker's, she may have died," Cherish said to Mamie in a congratulatory tone.

"I have learned to always follow my first instinct," Mamie replied. "Always remember if you follow your first mind, you usually won't go wrong."

"I just don't understand all of this. We went to church this morning. I felt real good and then came home to discover someone had been in my house. Then to find Mrs. Whitaker unconscious on the floor—I just don't understand."

"Well now, chile, you are seeing what it is like to serve the Lord. The Bible says that immediately the enemy comes to steal the word that was planted. And that is exactly what he tried to do."

"Are you saying that the devil is behind everything that has happened today?" Cherish questioned. "Wasn't it just an accident that Mrs. Whitaker fell off of that stool? That could happen to anybody, the stool slipping on the slick floor and you fall."

"Hum," Mamie grunted, "that is what the enemy would want you to believe. You see, he and his workers are *very* cunning. They do things that people just dismiss as coincidence and go about their business. But in reality the forces of evil have caused them to happen."

Cherish listened intently as Mamie explained some of the ways the devil and his cohorts operate.

"That is what makes them so dangerous. After awhile, people just ignore the happenings around them. This gives the devil more ammunition to use against them. Another thing that you should always remember is this: the devil knows *exactly* what button to push to get a person off focus."

"I see," Cherish replied, "but how will I *know* if it is the devil or just a coincidence?" Cherish wanted to know.

"That is easy. The Bible also says that every good and perfect gift comes from above. That includes everything we have and everything that we do. Everything is a gift from God: life, breath, strength, your mind, your health—everything. So if something happens that is not good, you can guarantee the devil had a hand in it somewhere."

Mamie's words were beginning to explain some things to Cherish, some things she had never considered before. *If what Mamie is saying is true?* Then there had been and probably were still a lot of demonic activity in Cherish's life. It seemed that everything in her life before she met Mamie had been bad. It wasn't until that fateful night on the bridge did things begin to change and Cherish's life began to take on a new direction. This thought prompted another question in her mind. *If God was good and everything that he gave to us was perfect, then how could the devil just step in and corrupt what God has done?*

There was still so much that she did not know about God, the Bible, and the devil. But she was hungry to find out. The little she had learned about the Bible and God from Mamie convinced her that there was a way that God could and would stop the evil and turn it around for good. Cherish just needed to find out how and what her part was in the great scheme of things.

She wanted to understand the whole of this mysterious battle that was going on between good and evil, to learn the secret to defeating evil and restoring good. It was going to take her many Sundays, Wednesday nights, and countless hours of personal study, but Cherish was determined to find the answers to her most pressing questions that she knew could only be found in the Word of God.

XXI

Looking at his watch, Hank saw that it was 2:45, one hour and forty-five minutes before Manny and his truck would be arriving out at the Rollins place. His conversation with Manny on Friday was, *to say the least*, not pleasant.

Hank began to worry about his newfound partnership and the person or persons that he had so willingly aligned himself. The conversation had also prompted Hank on Friday afternoon to check with the National Crime Investigation Center; he had entered the name Manuel Lopez into the NCIC database, and it had not returned a hit. This helped to ease Hank's mind somewhat; at least Manny was not a wanted criminal. He reasoned to himself that Manny was just a strict businessman and he demanded the best out of his workers. Still there was that gnawing in the pit of his stomach that things were not as they appeared. Hank had to get out to Nolan's and see if he and the boys were on top of things and that the corn would be ready by four or four thirty when Manny arrived. He guessed if it wasn't, he might have to pitch in and give the boys a hand to make sure. But first he had to go by and see Jack Sims; he hadn't heard a word from him in over two weeks. There was something not quite kosher about that.

Hank had been in the store on several occasions, and Jack was nowhere to be found; Michelle and Rachael had said that he was sick, *but for two weeks*? That didn't sound right to him. Today he was going to find out for himself.

Knocking on the door of the big Victorian house, Hank waited patiently for Jack to answer. He knew he was in there because he had gotten a glimpse of him peeking out of the window as he started up the steps. After about three or four minutes and several knocks, the door was finally opened, not by Jack, but by Rachael.

"Hello, Sheriff Wilson," Rachael greeted Hank from a partially opened door. The door was only open to a crack large enough for Rachael to stick her head through.

"Afternoon, Mrs. Sims. Is Jack in?" Hank asked.

"Well, yes, he is, Sheriff, but he is sick and can't come to the door right now. He is lying down upstairs."

She is lying, Hank said to himself. "Oh, really? I thought I saw him looking out of the window as I came up."

"Oh, yes, he did," Rachael, scrambling for an answer, replied. "He was laying here on the sofa, but when he saw you coming up, he didn't want you to see him in his weakened condition so he told me to tell you that he will call you when he is feeling better."

"I understand if he is feeling bad," Hank insistently stated, "but it is of the uttermost importance that I talk to him right now. I won't take up too much of his time, and I will certainly try not to disturb him unnecessarily."

"I really don't think that is a good idea right now, Sheriff. You see, we are not sure what it is that Jack has contacted, and we wouldn't want anyone else to come down with it. Believe me, it is not good."

"Mrs. Sims, I am not worried about catching anything. You have been here with him all this time and you don't seem to have anything. It is very important that I talk to Jack right now. It is a matter of business." Becoming increasingly more impatient and suspicious of Rachael's insistence on not letting him in, Hank pushed the door open and stepped into the house.

The inside of the house reminded Hank of a refugee camp that he had seen on CNN. There were sheets strewn around the living room. The windows were covered with blankets. The closet doors were propped shut with chairs, and there were pillows propped against the television, kind of like a barricade. There were various items that one could use as weapons laying around. These items were at the front door, beside the sofa, and at the bottom of the stairs. *What was going on here?* he thought to himself. The room was dark and musky. *This was more like a war zone than a refugee camp,* Hank corrected his thinking.

After surveying the room, Hank turned to Rachael with a questioning look on his face. Rachael, not being able to hide her emotions for another minute, burst into tears.

"Rachael, what exactly is going on here?"

"Oh, Hank, it has been horrible. I have tried to keep things under control. I didn't want anybody to know, but Jack is terribly sick."

"What? Does he have cancer or something like that?"

"No, if it was cancer there would be an explanation. But it is worse than that."

Suddenly, Hank heard a loud bang coming from upstairs, immediately followed by the sound of someone running down the steps. Turning swiftly, he saw Jack Sims looking like a madman, unshaven, hair wild and uncombed. His face was beginning to sink in. He looked like someone who had gone on a long hunger strike. If Hank had not have known this was Jack, he would not have recognized him. Jack came running toward him with a baseball bat aimed and ready to strike.

⚡

The hacking cough continued; one long retching spasm after another. With each episode, large amounts of bloody sputum would be coughed out of the lungs. Marge sat doubled over as the coughing spell literally took her breath away. Not only did the coughing cause pain in her throat, but the pain in her chest was unbearable. Looking down at herself, her dress was torn and bloody. She didn't have a clue what she would do next.

This had all began on Friday after the men from Dallas had left the house. Nolan was pretty beat up. She wasn't sure what exactly had happened out at the barn or why. But she knew something terrible was going on. Nolan had come into the house, bleeding from his lip. His eye was swollen shut, and he was holding his stomach. All Marge had done that day had been to ask Nolan what happened.

Nolan had become madder than she could ever remember. It was mainly because for the first time in his life, he had run across somebody that got the jump on him. He had never allowed anyone to physical beat him in a fight. This, mixed with the embarrassment that he was feeling, sent him in to a rage. He had beat Marge unmercifully; he had thrown her across the room into the side of the buffet table. He had grabbed her by the hair on her head and twisted it so hard she fell to her knees. It was while she was down that he stomped her repeatedly until she could no longer feel the pain. At one point, he had literally lifted her up by the neck and punched her in the face hard with his fist. Once he had gotten tired, she guessed, he left out of the house, mumbling something about getting the corn ready for Sunday, cussing Samuel and Brent for not being there and what they were going to get when they got home.

While Marge lay on the floor unable to move from the pain, the telephone had started to ring and ring and ring, but she was unable to reach it. It was taking all of her strength to try to crawl to the table and get the phone. By the time she had finally reached the table, got a hold of the receiver, it stopped ringing and there was only silence on the other end. Then suddenly, everything had gone black.

It was close to three in the morning before she regained consciousness. Nolan was not in the house; he was out at the barn. Marge, with strained effort, managed to stand to her feet. Looking out of the window, she could see Nolan working, feverishly filling the charred barrels with corn drippings. She knew she had to get away; it was now or never.

Going out the front door, Marge ran as quickly as she could in her condition; she managed to get into the wooded area in front of the house. She knew there was a trail that would take her to the West River Bridge. It was so dark

Marge could barely tell where she was placing her foot. In the darkness, there was no telling what would be out in the woods, but that was not her worry. Nothing in the woods could be as bad as what she had left at home.

She had to get as far away from Nolan as she could, but she had to get to a place where he would not be able to find her. She would hide out for a while until she was better, and then she would make her way into Hugo even if she had to walk. After walking for what seemed like an eternity, Marge finally found the sort of place she was looking for. It wasn't much, mainly just a shed, but at least no one would think to look for her there.

It was after she had settled down in the shed that the coughing had started. She was exhausted and scared, but there was nothing she could do but hope it would go away and she would be all right.

⚡

Ariel had followed Marge from West River Bridge; he had led her to her present location, all the while making sure that nothing happened along the way. Now he had stationed a guard right inside the door of the shed to watch over her as she slept. The guard would lead, direct, and protect her until she was stronger. Ariel would inform Raphael of Marge's location in due season so that he could help her to heal. Not too soon though, because if she healed too quickly from her injury, she would be tempted to return to Nolan and her life there. She deserved much better than to return to that life.

⚡

Phillip had just hung up the phone after talking with Mamie, a look of deep concern on his face.

"What's wrong, Phillip?" Sherri asked. "Did something happen?"

"Yeah, that was Mamie. She said that today after church, she had gone by Mrs. Whitaker's house to let her know about Bible study, and she found her lying on the kitchen floor unconscious. It appeared that she had fallen off a stepstool while she was trying to get something out of the cabinet."

"Oh, that's awful," Sherri said. "Do they think she will be all right?"

"Mamie doesn't know; she was taken by ambulance to Choctaw Memorial Hospital in Hugo. I guess I better go over there now and check on her. I guess I *am* her pastor, although she hasn't officially joined the church yet."

Sherri, thinking on a lighter note, interjected, "That could be because you didn't offer an invitation to join today, dear."

The truth of that statement hit home. "Oh my goodness, you're right. I guess I was so overwhelmed with the number of people in attendance, I forgot."

"But, honey, I am sure that Mrs. Whitaker would appreciate your visit. She probably intends to unite with the church. At this point, you are the closest thing to a pastor she has. It is my understanding that none of the people there today has been attending any church for a long time. You go now; the kids and I will stay here and play some games or read stories."

Reaching for his Bible, Phillip kissed Sherri on the cheek and prepared to exit the door.

"Be careful, Phillip," Sherri called after him. It was something she always said when he left the house, but in that moment, it seemed more appropriate than ever, though she didn't know why.

Gabriel, seeing Phillip pulling out of the driveway, followed along beside the car as he headed toward the highway and turned right toward Hugo. Phillip had only been to Hugo one other time; it was when he, Sherri, and the kids had gone there to one of Sherri's cousins' weddings. He wasn't quite sure where the hospital was, but he had no doubt he would be able to find it. After all, Hugo was not that large.

⚡

Foras was watching as Phillip's car was coming down the highway. *This would be the perfect time to eliminate that troublemaker*, he thought.

Calling out to his army of evil cohorts, he summoned the spirits of destruction and distraction. What better way to get rid of him than to have him destroyed in an automobile accident?

Phillip was driving along, praying and listening to the praise CD in his car. He was mainly just talking to God. Thanking him for all that he had done for him. Asking God to watch over and take care of Diana Whitaker, to place his hands of mercy upon her and to heal her of her injury.

Creeping up to the car and entering through the trunk so as not to be seen by Gabriel, the spirit of distraction made his way on to the floorboard of the passenger side of the car. Waiting for the signal from the spirit of destruction, he sat quietly. As Phillip got closer to the intersection of a dirt road leading to the right, the spirit of destruction stood waiting. A three-point small buck was grazing in a vacant hay field. Receiving the signal from the spirit of destruction, the spirit of distraction with one hand swiped the CD case that was lying on the dashboard to the floor, causing Phillip's attention to be diverted to the floor away from the road. At that exact same instant, the spirit of destruction scared the buck, sending him running on the highway. In a split second, a warrior from Gabriel's platoon stood on the highway and sent the deer around the other way. Phillip looked up just in time to see the deer as he ran beside the car on the passenger's side.

Panic struck deep into Phillip's heart at just the thought he had come so close to wrecking. He immediately began to thank God for having his hand of protection around him and his vehicle. The spirit of distraction knew he had better get out of the car now. He had been discovered. Gabriel had put his mighty hand through the windshield of the car and was attempting to pull the spirit of distraction out. The little imp managed to escape the grasp of the powerful warrior and retreated the way he had entered. However, all was not good.

As the little imp exited the trunk to what he thought was safety, a large warrior was there to meet him.

"What a minute," he tried to reason with the warrior. "I am not a worker; I am just support staff. I don't have anything to do with the hard stuff." But it was to no avail. The little spirit was banished with a swift and mighty blow.

⚡

Turning onto the Indian Nation Turnpike, Phillip headed into Hugo. The Indian Nation Turnpike turned into State Highway 70 just outside of Hugo. Following State Highway 70 into Hugo and turning on Jackson, he continued on to Fourteenth Street. Turning right off of Fourteenth, Phillip found himself right in front of the hospital. The hospital was small; the emergency room was not even equipped to handle major trauma. These would have to be sent into McAlester or to Paris Texas, but minor things they could and would take care of.

Going through the automatic doors, Phillip stepped up to the counter. The nurse sitting on the opposite side was busy charting in a patient's record.

"May I help you, sir?" she asked in a pleasant, friendly voice.

"Yes, I am here to see Mrs. Diana Whitaker. I believe she was brought here this afternoon from Evansville."

"Whitaker, Whitaker," the nurse repeated as she looked down the patient list. "Oh, yes, Mrs. Diana Whitaker. Are you a family member?" She wanted to know.

"No, I am her pastor, Reverend Phillip Fields."

"She is in room thirty, straight down the hall and to your left."

Phillip thanked the nurse and started in the direction in which he had been instructed. Coming to room thirty, he found Mrs. Whitaker lying very still in bed. Her breathing was even and unlabored. There was a bandage wrapped around her head. Looking down on her from the bedside, there were noticeable black circles around both eyes. Oxygen was flowing through a nasal cannula into her nose.

Phillip lightly touched her hand and prepared to say a prayer. Mrs. Whitaker gave no evidence that she knew he was there. Phillip prayed, *Lord, keep her in your grace. Give her favor, Lord. We know that your Word says that by your strips we are healed. I pray, Lord, that you would touch her body with your healing touch and restore her for your glory. Amen.*

Opening his eyes after the prayer, Phillip looked into the eyes of Diana Whitaker.

"Thank you, Pastor," her voice weak and low.

"You are very welcome, Mrs. Whitaker." He comforted her, "Now you get some rest, and you will be out of here before you know it."

Diana weakly nodded her head, turned it to the side, and closed her eyes. Phillip sat at her bedside for about thirty minutes. Then he left to return to Evansville.

The drive home was uneventful, unlike the trip to Hugo had been. Now Phillip was much more alert than he had been on the trip over, he was more observant of his surrounding and was prepared to stop if needed.

As he drove into Evansville's city limits, a strong feeling of dread hit Phillip, a feeling that he hadn't noticed while in Hugo. That was funny. It seemed as though when he was in Hugo, a burden was lifted off of him. Now that he reentered the city limits of Evansville, that old familiar feeling of depression or oppression swooped down and enveloped his entire being. *What is it about this place? Why is there such a forlorn atmosphere here?*

It had been a trying day for Phillip; he was looking forward to getting in and relaxing.

He needed to sit back and reflect on the activities that had taken place since he had gotten up this morning. He knew that God was trying to show as well as tell him something, but he wasn't too sure what that something was. Whatever it was, he hoped that he would be able to withstand the pressures and the demands that he knew was going to be placed on him, as well as his family.

His father-in-law had told him once that God takes a person through a time of trials to prepare them for their assignments. It depended on the severity of the trial, the importance of the assignment. If that was true, then God must be preparing him for a very heavy-duty assignment. He had had nothing but trials since he came to this place.

Although there were a good number of people in attendance at that morning's service, he still had worries and concerns about the upkeep of his family. There was not as yet an official financial chairman for the church, so Sherri had taken the money that was collected, counted it, and recorded it in the financial record. There was a total of two hundred and fifty dollars taken up. That would pay the utilities for the church and his home, but that was the extent of it. Phillip still had to figure out how they were going to buy food, gas, and pay the mortgage on their home. Once again, Phillip could do nothing but depend on God. Had not God stepped in and brought an increase to the church? Knowing in his heart that God would provide, it was still hard not to worry when you couldn't see an end in sight. Phillip asked a question of God: *How can I do great things for you when I can't support my own family?*

He was still thinking on this as he entered his home. Phillip was surprised to see Mamie sitting in the living room, talking to Sherri. He had not even noticed her car parked out front. *Boy, I'm really preoccupied;* that could be a very dangerous state to be in. He cautioned himself. Hadn't he learned anything today about preoccupation?

XXII

Belial was in a state of panic; he knew that His Highness would be showing up any time now. There had been far too many incidents where his forces were coming back defeated. Belial had no doubt that by this time His Highness already knew about each and every defeat that had come against his army.

What else could he do? He had implemented every scheme imaginable to either eliminate or otherwise hinder these *prayer warriors*, as they called themselves. But for some reason, they continued to keep praying. Belial was at his wits' end; he would have to go back to previous times and places. Times where there were hard resistances to deal with to find out what had worked. But in the meantime, he had to make sure that his crew would continue in their endless maneuvers. They would continue to fight. They could not give up now. He had to make sure that his human cohorts remained faithful to the Company that they continued to operate within the realms of his workers. He had to make sure that Hank

Wilson and the Rollinses remained loyal to his cause and that Mamie Webb and Phillip Fields were rendered helpless. Those two were his strongest opponent in this battle. He now understood that it was Mamie that had been the main instigator that called for help. It was then that Phillip Fields had been sent in.

If Belial and his crew could eliminate Mamie, then Phillip would not be a force to reckon with. He was weak and insecure. The forces had almost had him defeated until Mamie once again stepped in. Belial knew it would be no small matter to get Mamie in a state of despair. She had a hedge of protection around her that was almost impossible to penetrate. But over the years, Belial had learned that everybody had a point of weakness; now it was just a matter of identifying hers.

Phillip was extremely tired but understood the importance of being available when a member of his congregation needed to talk to him. Tonight was not the night that he really wanted to sit and listen to anybody else's problems. He may not be able to be objective when he was so tired. Nonetheless, he had to get in there and give it his best shot.

"Well, hello there, Mamie. This is a surprise."

"Evening, Pastor," she replied. "I hope this is not a bad time. I have been sitting here, talking with your wife, waiting 'til you got back from over at Hugo."

"Of course it isn't a bad time." Phillip tried to sound sincere, hoping that his tone did not belie his words. "What is it that you want to talk about?"

"You'll find out that I 'm the kinda person that comes straight to the point. I don't believes in beatin' around the bush. So I think there's some thangs that we really need to discuss."

"All right," Phillip stated a little bewildered.

"You see, I been praying for a long time that the Lord would send a strong pastor to this place, one that could handle the spiritual warfare that is goin' here."

"Mamie, you know that there is a spiritual battle going on all over the world. That was set in motion back in the Garden of Eden, and we are still fighting." Pulling out from his seminary training, Phillip wanted to sound as though he was *very* knowledgeable of spiritual warfare and the consequences of that type of battle. In reality, spiritual warfare was not a topic that carried a lot of weight in seminary.

"Pastor Fields, I don't doubt that you knows about spiritual warfare and where it comes from. What I wants to know is, can you stand under the pressure of the battle? You see, God don't want nor does he need no coward soldier."

"I'm not sure I understand what you mean, Mrs. Webb." A feeling of indignation was beginning to flare up in Phillip. *Is this woman calling me a coward? How dare she come in here and insult my intelligence?* He didn't care if she had gotten 3,000 people to come to church today. He was not going to allow her to start trying to take over and run things.

"Now I don't want you goin' and gettin' testy, Pastor Fields, but I just want to let you know that things here ain't as they appears. There is a strong demonic influence in this place, and lessen you are up to the challenge, then maybe you ain't the one that God sent to us. Maybe we needs to continue to pray and wait for the right one. It ain't about your bravery, Pastor, but it's about your staying power."

"All right, go ahead." Something about the way this woman spoke and expressed herself, carried a certain type of authority that one could not ignore or make light of. It was as if he *had* to listen to what she said, no matter how bad he wanted to turn away.

"Satan and his crew have literally taken over the town and the people in this place. When I was a young girl, my grandmother, a strong woman of God, recognized in me the ability to see into the supernatural. She said I had a gift from God. She also said that the ole devil was going to do everything he could to stop me. And you can bet he has tried; he took my husband and my kids. But still I keep right on praying."

"Mamie, when you say Satan has taken over this town, just what do you mean? And what is it I could possibly do to eliminate that problem?"

"That's the hard part, Pastor. Most people have no idea that Satan is working in and around 'em. They thinks it is just the way things are, but I know better. You see I have actually seen the little imps."

Phillip began to believe that Mamie really did have a mental problem of sorts; she was sitting here telling him that she had seen little imps. He didn't want to hurt her feelings, so he knew he had to patronize her. With a quick glance at Sherri, Phillip didn't comment on that statement. Instead, he just sat there, acting as though he was truly believing her story and wanting to hear more.

"What people don't understand is that the things that are happening to them and to their family are all by design. One of the devil's strongest weapons is to keep people stupid of what he is doing. Then he can continue to do whatever he wants. We got to remember that, just like in the book of Job, Satan starts at the bottom and works his way up. By the time he makes it to the top of the list of his attacks against you, your whole life is in a total mess. I guess what I am saying, Pastor, is that *unless* we—that is, those of us who know how he works—start to fight back, this whole place is going to be gone. It could possibly take a whole lot more with it."

"Okay," Phillip said, "what you are saying is that if we start to pray, that all of this will stop?"

"Yes, but not just pray. I mean we are going to have to all come together, pray, and pray hard. Do you actually think that what happened to Diana Whitaker was an accident? No sir, that was by design. You see, she is one of the strongest prayer warriors I know. Satan had to find a way to shut her up. And it didn't help any when you showed up. That made him real mad. Now he will do everything in his power to get rid of you. And remember, Pastor, don't take what happens to you lightly. Satan is trying to get rid of you."

For Phillip this was something entirely new. Although he was leery of what Mamie was saying, there was something inside of him that was in total agreement. Even though it sounded far-fetched, he knew in his spirit that she was right.

"Mamie, I will pray about what you have told me. We will see what God has to say about it. Then if he leads me, we will start a weekly prayer service."

"Pastor, please don't wait too long; if you do, that will give the devil room to come in and dissuade you."

"I won't, Mamie. I can tell that this is something that

is heavy on your heart. I am sure that God will give us the right answer."

Mamie said goodnight to Phillip and Sherri and prepared to leave. With what would seem an afterthought, she turned to Sherri and said, "You take care of yourself and the new baby."

Sherri, with a look of surprise, assured Mamie that she would. *How does this woman know that Sherri is pregnant? Sherri isn't really sure herself.* She hadn't even said anything to Phillip. She had decided that she wasn't going to say anything until she knew for sure. With the struggles that they were having, she didn't really know how to tell him or how he would react. She guessed she didn't have to worry about that now.

⚡

The furniture in the room went flying to one side. The walls were shaking; a rattling was heard as the windows in the old warehouse shook. There was a sound as if a large nuclear bomb had just gone off. Michael and his warriors instantly rose to attention. Even the cave in which they were gathered shook, sending small pebbles falling all around them. From their position, Michael's crew could see the activities of the Rollinses; spirits were scattering around. The mighty powers of evil shot into the air, causing an overcast appearance as the rumbling continued. Hank Wilson looked up into the sky, believing that there must be a real bad thunderstorm brewing. Other residents of Evansville seemed oblivious of the atmosphere and continued with their daily routines.

Phillip suddenly got a strong feeling of dread. The feeling was so strong he felt terror clutching at his throat.

At the same moment, Mamie, sensing impending doom, fell to her knees in prayer.

Rev. Potter, sitting at his breakfast table, suddenly experienced a crushing pain in his chest, a pain that caused him to grab his chest and double over.

⚡

There was complete and eerie silence in the office; a thick dark smoke filled the room. As the smoke cleared, Belial could see that in the place where his desk had sat was now occupied by a large, oversized throne made out of the richest onyx. A long charcoal colored carpet led up the four steps that encircled this large ominous piece of furniture. To each side stood two large creatures; each had three eyes that peered through slits that resembled a helmet. Their wings would span over eight feet when fully extended. Their bodies were covered with a thick, impervious armor, and at their sides, hung large double-edged swords. Their very breath was so hot and putrid that it could vaporize whatever and whoever it was aimed at. Belial stood as stone. He knew that any second His Highness would appear; then it was all over for him. The lesser demons were all crouched out of sight under whatever item they could find. Lesser demons were not allowed to be in the immediate presence of His Highness; if they were discovered, they would be instantly annihilated.

Before Belial had time to regain his composure from the appearance of the throne and the armor bearers, His Highness was sitting on the massive throne. With red eyes that would literally burn a hole through his adversary, His

Highness was staring at Belial. Instantly the demon prince bowed in homage to his king.

"Stand up, you bumbling fool!" His Highness demanded

Belial, in a total state of fright, did as he was commanded. Unsure of what to expect, he stood, looking at his king with the eyes of a scared hound.

"What is so hard about this operation that it seems nobody is capable of keeping things running in an appropriate manner?"

"I don't know, sir."

"I sent you here because Jesse didn't seem to be able to maintain the operation, but now you can't seem to do any better."

"Yes, sir."

"I have heard from my informants that there is a large group of the heavenly host here and they seem to have gotten the upper hand on you and your useless group of incompetents."

"That is simply because they are sneaky. They just come out of nowhere before we know it they are there, sir," Belial nervously replied, attempting to shift the blame from himself.

"That is why I found it necessary to come here myself—to make sure that this operation is not foiled. I hear that the mightiest of the host of heaven have been commissioned here. With that type of power, only equal power can defeat them. This is not a battle that can be fought with the weak," His Highest declared.

Belial was beginning to feel somewhat better; maybe it wasn't that the king thought he was totally incompetent, but rather he knew that Belial didn't have the warrior power to compete.

"I will need every imp, prince, spirit, and principality that you have on this job. I want the main support people of the heavenly host silenced, and I mean quick.

"I have brought the warring beasts with me, and they are out there right now, searching for the heavenly host and their warriors. But Michael I want for myself. Do you understand that?"

"Oh, yes, sir, Michael is yours and yours alone." Belial knew he had to agree with whatever the king said; he knew that if he didn't, he would be removed to the realm of no return.

"Now, my friends, this war is officially declared." Pointing to the back of the room with his long talon, His Highness asked the question, "Has anyone taken the time to notice the spiritual clock on the wall and seen what time it is?"

Belial, who had been joined by Astaroth, Azazel, Foras, Mastema, and Jesse, looked in the direction that their king was pointing, and to their amazement, they noticed that the spiritual clock had moved forward another year.

⚡

Michael and the other archangels knew exactly what all the commotion was about. The king of the powers of darkness just made his way on the scene. This was not something that the archangels had been expecting. They should have expected it though. Once they had gotten the true understanding of what it was that he was trying to accomplish here in Evansville, they should have realized there was no way he was going to allow his underlings to handle it alone. The king of darkness had lost too many battles by letting the lesser demons handle situations. This project was the one that could turn around the whole world for a third time, and he was not about to lose gracefully.

Calling the angels together, Michael had to prepare them for the fierce and relentless attack about to be waged by their enemy.

"As you all know, it appears that the king of darkness has arrived in Evansville," Michael informed the crew. "This means that we are getting ready to be engaged to the fullest extent.

Whenever he shows up, he brings the biggest and vilest of his dark crew with him. We have all at one time or another battled this bunch, so we know what to expect."

"Michael, from what we have learned since we have been here is that the power source for us is few and far between. It has taken everything we had to defeat some of the little spirits and imps. How are we expected to battle these monsters?" Gabriel asked.

"The one advantage that we have is that we know his tactic. They have not changed over the centuries. He may go about them differently, but it is always the same. Like us, they have to have human participation in any endeavor they attempt. The first thing they will attempt is to weaken those that are on our side. We know that he will use any method he can to do so, including death. It is our position then to make sure that no matter what he does or what weapon he and his cohorts use against our people, we turn it around for our benefit. In other words, we need to use his weapons against him. Make his attacks push them deeper into prayer."

"If I know the king of darkness, he has his goons out right now performing their evil tasks, so we better get started now," Ariel stated.

"You are so right," Carmuel agreed.

"Let's go, and remember, be careful; do not let them catch any of us alone or during a time of weakness. Raphael, this is the time that you and your platoon will be of the greatest value," Michael said.

One weapon that the heavenly host had that their enemy didn't was their ability to become transparent. When the heavenly host wanted to go around undetected, they could simply become invisible to even the sons of darkness. This ability had worked to save countless numbers of potentially disastrous situations.

The king of darkness thought he knew everything that there was to know about Michael and his warring angels, but this was one thing that he was totally oblivious of. When the angel wanted the demon to know he was there, he would materialize.

Of course, there were also the times that an angel had encountered a demon in his material state before he had a chance to become invisible. When this happened, the angel had to fight; he couldn't become transparent.

As the angels ascended out through the top of the cave, they formed an angelic formation to begin their search for the meanest of the mean in the kingdom of darkness. They had to know where they were and what they were doing. The angels could not take the chance of them hindering the prayers that were so much needed. Raphael headed toward Hugo; he had an appointment at the Choctaw Memorial Hospital.

⚡

Mamie had been praying ever since she had gotten that feeling of doom early that morning. She spent over an hour interceding for the town and the people in the town. She didn't know exactly what, but she knew something big was getting ready to take place. She prayed that God would instill the importance to Rev. Fields and he would follow the leading of the Lord. Even the air outside held heaviness, a heaviness that was stifling.

Mamie now had to call Bertha and the other prayer warriors; they had to have intercessory prayer and the sooner the better. There was a call for action, and the action had to be now. If there were going to be some changes in Evansville, they had to start now or the consequences would be devastating.

XXIII

Ever since that day at his house, Hank had been terribly concerned about Jack. That was a situation that could have turned bad quickly. Jack seemed to be inhuman; after a brief struggle, Hank had managed to get the bat away and subdue him. He was not sure what was causing this behavior in him, but Hank knew there was something badly wrong.

He had questioned Rachael at length about when this had all started. She told him that Jack had been acting differently really ever since they had moved into the house and he had taken over the store. She said she at first just thought it was the pressure of trying to get the store out of the red into the black. But even after the business had picked up and they were making good profits, there was still something wrong. Rachael related to Hank how Jack had started to drink very heavily; he was drinking anywhere from three to four bottles of the Rollins Royale a week. Before he started drinking the

Royale, he would drink Hennessey, but she had never seen him drink that much before.

It had been Hank's suggestion to Rachael that she not give him any of the Royale and see if he would gradually come back to normal. He told her he felt that by the Royale having such a high alcohol content that Jack could have alcohol poisoning. If this didn't seem to work, then maybe she should take him to a doctor. The last thing Hank wanted was for Jack to go to a doctor and they find out that he was alcohol toxic; he didn't know exactly why, but he felt that could have dire consequences for himself. He had to help Rachael get Jack sober. Then they would see what happened. Hank had reassured Rachael that Jack's condition was strictly between them.

If she needed him, no matter what time of day or night, she could just call, because after all, Jack was his best friend.

Hank made his way to the courthouse. Lewis Walker and Terry Stevens were to be arraigned before Judge Hanes that morning. They had both been in the county jail for three days, but they still didn't seem quite right. They were jittery and nervous. Lewis Walker would sit in the corner of the cell and just rock back and forth. Terry Stevens would just pace back and forth.

The day before, when Randy had gone in to take their food, Lewis was begging him to get him something to drink, something strong. Randy said he believed both of those boys were going through the delirium tremors. It was odd because neither one of those two were known to be big on drinking. Of course, they would go out on Friday or Saturday night, have a few drinks, shoot a little pool, but that was about the extent of it. It was baffling to the deputies and the jail staff.

Hank remembered when Manny had told him about the product; he had said that the energy substance that he had would make people want to drink the Royale, and before they knew it, the Rollinses, Jack, and himself would be rich. Hank also remembered telling Jack that it would be something that people would have to have. They may not want it, but if they had to have it, they would buy it. Hank was going to have to talk with Manny about this new energy drink. Could it be that the energy substance was having an adverse affect on people? Hank needed to know what that energy product was. He had to know so he could prepare himself if anything came up and he had to protect himself. Then Hank remembered something, something that was upsetting; he had taken his mother a bottle of the Royale, because she said she felt like she was coming down with a cold and needed to make herself a little toddy.

He had to get in touch with Manny as soon as court was over today. They were going to have a serious talk. There needed to be more testing done on this stuff. It could be that the alcohol and the energy substances were incompatible, that the mixture was causing some type of toxic substance to be released into the body. Why hadn't he thought of that before? He was so desperate to get out of debt and live the good life, he never thought about what the stuff could do to people. This stuff was being shipped to Texas and Oklahoma; Manny said they were working on getting some liquor store contracts in Missouri and Arkansas.

If it were determined that this stuff was bad for human consumption, he could possibly be named in a multimillion-dollar lawsuit. *Not good, not good at all.*

Hank sat through the court proceedings, preoccupied with the situation with the Rollinses and Manny. It wasn't until he heard his name that he snapped out of his deep train of thoughts.

"Sheriff Wilson?" the judge was saying.

"Yes, Your Honor?"

"I was asking if you had any objections to these two young men being sentenced to community service? That would require you to be responsible for overseeing their progress."

"No, sir, no objections. That will be fine."

"All right then, I sentence you both to one thousand hours of community service for a total of six months. To be served at the discretion of the county sheriff. This sentence will commence on the first day of next month. If there is nothing else to come before this court, then I declare court is adjourned. Sheriff, I would like to talk to you in my chambers."

Hank hoped that whatever it was that the judge wanted to tell him wouldn't take too long; he had a lot of stuff to do today. Hank kept a watchful eye on Lewis and Terry. They still were not acting the way normal people would act. It was as if they had been on another planet during the trial. Hank wasn't even sure if they understood what they were sentenced to or what was expected. At least with them serving their sentence under his supervision, he could watch over them and hopefully keep them off the Royale.

Entering into Judge Hanes' office, Hank broke the silence.

"You want to talk to me, Judge?"

"Yes, I do. Have a seat, Hank. It has come to my attention that there is something going on in this town that I have been unaware of. I am not sure whether you know anything 'bout it or not. But if you don't, I think it is about time that you checked around and see what you can find out."

"Something like what, Judge?"

"Not real sure myself, but it has something to do with the Rollinses and their *enterprise*."

Hank felt an uneasy feeling, fright, creeping up on him again. It sure had been a day for him; it had been one thing after another to make him question his affiliation with Manny and the Rollinses. He was thinking that maybe he had better get out while the getting was good. Now the judge was asking questions. How much did he know? Was he watching his activities or was he just fishing? At any rate, he was going to have to keep a low profile with the Rollinses for a while.

"All right, Judge, I will see what I can find out. I will make it my own personal business to check into whatever it is or may be happening out at the Rollins.'"

"Good, see that you do. And, Hank, maybe you shouldn't be spending quite so much time out there." Judge Hanes concluded with an all-knowing look.

Without speaking, Hank left the judge's office, put on his cowboy hat, exited the building, got into his cruiser, and headed east.

⚡

Randy Baker had been true to his promise of patrolling Cherish's house every night. He would drive by her house two to three times during his shift. Randy had known Cherish in school—until she dropped out in the ninth grade. He had always had a secret crush on her but would never let anybody know about it. If the other kids in school had known how he felt, he would have been teased to no end. The guys at school had all classified her as just a no-account Rollins. Anybody that wanted to date her for anything other than a good time was *out of his mind*. Randy had kept his crush a secret from Cherish and everyone else, but that was a long time ago.

Now things were different; they were both adults. *What difference does it make to other people what I do?* But then there was the problem with her having a child. Nobody had the slightest idea who the father was. Some people in town suspected that she had been selling her body and got knocked up. And then there were those that said she had probably been fooling around with some circus freak over in Hugo. Not knowing who the child's father was could pose a problem if Randy ever decided to start seeing Cherish on a regular basis. He would just take it slow and see what developed.

⚡

Randy possessed an array of good looks. He had a head full of thick, dark brown hair. He had sexy eyes with thick dark eyebrows that spoke a language all their own. He had a nice smile that revealed straight white teeth. He would be a catch for any woman. And Cherish knew that he was not married. He was exactly the kind of man that she felt she would like to have in her life.

While she was at home, her father and brothers would never allow anybody to come calling. She wasn't even allowed to receive phone calls. This wasn't all bad because Cherish would have never wanted anybody to come out to her house anyway, not that anyone ever would. She was treated as a servant at home; she was useless except for cooking, cleaning, and fetching for her father and brothers. Her mother had always told her to that someday she would be free and she could leave there and make herself a real life. Cherish just never imagined that the life would be there in Evansville and she would be a single mother raising a little girl.

Thinking about Hope, Cherish knew that she was the most important thing that could have ever happened to her, regardless of the circumstances. Hope was hers. Somebody that loved her for who she was; somebody that no one could take away. It was while she sat there thinking about her life, past and present, that she saw the sheriff's department cruiser coming down the street. Tonight Cherish had decided to go outside and wave at Randy. Maybe he would stop and she could offer him a cup of coffee.

Seeing Cherish waving from the porch, Randy whipped into the driveway. Instinctively, his hand went to his revolver as he got out of the car.

"Is something wrong, Ms. Rollins?"

"No, nothing is wrong. I just thought I would wave as you drove by to let you know that I was appreciative of you patrolling my house."

"I thought that something or someone had managed to get into your house and I didn't see them." He laughed.

"No, I am sure that nobody is going to try and get in again. They know that you have a close watch on the place, and they would be stupid to try." *Now was the perfect time to invite him in,* Cherish thought. "Would you like a cup of coffee, Deputy Baker?"

"Randy," he corrected Cherish. "We have known each other too long to be so formal. Yep, a cup of coffee would be nice. I'm sure it is a million times better than that tar we have at the station."

"All right, Randy, come on in."

Cherish's house was immaculately clean; everything had a place and everything was in its place. Although it was an old house in much need of repair, it had a calm and peaceful atmosphere. It felt like home, the kind of home that Randy longed to have.

Cherish and Randy sat at the kitchen table. She had given him a piece of pound cake to go along with his coffee. It was a little awkward at first, but soon they were laughing and enjoying each other's company. After about forty-five minutes, Randy knew he had better get back to his rounds. If anyone questioned what had taken him so long, he would say that he had stopped to get some coffee and something to eat, which in reality was true. It just had not been a planned break.

Getting up to leave, Randy stopped. "Did you hear that?" he asked Cherish.

"No, hear what?" she answered, a little nervous at the way he was acting.

Going to the kitchen window, he looked out into the backyard.

"What is that you have back there in the yard?"

"Oh, that is just an old shed."

"You got anything in there?"

"Not really, just a few things that Mamie gave me when we moved in that I haven't got room for in here. Why?"

"You stay in here. I'm going to check it out. It is probably nothing—maybe a stray cat or something, but just to be on the safe side, I will find out." With his hand on his revolver, Randy slowly made his way to the shed.

⚡

Her body was shaking uncontrollably. The cough was getting worse and worse. By this time, Marge was way too sick to even get up off of the makeshift bed she had concocted. The fear that she was going to die was overwhelming. Unless someone came out here by accident, she could die, and no one would be any the wiser. Her bones could lay in here for years. This was not what she had hoped for the night she ran away. She had hoped to get far away from Evansville and start a new life in a place that Nolan would never find her. Evansville was like a tomb; it would embody her forever. No matter how hard she tried, she could not get away from this place. It was almost as if it had arms that held her until it squeezed the life right out of her body.

Marge was alone and scared. She hadn't eaten in two, maybe three days. She knew she needed some medicine but had no way of getting any. If she came out and went to find help, she was afraid that whoever she went to would call Nolan. Then he would only come get her, take her back, and beat her again. If he ever got a chance to beat her again, she knew it would be the last. He would *truly* kill her next time.

⚡

Slowly Randy opened the door to the shed. He could make out the figure of a person lying on a pile of old pillows covered with what appeared to be curtains. Shining the light, he saw it was a woman, but not just any woman. Calling back over his shoulder to Cherish, Randy instructed her to phone for an ambulance, and after she had done so, he thought she better come to the shed.

Oh my God, what could it be, or who could it be? Randy wouldn't ask me to call an ambulance if it wasn't somebody, she reasoned. Hands shaking so hard she could hardly hold on to the phone, Cherish dialed 911. When the operator answered, she gave them her name address and told them that Deputy Baker was there and he needed an ambulance.

"Is it the deputy that needs an ambulance, ma'am?" the operator asked. "Is he hurt?"

"No, it is not deputy Baker that needs an ambulance, but he said to send an ambulance. It is for somebody else."

"Do you know the victim's name and what happened?"

"No, I have no idea. I am just doing what he said. Hurry."

"We have a unit on the way, ma'am."

Hurriedly hanging up the phone, Cherish ran out of the back door and to the shed. Inside, she saw Randy kneeling beside the form of a person. Moving closer where she could see, Cherish put her hands over her mouth as she let a scream of pure anguish.

"Oh my God, *Mama!*" she screamed as she fell down beside the listless body. Cherish lifted her upper body in her arms and held on tight. On the floor around the pallet were a plate, cup, and an empty bowl that held homemade spaghetti. Randy exited the shed as he heard the sound of sirens approaching the house; he would have to direct them around to the backyard.

⚡

Mamie was tired from the day's activities. Sitting in her favorite chair, she was reading in the book of Psalm. The silence of the night was interrupted by the sound of sirens. The sirens seemed to be getting closer and closer. Looking out of the window, Mamie watched them as they pulled up to Cherish's house. In a state of panic, Mamie hurriedly grabbed her sweater off the coat rack and started toward Cherish's house, praying as she went: *Please, Lord, don't let anything be done happened to Cherish and little Hope, please, Lord.*

As Mamie came through the gate to the backyard, she could see the paramedics loading someone on the gurney. Looking around, she saw Cherish crying hysterically. Whoever was on the gurney was far too large to be Hope. Mamie let out a sigh of relief. At least it wasn't Cherish or the baby. Just who it was she didn't know. Another thing she didn't know was why were they in the backyard? Could this be the person that had broken into Cherish's house? Had they come back and the deputy had to shoot them? All of these questions were going through Mamie's mind as she watched from a distance as the paramedics placed oxygen on the person and hung a bag of IV fluid on the pole of the gurney.

Looking down into the face of the person as the gurney passed by, Mamie recognized the person on the gurney as Marge Rollins.

"Oh my Jesus, what has happened here?" she asked.

"Oh, Mamie, it's Mama. Randy heard something coming from the shed. So he went to see what it was and found her lying on some pillows covered up with those curtains that we took down from the windows. She is real sick, Mamie."

"Just you calm down now. They will get her to the hospital, and she will be just fine. Go get Hope and your sweater, and I'll go get the car. I'll be right back."

⚡

For Cherish, the ride to the hospital was the longest ride she could ever remember taking. Mamie was getting old, and her eyesight was not as good as it had been. At night, she had a real hard time judging distance. Cherish knew how to drive, but she had never gotten a license, so she couldn't legally drive. It took them what seemed like an hour to get to Hugo, a mere twenty miles away. Pulling up in front of the emergency room, Cherish had gotten out of the car almost before it was fully stopped. Mamie told her to go on in, and she would sit in the car with Hope who had gone to sleep in the backseat. Mamie knew she would continue to sleep.

Working at the hospital, Cherish knew where every room was and who every doctor was. She even knew every housekeeper, or environmental specialist, as they were called now. Rushing over to the emergency room's admitting clerk, Cherish frantically inquired about her mother's condition.

"Cherish, the doctor is in there with her right now, and it will be a few minutes before we know anything. In the meantime, there is some information that we need about your mother."

It seemed that the battery of questions was never going to end. Cherish answered as many as she could. But the rest, she told the clerk, she would have to get from her mother when she was able to talk.

It had been almost thirty minutes before the doctor entered the waiting area with news about her mother's condition.

"Cherish?" It was Doctor Johnson, the resident physician on call.

"Doctor Johnson, is my mother going to be okay?"

"She is a very sick lady. But I believe after a few days, she will begin to show some improvement. What exactly happened tonight? Was she in an accident or something?"

"I am not sure. You see, Randy—Deputy Baker," Cherish corrected herself, "heard a noise coming from a shed in my backyard, and when he went to see what it was, he found her laying in there. Tonight is the first time I have seen my mother in almost four years, Doctor. I really don't know what has happened."

Cherish believed that she did know what happened, but now was not the time to start making accusations. She would have to hear it from her mother. If it was what she thought or knew it was, then this time something had to be done.

"Can I see her now, Doctor?"

"Only for a few minutes, she really needs her rest. I gave her a sedative, so she probably won't even know that you were there. Most likely, she will sleep through the rest of the night and well into the morning."

XXIV

Hank sat impatiently at his desk. He had tried all morning to get touch with Manny, but every time he had, the phone would ring until it went to voice mail. Hank had left several messages for Manny to call. It had been well over an hour, and there had been no word from him.

Hank knew that Manny went nowhere without his cell phone, so he had to have gotten his messages. He only wished he had another number to call Manny's office, home, or anything. The office number he had called the first time was now out of service. But Manny had conveniently not given him the new number. That is, if there was a new number.

It was beginning to really make Hank angry. There were too many people acting strangely. Judge Hanes was putting pressure on him, demanding he be informed about the 'happenings at the Rollins' place." Manny was not returning his calls. The Rollinses were slacking in their duties. Hank was getting sick and tired of this mess; he would have to handle this thing his way.

Getting up, he prepared to leave the office, but he needed to give Mabel some type of explanation as to where he would be in case he was needed.

"Mabel, I will be back. I need to go over to check on my mother. She hasn't been feeling well, so I am going to see if she needs anything. If you need me, call my cell because I won't be able to hear the car radio."

"Oh, all right. Tell your mother I said hi and hope she is feeling better," Mabel replied.

While he was out, Hank decided he needed to also check on Jack. Maybe now that he has been off the sauce for a few days he was beginning to get better. Rachael hadn't called him, so he felt that was a good sign. First, he would go see about his mother; he hoped that she had not had any bad affects from that bottle of Royale. He had only taken her a half-pint that shouldn't be enough to do any real harm.

Walking up on the porch, Hank retrieved the mail from the box, picked up the newspaper, and knocked on the door. After about three minutes, he decided to just use his key and go on in. Mildred was probably glued to the television and couldn't hear him. Calling out as he entered the house, Mildred didn't answer. The house was quiet; no sound was stirring. That wasn't like her. She always had the television on maximum volume. Fear began to set in as he began to go from room to room calling out for his mother. Entering the bathroom, he saw Mildred lying on the floor between the sink and the commode.

Immediately placing his fingers to the left side of her

neck, feeling for a pulse, Hank determined that she was still alive, and he frantically phoned 911.

After calling 911 and waiting for the ambulance, Hank made a quick search through the house. He needed to find that bottle of Royale. He had to know how much of that stuff his mother had drunk. When he was a child, he remembered his mother would keep her bottle of medicinal booze in the pull-down floor bin of the old pie safe cabinet. This would be the best place to look now for the bottle. As he had believed, there in the bin was the bottle of Royale. Holding up the bottle, Hank estimated there was only about two or three ounces of the stuff gone. With a feeling of relief, Hank returned the bottle to its place. At least his mother hadn't drunk enough of that stuff to get sick; there had to be a legitimate medical reason for her unresponsiveness.

⚡

The emergency room nurse was writing down the report from the paramedics as Doctor Johnson entered the enclosed area of the department. "Doctor, the paramedics are bringing in a sixty-five-year-old female, possible CVA. Their estimated time of arrival is ten minutes."

"All right, is exam room three ready?"

"Yes, everything is in the room."

"Did they say whether she was stable?"

"They said her vital signs were stable, but she was unresponsive to tactile and verbal stimuli. Her vital signs are blood pressure 115/62, respirations 12, heart rate 80, temperature 98.6."

"Where are they en route from?"

"Evansville."

"Evansville? This is about the third or fourth person from there this week. What is going on over there?" Doctor Johnson inquired.

⚡

Michael was cautiously sitting in the tree at the side of the house as the paramedics removed Mildred Wilson from the house. He watched as Hank Wilson exited and prepared to follow the ambulance to Hugo. This was a very dangerous mission. Hank was one of Belial and his crew's most dedicated followers; it took much tact and discretion to make contact with him.

⚡

Phillip had a troubled feeling in his spirit. He kept going over in his mind what Mamie had said to him on Sunday night. He had heard about preachers that went into spiritual warfare, but he had never had a desire to fight demons. This was not, he believed, his calling. He believed that there were demons, because the Bible spoke of the fallen angels that followed Satan when he was banished from heaven. But in all actuality, he wasn't real sure whether those demons actually were walking the earth and influencing the lives of man.

Mamie had made it very plain that she believed that there were demons and evil forces in Evansville controlling the ways of life and the people. Once again, it could be the ramblings of a slightly deranged person. In his psychology class, he had learned that, more times than not, a person with a mental illness would go either one way or the other. They would either become extremely religious to a point of being fanatical or they would become overly occupied with their sexual nature.

Anyway it would not hurt, Phillip thought, *to read up on the world of demons and demonology.* Surfing the Internet for articles, documentaries, or any other information on demons, Phillip found several interesting sites. Some described the working of demons; others, the names of demons. Some described the classes or rankings of demons. There were sites on exorcisms and demon possessions. There were sites that contained articles relating the biblical significance of demons. Then there were those sites that completely dismissed demons altogether.

Studying through several sites and running a cross-reference, Phillip began to think that maybe Mamie wasn't too crazy after all. Phillip was just not prepared to be engaged in a spiritual warfare. In actuality, the thought of an encounter with demons frightened him. He never wanted to be the type of minister that went after demons on a personal level. He never considered himself as a demon buster. Phillip's experience in the realm of demons was very limited. He had only heard about how demons could possess a person. He had read the stories in the Bible about Jesus and the apostles encountering and casting out demons, but Phillip had never talked with anyone that had actually encountered or in any way dealt with a demon.

This is getting too far-fetched. This is almost as bad as the Salem Witch Hunts. I'm a rational person; I cannot allow the superstitions of an old woman to influence my thinking, to be out there, searching for something that in all probability does not exist. He reasoned that the things that were happening were happening because of the will of man. God honored man's free will, and it was man that caused the things that were happening around them. It was due to the sin nature that man allowed things to influence them—greed, power, lust, and pride.

Being satisfied with his conclusion, Phillip determined that his next sermon and possibly at Bible study that night, he would teach on those subjects. Maybe that would help to dissuade any further thinking about the devil and demons taking over.

No matter how hard he tried to remove the topic of demons from his mind, it seemed it always was popping up. One minute he convinced himself demons didn't exist—at least, not in the way that Mamie believed. The next minute he caught himself wondering if maybe they did. It was very unnerving for Phillip.

If it didn't stop, he was going to find himself locked up in the Looney Bin. Since his latest conversation with Mamie, there were times he would wonder about everything that happened, wondering if it was a direct result of a demon. If he lost something, he was thinking that a little imp had stolen it. If he accidentally cut himself shaving, he would envision an imp controlling the razor.

This is stupid. Phillip was sure that the devil and his imps had more important things to do than steal pencils or cut his face while he shaved. The image that he had conjured up was that of a mischievous child playing pranks. But he was well aware that Satan was not a prankster but a master deceiver that wanted to rule the world and the people in it. Phillip was beginning to do what he had spoken against on Sunday. That was "not to look for demons under every rock and around every corner." He had assured the congregation that demons were indeed real, and they were on the earth. They indeed had a job to perform. They could make certain things happen and control some aspects of one's life. But they were not just sitting around waiting to pounce on you from a tree as you passed by. *Or were they?* He began to wonder.

As Phillip sat in his office continuing to read some of the articles on demonology, the phone began to ring. *It was a blessing,* he thought, *that God had given someone the wisdom to invent caller ID.* Now he could see who was calling and possibly get a vague idea of what to expect when he answered the phone. The caller ID said "Mamie Webb." Phillip wasn't sure he wanted to talk with her just right now. Maybe he would not answer; he didn't really want to hear about demons and what they could do at this moment. But then again he had to answer. She maybe calling saying that she wasn't coming to Bible study tonight. Reluctantly, Phillip picked up the phone.

"Hello, this is Pastor Fields," trying to project a tone of cheerfulness.

"Hello, Pastor, I was calling to ask you to pray. Mildred Wilson was rushed to the emergency room a little while ago," Mamie reported.

"Oh, I hate to hear that. Do you know what was wrong?"

"Only thing I know is that her son, Hank, went to check on her, and he found her unconscious on the bathroom floor. They think she may have had a stroke."

"Of course we will be in prayer for her and her family that the Lord will raise her up off of her bed of affliction, that she will not have any residual effects of this stroke."

"And also, Pastor, I don't know if you have heard, but we also need to be in prayer for Cherish."

"What is wrong with Cherish?" Phillip asked.

"It's not Cherish; it is her mother, Marge Rollins. She was found in a shed last night, a shed behind Cherish's house. She was in pretty poor shape, and she is in the hospital also."

This information was more than Phillip could swallow all at one time. In the last week, there had been more and more occurrences of illness, crime, and disaster than there had been the whole year that he had lived here. Not to mention the things that had happened to him personally. What was going on?

"Thank you, Mamie. I will go into prayer when we get off the phone. Is Cherish all right?"

"Yes, she is fine. She took off a few days so she could stay there with her mother. She left Hope with me."

⚡

Hanging up the phone, Mamie stated out loud, "Lord, please turn his heart and open his eyes that he may see what you are trying to show him."

⚡

Phillip was in a total state of disbelief of the news that he had just received. There had to be a rhyme and reason to what was happening. There had to be a solution, a logical solution to the events. He now believed that he had to get out and reach the people of this town. Convince them that it was time to change their lives. Then the conditions would change in the town. It wasn't, in Phillip's opinion, until the people turned from their present state of spiritual health that things would begin to change. If not, they were destined only to get worse.

With this determination in mind, Phillip began to study on repentance and deliverance from sin. He would teach that subject tonight; he would also emphasize the importance of going out into the community and witnessing to the people, trying to bring them into the fold of safety. He would start an outreach ministry designed to spread the gospel into the streets. That is where Jesus and his disciples were: in the streets. They were not closed up inside a church building; no, they were out among the people, people that needed them and their message of hope and salvation. That is where Phillip was going to be: in the streets. If he was truly going to be a minister of Christ or Christlike, he needed to do what Christ did. Still Phillip's thoughts went back to the subject of demons and their activities. *This has got to stop*, Phillip once again cautioned himself, *and it has got to stop now*. "Lord, please ease my mind. Remove these thoughts that have been planted."

⚡

Rachael, feeling the effects of the last few weeks on her body, finally had gotten a chance to lie down and get a little rest. She knew she couldn't sleep long, only as long as Lucas slept. The last few days she thought she could see a little improvement in Jack. Once she had convinced him that there was no more Rollins Royale at the store. It was on back order and would not be in until late next week. Jack had gradually begun to calm down.

It had taken about three days, but now she believed that there was some improvement. This was reflected in the fact that he had started to sleep more; he wasn't rambling through the house as he had before. He would actually sit and watch television for a short period of time.

Maybe Hank had been right; Jack probably had alcohol toxicity, and now that the vile stuff was coming out of his system, he was slowly returning to normal. What she didn't know was just how long it would be before he was back to the Jack she had married. *What if he had residual effects from this? What if he never returned to normal? Then what would she do?*

When she woke up, she would call Hank and let him know how Jack was progressing. She hadn't talked to him since the day he had been at the house and had to physically restrain Jack.

Rachael had never believed that her life would have taken such a drastic turn. There had to be something that could be done, something she could do that would restore hope in her and in Jack. Something that would alleviate the pain and suffering that she had endured for the past few months of living there in Evansville. She hated the place. It was little, broken down, and horrible. There was nothing to do, nowhere to go, and she had no friends. She had no one to talk too. The last few weeks she had felt herself falling into a deep dark hole. A hole that had no bottom; she was just falling. She had lost all interest in her appearance, and her self-esteem had diminished to nothing. Just thinking about these things, the tears started to flow onto the pillow, tears that she could no longer restrain, tears for herself and her seemingly hopeless situation. *What can I do? Where can I go to escape this prison I've found myself in?*

⚡

Sleeping soundly in the recliner at the bedside, Cherish was deep into a state of dreaming, a dream that had haunted her for a while. She had a reoccurring dream that she was in the barn; her father had tied her up by her hands, and she was hanging there, not unlike a side of beef. She envisioned herself naked. She could hear the sound as the bullwhip cracked toward her body. Even in her dream, she could feel the sting as the leather made contact with her already bloody skin. Being jarred awake from the dream, looking around, she had to regain her bearing. Then she remembered she was in the hospital with her mother. She wondered if she had made any noise while she was asleep. *Did she say anything, and if she had, did anyone hear her?*

Letting the recliner down into the chair position, Cherish went to the bed. Looking down at her mother, she could see the scars and bruises that covered her face, neck, and arms. The bruises had taken on a green and yellow coloration as they began to fade. Pulling back the covers, Cherish followed a tube that was placed into the right side of her mother's chest down the side of the bed into a plastic container. It was a chest tube, applied to re-inflate a lung that had collapsed. There were about one hundred millimeters or three ounces of bloody drainage collected in the container. The IV was connected to a pump and was infusing at one hundred fifty millimeters an hour. Marge Rollins was still unresponsive from the analgesic and sedatives the doctor had prescribed. Looking at her mother in her weakened condition, Cherish made a vow that she would never let her father hurt her mother again. "God, please don't let my mama die. Let her get all right. I promise, Lord, I will take care of her. She will not have to go through this ever again. Lord, if you will heal her, I will do whatever you need me to do as long as you need me to do it," she prayed.

"Good morning," the doctor's voice interrupted.

"Hello, Doctor," Cherish replied.

When she had brought her mother in last night, Doctor Johnson, the resident had admitted her to the hospital. He had given the initial orders for treatment then assigned her continued care to Doctor Wheeler. "I was going over your mother's records, and I see that she had to have a chest tube placed due to a collapsed lung. Also the physical assessment reveals there are numerous bruises and cuts on her body. Do you know how she got those bruises and cuts?"

"Not really. I hadn't seen my mother for a while. Actually, last night is the first time in a long time. I have no clue what happened to her." Cherish knew full well that she couldn't tell the doctor what had happened—at least not until she had heard it from her mouth's mouth.

"Well, Cherish, there has to be a reason for a person's lung to collapse. There have been cases of spontaneous deflation, but those are very rare cases. From the X-ray, we have found out that your mother sustained a fractured rib that in turn punctured the lung, causing it to deflate." Cherish listened carefully as Doctor Wheeler explained the cause and effect of her mother's condition.

"Our main concern at this point is to get that lung reinflated. We are also giving her some antibiotics because her white blood count is up to four thousand. That tells us there is an infection somewhere. Once we have those two things resolved, I believe that she will be fine, unless of course there are other injuries that we don't know about."

"Do you think it will be a long process of her getting better, Doctor?"

"It has been my experience that it usually takes three or four days for a lung to re-inflate, and the antibiotics should start working in twenty-four to forty-eight hours. I would say she should be better and ready for discharge by the end of next week or maybe the first of the next. That is once again, if everything goes all right."

"Thank you, Doctor." Cherish was indeed relieved to know that the doctor did not believe that her mother's condition was so serious that it would take months to get over. She silently said a prayer of thanks.

XXV

Manuel Lopez, whose real name was not Manuel Lopez, but Ricardo Almendarez, was on top of the game when it came to racketeering. He had been successfully avoiding any form of suspicion for years. He surely was not stupid enough to use his real name with these stupid people over in Oklahoma. That would be like signing himself into the closest state or federal penitentiary. As far as anyone in Dallas knew, he was a legitimate businessman. As a matter of fact, Ricardo was hardly ever in his places of business. He left that to the managers and his top men to do. He led a very routine life. He got up every morning at five thirty, ran a mile, then returned to his large eighteen-room home, read the paper, made some phone calls, and then spent the rest of the day doing pretty much as he wanted to.

To all outward appearances, Ricardo was a perfect husband and father. He and his family attended St. John's Catholic Church every Sunday. He made major contributions to the church to help with the school, orphanage, and hospital. He was held in the highest regards by the parish priest. There was nothing to suggest that Ricardo Almendarez was anything but on the up-and-up.

Ricardo knew that until he was sure that everything was going the way it should, he was going to have to take a personal interest in the affairs over in Evansville, hence the name Manuel "Manny" Lopez. They were a group of backwoods hicks that didn't have a clue about anything. They were only looking at making money and being able to brag about the moonshine that they were making. *Give them a few hundred dollars, a new truck, and a few gold chains, and they were on top of the world,* he thought.

The problem was he didn't want too much bragging. After all, it was loose lips that sank ships. He didn't want anything to go wrong. The operation was too important for that. He had the best of all worlds; here he was, supplying some of the purest uncut cocaine in the world, and it was being distributed across two states without the authorities having a clue. It was being sold right under their noses, and they were totally oblivious to the fact. Who knows? Some of them may have purchased it and sampled the wares themselves. Wouldn't it be funny if these almighty officers of the law had to have a drug test and it came back positive and they not have a clue how? This stuff could be sold to doctors, lawyers, school teachers, police officers, even FBI and DEA agents, and there was no way they could ever trace it back to him. Rollins' Royale could make its way into the homes of the country's and the world's highest officials. Even if it was discovered that there was cocaine in the stuff and they went to bust the good citizens of Evansville, those illiterate fools would instantly begin to blame everything on Manny Lopez, a person who did not exist, and his distillery and bottling plant that also did not exist. Ricardo was proud of himself for coming up with this dynamic scheme; it was pure genius. The days of selling drugs on the street with a drug dealer and runners were over for him.

He would leave that to small-time people. He was going to be the biggest drug distributor in the world. Now it was just the matter of keeping production running and the merchandise coming in.

Ricardo was certain that after his last visit to Evansville, there would be no more trouble with getting the supply to meet the demand. Looking at his cell phone, he saw that Hank Wilson had phoned again. Ricardo didn't have time to mess with him right now. He probably was calling to whine about some minute little something. He would just have to wait. Ricardo was in the middle of negotiating a contract with a major liquor distributor in Missouri. That was much more important than what this little worm could want.

⚡

Uriel was standing guard at the entrance to the church. Things were heating up so much that he knew the church would be the first line of attack from the king of darkness and his vile army of slime. Uriel had a sense of dread the people were not praying as they should. Of course there were the daily prayers going up, those of thanksgiving and petitions, but true heartfelt intercession *had not* yet occurred. He and his crew were hard at work planting the seed of faith and prayer among the people, but as yet there was still a lacking.

Michael informed his warriors not to interfere in certain actions of the sons of darkness; he felt that if enough bad things happened, then the people, if out of nothing but sheer desperation, would begin to cry out for deliverance.

Gabriel had been hard at work with his platoon, guarding over Phillip, Mamie, and Cherish. Once he had received confirmation, he would once again attempt contact with the Rev. Potter. Being a called minister of God, Rev. Potter couldn't help but know the signs of the times, regardless how indifferent he may appear or how complacent he had become. The calling on his life was far too strong for him to ignore, especially at a time like this.

Although the situation was looking a little bleak, all the archangels knew that in due season all things would work out for good. But in the meantime, there was still a lot of work to be done and a lot of battles to be won. But in order to win a battle, the angels had to have the right ammunition and power.

In the old warehouse at the far south end of town, the King of Darkness was holding a meeting, preparing all of his soldiers for a major attack. An attack he would assure them was nothing to fear. "Now that everything is in order, we cannot afford for anything to go wrong. I want to get a report of all the activities up to this point to make plans for the next step. Let's begin with the Rollinses."

Jesse stepped forward to give an in-depth report of the activities and mental state of the Rollins family. "Your Highness," Jesse addressed the Chair. After receiving the nod, he continued.

"Once the Rollins boys got out of jail, they returned to work. They understand that if they didn't keep up production, they are in for a real bad time. Nolan is driving those boys with a sharp iron prod. Nolan has the idea that he will get even with Jason for beating him up, and this only gives him more determination and makes him work even harder. Of course, we know that nothing he can devise will work in the way of revenge, but he doesn't know that. It is just a catalyst to keep him functioning at high speed." Jesse was about out of air after his long monologue.

"Is that all?" the king of darkness inquired. "There is nothing of a threat to us out there, is there?"

"Only one tiny thing, but it is really nothing to worry about," Jesse stuttered. "Marge Rollins has disappeared."

"Disappeared how?" His Highness asked with the familiar tone of anger.

"It seems that after Nolan's encounter with the boys from Dallas, he was so angry that he went in and took his frustration out on Marge. Then sometime during the night or early morning hours, she left."

"Now just where might she have gone?" the king asked in a tone of sarcasm.

"I'm not real sure, sire," Jesse answered, fear clutching him like a belt. "I have had a troop out looking everywhere, trying to locate her, but we still haven't found her."

"That tells me that the heavenly hosts are behind her disappearance. I want her found, do you understand? I don't care what it takes. Get her back!"

"Yes, sir," Jesse replied and took out in search of Marge. Jesse was afraid; he was afraid of the mighty warring angels, and he was also afraid of the king of darkness. With either opponent, he was subject to come out as a faint memory in the kingdom of darkness.

Continuing with his meeting, the king proceeded to his next topic.

"What about Hank Wilson? Are there any problems with him?"

"No, not now, sire." It was Faros that spoke up. "There was a small problem with him. He had started to question the operation; he was beginning to wonder about the long-term effects of his continued involvement with it. So we had to eliminate those thoughts."

"Good. What did you do?" The king was pleased with this response; it always pleased him when his crew could eliminate any form of good.

"We made sure that no matter how he thought he wanted out, he would have to continue. It is always just a matter of money," Faros continued.

The king, openly pleased with the report, smiled a large toothless smile.

"We arranged for his mother to suffer a stroke. Now he will be facing huge hospital bills, and he will need every dime he can get, and on his salary he would never make it."

"That is the kind of thing I want to hear. Next, what about Rachael Sims?"

"Rachael is a little iffy, sire," Astaroth announced. "One minute she is going right along with the plan; the next she is crying. It is when she starts crying that we worry because she starts to question. It has been proven over the years when a human gets fed up and starts to question, the next thing they will do, even unaware, is pray."

"Keep the spirits of pride and rebellion close by her at all times. With those two spirits lingering with her, she will lose all desire to question. With no questions, then there will be no prayer. Since we are on the subject, what's going on with Jack Sims?"

"Right now he is coming around to our way of thinking. Of course we had to make sure that he would go along with the plan, so we put him in a state of confusion with hallucinations, and now that he is coming out, he will be more susceptible to our influence and suggestions." Astaroth, now finished with his report, resumed his seat.

"All of that sounds promising and except for that Rollins woman we seem to be doing just fine," the king stated. "Now that I know where our allies stand, I need to know what are we doing about that troublemaker, Mamie, and her little puppets, Cherish, Phillip, and the rest of those self-proclaimed *prayer warriors.*"

There was silence in the room; everyone was sitting as though they were in deep thought. It was Belial that finally broke the silence.

"Sire, we have set plans in motion to eliminate those people. We already have accomplished one victory: Diana Whitaker. It was arranged that she would take a nasty little fall. Now she is in the hospital in a semi-comatose state," he concluded.

"That's fine and good, but what about Mamie?"

"We are working on that, sir. It's just that..."

"It's just what?" the king growled.

"Well, we can't seem to get close to her; she is so well

protected. Some of the largest angels of heaven have her under constant guard."

The king sat totally still; the demons in the room became increasingly nervous, wondering what his next words would be. Would he, with one swipe of his hand, send them all flying into an unknown realm? Would he allow his two gigantic armor bearers to send their fiery breath out and vaporize them? They were all unsure of their fate within the next few minutes as they waited for his response.

For what seemed to those in anticipation of his next words an eternity, the king finally opened his mouth. With breath that would melt glass he shouted, "I want those miserable good-for-nothing prayer warriors *stopped*! I want them stopped no matter what it takes. I want it done *now*."

The force of his breath sent those immediately in front of him sprawling backward.

"I want all of the princes and principalities to pull out all your imps and spirits. Get them put on these prayer warriors immediately. I want you looking under every rock, in every ditch, and behind every door until each and every one of them have been identified. I do not want one to slip through the net."

"Yes, sire," all the demons said in unison.

"I want every demon and spirit imaginable—the spirits of self-will, strife, bickering, hurt, spite, hatred, stubbornness, accusation, criticism, rejection, insecurity, rejection, inadequacy, and fear. Do you understand what I am saying? I do not want *anything* left undone. I want that scum to be attacked from every inner and outer source. I want them to be so confused and miserable that they will have no desire to pray or the unction to utter even an Amen. And do not forget the spirits of lust and greed."

"We understand, sire, but those people have a strong hedge of protection around them. They have some of the mightiest archangels known protecting them," Azazel spoke up.

"You don't worry about the archangels. *I* will take care of them. You just take care of the little things like emotions, feelings, and physical condition. Believe me, you will have no problem getting through the defenses."

Listening to the king gave the demons imps and spirits a boost of confidence. They now felt with the most powerful beasts of darkness there to watch their backs, there was nothing that they could not do.

The first course of action would be to draw the archangels out to be destroyed by the mighty beasts of darkness. Once this was accomplished, the rest would be easy.

With a flurry of wings fluttering and a deafening chatter, the demons exited the old warehouse. Now with a newfound energy and determination to whip the heavenly host and to push their operation into full gear, they flew out into the town of Evansville. It wasn't necessary any more to hide from the warring angels. Instead, it was their job now to pull them out in the open.

Astaroth's first destination was to go to Mamie's house. He wanted to be the one that caused her to stumble, to render her defenseless. If he could accomplish this feat, he would certainly gain the respect and admiration of the king and could be promoted to a higher level with more important responsibility.

Mastema, having the same idea, also set out to go to

Mamie's house; he was, after all, the one who originally got the plan rolling. He definitely could not allow someone else to steal his moment of glory.

Azazel instantly headed to the New Life Christian Fellowship. He was certain this is where he would find his nemesis, Gabriel. It would be a true pleasure to see him squirm under the pressure that would be applied to him by the mighty beast of darkness.

This was one of the happiest days that the sons of darkness could remember. This would be the day they would actually defeat the heavenly host and become the rulers of the universe.

⚡

Carmuel, sitting quietly in the rafters of the old building, had heard everything that the king of darkness had reported to his workers.

He now had to get to the cave and report their activities to Michael. With lightening speed, he flew to the cave. With his power fading, he was worried about his ability to remain transparent. Managing to make it to the cave in the nick of time, Carmuel addressed his leader. "Michael, I just left the old warehouse. The king of darkness has instructed his imps and demons to wage all-out attacks on the prayer warriors and the Rev. Fields. He has sent for the spirits of self-will, strife, bickering, hurt, spite, hatred, stubbornness, accusation, criticism, rejection, insecurity, rejection, inadequacy, fear, lust, and greed, among others. He has called for all the forces of hell to help with this battle. He is having them released right now."

"We need to be prepared. Those can be very dangerous spirits," Michael stated. "We better get ready to ascend to the call."

"Wait, Michael, there is more. The demons are going to attempt to pull us out into an open battle with the beasts of darkness in order to have free reign with the warriors. He also has sent out a search party to find Marge Rollins to make sure she does not mess up their whole operation. Now this is the worst part: the king of Darkness has declared that none of the other demons, imps, or beasts is to confront you. You he wants for himself."

"I am not surprised at that declaration," Michael admitted. "He has wanted to have face-to-face combat with me for centuries. There is only one thing I have a concern about: if the prayer warriors are unarmed, that means we will be defenseless against these vile and putrid creatures.

Unless we have our energy source, our power will be extremely limited." Looking around at his warriors, Michael recognized that there wasn't enough power among them all to defeat one of the princes of darkness, not to mention one of the beasts of the deep.

"I have no doubt that they are headed to Mamie's house as we speak," Gabriel volunteered. "She is the strongest weapon we have in this place. Without her, the others would crumble in a heartbeat—that includes Phillip."

"You are so right," Uriel interjected. "Phillip is already having difficulty believing that there truly is a spiritual war going on all around him. It would not take but one small insignificant imp to turn him completely around."

"Phillip has always had a fear of rejection and humiliation. The one thing he will avoid at all cost is conflict. What he doesn't understand is that the worse conflict that he will ever encounter is the one he cannot see," Michael said.

As Michael was speaking, there came an urgent call from headquarters. "Michael, the battle has begun. The sons of darkness are all over the town of Evansville. They have spirits attacking any and everyone they come in contact with. One of the bad things is that the spirits are using their power of transference to go from place to place," headquarters reported.

All of the archangels and warring angels knew what that would mean. Like the angels' power to be transparent, the demons had the power to invade a person's body and then be transferred to someone else simply by touch. They had been known to pollute whole countries that way. The King of Darkness was truly playing for keeps with this one.

The angels all knew that they would be victorious in the end, but what would the collateral damage consist of?

XXVI

The forces of hell were in full operation, busy causing havoc and chaos throughout the town of Evansville. Mamie was sure that things were coming to a boiling point. She could feel the presence of evil everywhere she went. She had been in prayer all morning, prayers of intercession for the town of Evansville, Marge Rollins, Diana Whitaker, and Cherish. Being on the road of intercession as long as she had, Mamie was pretty familiar with the wiles of the enemy. She understood that he did not play fair nor did he surrender easily.

Looking toward the ceiling, Mamie thanked God that it was Wednesday and they would be going to church tonight. What Rev. Fields intended to be Bible study she asked the Lord to redirect into intercession. Mamie was well aware of the fact that Rev. Fields did not believe in the actual existence of demons and spiritual warfare. But Mamie reasoned with God, "Thomas didn't believe that Jesus had arisen until you made a believer out of him, so I'm asking that you make a believer out of Pastor Fields, Lord. I'm asking that you do it fast."

With the presence of this much evil, Mamie also knew that she would come under numerous and possibly strong attacks. She prayed that the Lord would give her the strength to withstand whatever it was that the devil threw at her. She prayed for the strength of all the intercessors. She knew that all were not as strong as she was.

They would need extra help in this time of trouble. Now it was time for her to get busy; she had to make contact with all those she knew she could count on to be at church that evening.

⚡

Hank Wilson had been told that it was very likely that his mother had suffered a cerebrovascular accident, better known in layman's terms as a stroke. This stroke had affected the left side of her body. With the proper treatment and extensive physical therapy, the doctor believed she would be able to regain most if not all of the functioning of that side.

Driving home from the hospital, thinking about what the doctor had said, unbeknownst to Hank, he had a front and a backseat passenger. The spirit of worry was riding in the front, and the spirit of self-pity was the backseat passenger. While he drove along, they struck up a conversation that Hank believed were his thoughts coming to the forefront of his mind.

"Physical therapy will cost a mint," the spirit of worry stated.

"I don't know what he can do. He doesn't make enough money to pay for that," was the spirit of self-pity's reply.

"What if the therapy takes months? How will the bill be paid?"

"Hank is the only one to look to for payment. He is her only child."

While the two spirits were interjecting these thoughts into the mind of Hank Wilson, they were then joined by the spirit of hopelessness.

"There is only one way to get the money for these medical expenses, and that is to make sure that the Rollins' Royale continues to sell," the spirit of hopelessness added to the mind game.

"What about the bad side effects that are cropping up with that stuff?" the spirit of worry mused.

"What other option is there? There is nothing else he can do. Nobody else can or will do anything," was the spirit of self-pity's addition.

"It doesn't matter; at this point, you got to do what you got to do." The conversation ended with the spirit of hopelessness instilling the final decisive statement. With this mission accomplished, the three spirits retreated to their next assignment.

⚡

Phillip was struggling with the thought of spiritual warfare and demons. No matter how hard he tried, he could not seem to get the subject off his mind. Being confused without any plausible solution, he had phoned his father-in-law to pick his brain on the subject. What Phillip learned was astonishing.

When he asked his father-in-law what he knew about

demons and spiritual warfare the first question out of Robert Johnson's mouth had been, "Why? What is happening?"

Phillip thought that was strange. He hadn't said anything was happening; he just wanted to get some information on the subject. But not wanting to sound totally ignorant of the subject himself, Phillip related that there were some things happening but he couldn't attribute them to demons. He then explained to Robert his conversation with Mamie. Robert listened intently as Phillip related the whole conversation. He also told Robert how Mamie had appeared at the church, and then the next Sunday, she was instrumental in bringing almost fifty people to service. Still, Robert listened without speaking. After rattling on at length with Robert not saying a word, Phillip was wondering if Robert was still on the line or if they had been disconnected.

"Hello? Are you still there?" Phillip inquired.

"I'm here," Robert replied. "I was listening to your story. You say this Mamie is a black lady?"

"Yes, she is."

"And you say she said that there are a few that have been meeting, waiting on the Lord to send them a pastor?"

"That is what she said. But remember now; people here say that Mamie is a little touched in the head. I have reason to almost believe them, because she told me that she has seen the little imps." Phillip chuckled at that last comment. But there was no sound of laughter coming from the other end.

"Son, you obviously called me to get some information. Also I believe you called to get a second opinion on your own state of mental health. Because in your heart you do believe that this story of Mamie's is true, but your logic tells you that it is far-fetched. Am I right?" Robert asked.

"Yes, I guess that could be true. I needed to find out from you about this demonology stuff. I have researched it on the Internet and have found so many conflicting theories I don't really know what to believe."

"What I am going to tell you may or may not be what you want to hear, but I believe either way it will help you. After I have told you what I am going to tell you, then I want you to go into prayer and see if God will confirm or reject what I have said, all right?"

"All right," Phillip agreed.

"First of all, never underestimate the wisdom of an old prayer warrior. You see, they have been on the battlefield for a long time.

"One thing you will learn as you mature in the ministry is that God reveals things to the intercessor a lot sooner than he will reveal it to you. It is the intercessor that is the biggest help a minister can have. The sad thing is that so many pastors, preachers, and ministers refuse this help that God sends due to pride. They will believe the intercessor is attempting to take over or that they are trying to usurp the pastor's authority. But in reality the intercessor is there to make sure that any type of evil is recognized before it can do temporary or, in some cases, permanent damage." This remark stung Phillip to the core. He had felt that Mamie was trying to come in and take over, that she was trying to run things.

"And as far as her saying that she could see the little imps, don't make light of that. There is a very real possibility that she can." Robert continued, "Now I will tell you a story that happened to me when I was young in the ministry. I had been asked to come and speak at a woman's home Bible study, in a little town set off deep in the southernmost part of Oklahoma, almost on the line of Texas. This meeting was at a lady's home who lived quite a way out in the country.

"Before I went, I had told the members of my church about this meeting and where it was going to be held. There was one elderly lady, an intercessor, in the congregation, and after service, she came up to me and asked if I minded if she went along with me. I told her no, I didn't mind. This was something that was a little strange, but I dismissed it as an old lady just wanting an opportunity to get out of the house and go somewhere different. It was as we were on the way to this meeting this old lady, my wife and me, that she explained her reasons for wanting to come along.

"She said the Lord had shown her that when I got there, I was going to be confronting the very forces of evil and that she was to go to give me a prayer covering that would usher in the warring angels. Being young like you, I felt this old lady was probably senile and I needed to patronize her, so I merely said I appreciated that and once again dismissed it. While I was ministering at this meeting, there was a woman there who just kept staring at me. I avoided looking at her because her stare sent an odd feeling through my whole body. I noticed that the old lady from my church after a while had made her way over to this woman and sat down right next to her. About halfway through my lesson, this woman started to question some of the things I was teaching; she was very disruptive, anyway, to make a longer story short." Robert laughed, knowing that he had gone on and on but needed to get the point across to his young son in the ministry. "Before the night was over, it was discovered that this woman was actually demon-possessed. We ended up performing an exorcism right there in the lady's living room that was holding the Bible study."

Wow was all Phillip could say.

"So believe me, son. Never underestimate the wisdom of an intercessor, especially one that is seasoned and mature in the Word. If Mamie says there is evil taking over Evansville, my advice is to listen to her and do whatever it is the Lord has told her to do."

"Thank you, Dad. I really don't know much about the activities of the spiritual realm, and I have no idea how to fight a spiritual battle."

"You will learn. I believe that you have a good teacher right there with you. But if there is anything I can do to help, just let me know."

"I will, believe me."

After hanging up at the end of his conversation, Phillip was more perplexed now than he was at first. If his father-in-law, a mature minister, said he should believe Mamie and follow her lead in this matter, then he had no choice but to listen. Just the words "war" and "battle" made him uneasy. He knew that there were always casualties in any war and wounded in any battle. Phillip was now wondering if this was what the Lord had sent him here to do, to fight a spiritual battle. *What does he do now?* He would really need the help of someone more experienced in this area than he was. Tonight would be the beginning of a totally new experience.

Gabriel had his crew stationed around the church. Tonight was very important to the upcoming confrontations; there was no way that the sons of darkness could get the chance to hinder the progress of this encounter.

Azazel, watching from the shrubbery at the edge of the property, was feeling very cocky. He just knew this was his chance to settle a long score with the angel of inspiration. All Azazel had to do was make himself known; then he would have Gabriel right where he wanted him—out in the open and right into the hands of the mighty beast. With courage increased, Azazel casually strolled up to the door of the church. The atmosphere that was coming from the inside was more than he could tolerate. But he knew the only way he was going to accomplish what he had set out to do, was to venture into the building.

With unparalleled speed, the warring angel flew toward Azazel with sword drawn. Azazel shot backward, barely missing being cut in half. Azazel fled from the church with the warring angel in close pursuit. The beast of darkness flew down from the tree as if a fiery comet headed straight toward the warring angel, slashing his lethal sword crisscross through the air. The tip of the beast's sword cut a gash in the left bicep of the warring angel.

The angel, with the speed of light, flew high up into the air. With the advantage of height on his side, the angel turned. Like a streak of lightening, he charged toward the beast, sword pointed out straight. Being caught off balance from the impact, the sword penetrated the beast through the tough armor of his chest. Wings crumbled beneath him. Legs twisted, the beast lie on the ground with the large warring angel standing as a mountain of light over the pathetic creature. Pulling his sword from the chest, he plunged it deep into the abdomen of the disgusting creature. With a screech, the monster evaporated into a red sulfuric smoke.

The prayer warriors gathered in the church got an urgent unction to begin to pray, to pray with an earnest dedication for something to manifest. With the prayer warriors praying, the warring angels were gaining more and more strength, allowing them to fight the spirits, imps, princes, and beasts of darkness that were waging an all out attack.

Making his way silently under the seats of the sanctuary, the spirit of discontentment crawled toward the person praying on the front row. Gabriel, noticing this slimy little scum, positioned himself directly in front of the prayer warrior, awaiting the spirit to emerge from under the seat. Coming out from beneath the seat, the creature was looking up at the prayer warrior. He was prepared to invade their person for later transference.

Turning around to see if the coast was clear in front of him, he saw large muscular legs and feet shod in the iron armor of battle. Following the legs up with his eyes, fear struck his heart as he saw the piercing eyes of Gabriel standing before him. Before the spirit had a chance to move, Gabriel grabbed him up by his neck and flung him into the wall. Making contact with the hard surface, the spirit dissolved into black chalk.

Raphael, feeling that there was a major emergency

developing, knew that he had to restore Diana Whitaker as soon as possible.

Entering her room, the guardian angel that had been left to protect her was silently standing at the head of the hospital bed, wings outreached, forming a canopy over her sleeping body. Raphael moved to the side of her bed. He lightly laid his hand on her forehead. Instantly, her eyes opened.

Diana, looking at her arm, saw the tube that was connected to her right arm leading to a machine to the side of her bed. Looking down, she saw the shape of her body covered with a white blanket and sheets. Trying to remember what had happened, she vaguely recalled standing on a stool to get a can of salmon. She remembered feeling herself losing control, falling backward. After that, she had no recollection of the events that occurred next.

Finding the nurse call, Diana pushed the red button. Within a few minutes, a nurse entered the room.

"Well, hello there, Mrs. Whitaker," the nurse said with a large smile. "How are you feeling?"

"I'm not sure. I don't seem to have any pain."

"That is great," she was saying as Doctor Wheeler walked in.

"Mrs. Whitaker, I am so glad to see you have come around." Pulling the stethoscope from around his neck, he began to listen to Mrs. Whitaker's lungs and heart. He felt her head for soreness. "Do you think you can walk?" he asked.

"I can try."

"Nurse, let's help Mrs. Whitaker to stand."

Sitting Mrs. Whitaker up on the side of the bed, the nurse slowly assisted her to a standing position. After waiting for her to regain her strength, she held her arm lightly as she walked to the door and back to the bed.

"Do you feel all right?"

"I feel fine."

"The results from every test we have run have all come back fine. So if you feel like it, you can go home later this evening."

"I really would like to go home. I believe I'm fine."

"All right, I will write the order, and you can go home as soon as the nurses get everything ready. Do you have a way to get there?"

Diana hadn't thought about that. Who could she get to come and get her? Raphael instantly whispered into her ear the name of a person that would come and pick her up. Thinking that the thought was hers alone, she informed the doctor yes, she did. If she could get someone to call Rev. Phillip Fields, he would come and get her.

Before leaving the hospital to return to Evansville, Raphael had one more stop to make. It was now time that Marge Rollins was allowed to come out of her lethargic state and begin the healing process. Although it was not time for her to return to Evansville—that would be more like a week away—it was time she was able to talk to Cherish, the doctors, and nurses. Raphael leaned down to Marge's ear and instilled into her a word of wisdom regarding her future life.

As Raphael was leaving the room, he glanced back as Marge began to stir in the bed, showing signs of awakening.

⚡

Evansville was a hot bed of activity. Unseen by the human inhabitants, there were bodies flying through the air, lying on the sidewalks; the wounded were crawling, attempting to find shelter, and warriors were waging hand-to-hand combat, swords glistening as they were swirled through the air. This was a literal battlefield right in the middle of Evansville, all unknown to those around.

Michael, watching all the activity from his post at the cave, was pleased with the progress so far. He had learned not to get overly confident this early in the war. There were destined to be times that some of the sons of darkness would actually come out victors. Michael knew he had to maintain a constant line to headquarters.

XXVII

Ricardo was on the top of the world. Nothing could stop him now. He had managed to get a contract with one of the largest liquor distributors, not only in the state of Missouri but in the whole Midwestern United States. This was more than he had ever imagined. It was all downhill from there. It was time to return the good sheriff's call.

"Hank, this is Ric—Manny. I see that you called," Ricardo said with an attempt at correcting the slip of the tongue as he spoke to Hank. "Was there something that you needed?"

"No... I was just calling to see when you would be coming to get the shipment." Hank knew now with his mother's medical expenses he was in no position to question Manny about the possible danger of the Rollins' Royale. Anyway, it didn't matter. He wasn't going to be drinking the stuff.

"Well, as a matter of fact, I was going to let you know that I will be sending the trucks down there this weekend. I have a new contract, and I will need to have the stuff bottled and ready to deliver by the end of next week."

"That is great, Manny. How much are you going to want to pick up this weekend?"

"I expect to pick up at least seventy-five barrels. That will make about one hundred thousand bottles of finished product."

One hundred thousand bottles of Rollins' Royale. That was enough to annihilate the better half of the country, Hank thought.

"I see. So exactly what day will you be getting here?" Hank needed this information; he was not sure exactly how much the Rollinses had made, but this was a big order. Hank wasn't even sure if the Rollinses could turn out twenty barrels of the stuff, let alone seventy-five.

"I won't be coming personally. I have a lot of things to do here getting ready for this new contract. I will be sending two—no, better yet, I will send one eighteen-wheeler. That way, it will be large enough to hold the whole shipment. Jason will be coming in my place. And, Sheriff, a word to the wise: I expect all the stuff to be ready when my driver arrives. The Rollinses have had a total of three weeks to produce the corn. It only takes a week to produce sixty barrels. They should have at least ninety barrels, but I will only *expect* seventy-five this week. Next week, I will pick up the other seventy-five, fifteen from this batch plus the sixty from next week. I get real upset when somebody tries to get to me. And when I get upset, someone *will* have to pay, you understand?"

"I do understand, but, Manny, just for your information, I take offence when somebody hands me threats. So we both have our own little idiosyncrasies," Hank replied with a tone of indignation in his voice.

"I see. Then in order for both of us to be happy, things best go as planned. Am I right? And by the way, Sheriff, that was not a threat; it was a promise. Good-bye now." The phone line went dead as the call disconnected.

Hank had a strong feeling that Manny was not who he portrayed himself to be. Although the background checks had not revealed anything, the law enforcement officer in Hank told him that things were not what they appeared to be. If Hank could just get through the next month and a half doing business with this lowlife, he would have enough money to pay the medical bills and he was cutting out of this operation. *No, better yet*, he reasoned, *I will take it over myself.* It was beginning to have a dangerous overtone, and Hank didn't like that. Once Manny was out of the picture, Hank was sure he could work out a deal with Nolan. He would be able to take over the business without a problem.

⚡

Jack had gone for almost a week without a drop to drink. He had gotten up that morning, shaved, ate breakfast, and then gave the impression he was going into the store. Rachael wasn't sure if that was a good idea. What if he got over at the store and started acting strangely again? But she wasn't going to risk making him mad by telling him he couldn't go either. She would just have to go along with him. If there were any signs of him getting strange, she could bring him home. After breakfast, Rachael got Lucas ready; then all three walked over to the store together.

Since Jack is here today, Rachael thought, *I will give Michelle the day off. This will let her have some time at home.*

That way, if Jack began to act suspect, there would be no one to witness it but her. Rachael told Michelle that she and Jack would run the store today but they would see her tomorrow. After speaking to Jack and asking him how he felt, Michelle gladly left. Not sure what is was that Jack intended on doing, she went about checking the inventory and rotating the merchandise on the shelves. Jack just sat behind the counter, watching out the window as if he was expecting someone or something to come through the door.

It was nearly one o'clock, and everything had gone fine up to that point. Customers had come in, and Jack rang them out and talked in a normal way. Rachael was feeling that everything was going to be fine after all. Hank had been right; it was the whiskey. Jack had possibly had an allergic reaction to the stuff, and as long as he stayed away from it, he would be fine. The rest of the day went uneventful; they closed the store at nine o'clock and returned home. It was now as though nothing had ever happened. The past three weeks had been only a figment of Rachael's imagination. Rachael got busy making dinner as soon as she got in from the store. Jack sat at the kitchen table while she cooked. It was the first time in almost a month that he had sat and talked.

"Rachael, what exactly was I doing while I was out of my head?" He wanted to know.

"You just don't worry about that now. It is over. Let's try and forget about it."

"No, let's don't. I want to know. What was I saying? What was I doing? I need to know." There was urgency in his voice, almost a plea.

"It wasn't really anything you said exactly; it was more of the way you were acting."

"You say that I said nothing exactly. What did I say in particular?"

Rachael was beginning to think that Jack thought he might have said something that he shouldn't have said. Trying to think back, she tried to remember anything that he said that would be important. "You didn't say anything in particular. Really, it was just ramblings like 'They going to come and get me.' You said that 'everybody had found out and now they were coming after me.' Just stuff like that," Rachael carefully related, trying to reassure Jack that he hadn't said anything, that he hadn't revealed any deep dark secrets.

"Jack, it was just that Rollins whiskey. You had a real bad allergic reaction to it. Hank said it was probably too strong for you. Now that we know that, it will never happen again."

Although Rachael didn't know it, Jack had revealed a secret that had haunted him for almost twenty years, a secret that only he and Hank Wilson shared. Now that his mind was cleared, Jack knew that he had to get the burden of the secret off him. He had to let Hank know that he no longer was going to go along with any more of his schemes out of fear that Hank would someday reveal the nasty little secret they both shared. Enough was enough, and Jack was not going to be held in bondage any longer. He would not have Hank holding it over his head just to get him to go along with whatever Hank had up. Jack knew what he needed to do, and there was no one that was going to be able to stop him.

⚡

Marge Rollins was now alert and oriented. The nurse's aide had helped her with her bath; she was now sitting up in the bed, eating lunch as Cherish came through the door.

"Hey, you're awake," Cherish exclaimed with a tone of relief in her voice. "Mama, I have been so worried about you." Cherish hugged Marge, not too tightly, not wanting to hurt her in any way and not to disturb the chest tubes that were still attached and draining.

"Oh, thank you, baby. I hate that the first time we see each other in years I have to look such a mess," Marge apologized.

"You look just fine, Mama," Cherish lied, not wanting to hurt her mother any more than she already had been. "But I do need to know what happened to you."

Marge sat, picking at the food on her tray, not answering the question.

"It was Papa, wasn't it? He did this to you. I know it." Anger was welling up in Cherish, an anger that she had carried around so long it had morphed into hate.

"Now, Cherish, you know your father. He has certain ways he wants things done and certain ways he wants you to act. When we don't act in those ways, he gets angry. If I had not acted in the wrong way, he wouldn't have gotten mad and he wouldn't have had to hit me."

"Mama, you cannot take the blame for that man's stupidity. He does not have the right to hit you. I don't care what you have or haven't done. He only does that because he is too afraid to hit a man. You could have him thrown in to the state penitentiary for hitting you. Do you know that? There are laws that protect woman from men like Papa."

Marge listened while Cherish was talking. *Could this be*

my daughter? Is this the same girl that Nolan beat whenever he wanted to, the same girl that he threw out of the house? Now she is saying that no woman has to take that from a man. Cherish has really changed in the four years she has been gone.

"Cherish," Marge said, "that is easy for you to say. You got away. You don't have to live with him. If I just thought about calling the police, Nolan would kill me."

"Not if he didn't know where you were. Then he couldn't."

"He would find me. He would hunt until he found me, no matter how long it took. And when he found me, he would kill me."

"What did you do that was so bad this time that he punctured a lung and fractured several ribs? And just how long had you been hiding in the shed behind my house?"

"That shed was behind your house?" Marge was shocked.

"Yes. You didn't know?"

"All I knew was that I had to get away, so when I got my chance, I left. I ran through the woods, and, Cherish, I would swear that there was somebody there helping me get through there. I never got lost or tripped over anything. I just made my way through there like it was daytime, and it was in the dead of night. Anyway, after I crossed over West River Bridge, I didn't know where to go, and something said just go straight. I was hurting so bad. When I got to the edge of town, I didn't want anybody to see me, so I went through the backyard of the houses, and then I saw this shed. It was right there in front of me. It didn't have a lock, so I went in to lie down. That is when I started to cough. I was coughing up blood."

"You haven't told me what you did that was so bad that he beat you like this."

"I really can't tell you why. But let's just say I was butting in where I shouldn't have. And he was already mad at somebody else. He didn't need me making things worse."

"So you going to tell me that Samuel and Brent just stood there and let him beat you like this? They didn't do anything?"

"No, your brother's weren't there. They were over in Hugo. They had gone over there to go to the Silver Dollar; it was just me and your father there until the men from…" Knowing she was saying too much, Marge stopped talking.

"What men? The men from where?" Cherish probed Marge. "Mother, the men from where?"

"It doesn't matter now; it is done and over. I just need to get well, get these tubes off of me, and get out of here. How long you think they will keep me here?"

"Probably could be another week, maybe longer."

"How can you be so sure? Has the doctor been talking to you?"

"Yes, that too, but I also work here, so I can pretty well tell you that you will be here at least another week."

"Are you a nurse?"

"Not a licensed nurse—not yet, anyway. I am going to start school in the fall and get my license, but right now I am a nurses' aide."

"Cherish…?" A question that Marge had to know the answer to formed on her lips. She had to find out.

"When you left home that night, you was pregnant."

"I know, and now I have the sweetest little girl. Her name is Hope, and she is almost four. I will bring her up to see you tomorrow, now that you are alert."

"I also heard that you had stayed with Mamie, that black lady everybody says is a witch."

"I did, and no, Mamie is not a witch. She is the nicest, sweetest, smartest person I know. It is because of Mamie that I am where I am today. If she had not stopped me from jumping in the river the night Papa threw me out, Hope and I would be dead. She has done more for me than anybody else ever has. She has been right there whenever I needed her; she has taken care of and protected Hope and me the whole time.

"As a matter of fact, she is the one that delivered Hope. If it had not of been for her, Hope would have died. I am not ashamed that I stayed with Mamie. That is the best thing that could have ever happened to me."

"I know. Mamie is a great person."

"You know Mamie?"

"Yes, she has been around here for a long time. A long time ago, when women didn't have money to go to the doctor or hospital, Mamie would deliver their babies for them. She had been licensed a midwife back in the early 1950s by old Doc Wilson. Mamie delivered you."

"She never told me that. So that is how she knew who I was that night on the bridge. And that would also explain how she knew I was pregnant; she is a real midwife."

"Mamie can tell if a woman is pregnant sometimes even before the woman herself knows. Many a woman has gone to Mamie to find out if they were pregnant."

"Mama, you need to rest now. When you can leave here, I am taking you home with me. There will be no more of Papa beating on you. The Lord works in mysterious ways. I will never believe it was an accident you ended up in my shed.

I believe you were led there. And by the way, did you ever come in the house?"

"I was hungry."

Cherish laughed, leaned down, kissed her mother on the forehead. "I'll bring Hope tomorrow."

⚡

The Wednesday night prayer service lasted a lot longer than any service Phillip had conducted. He was used to an hour, no longer than an hour and a half. This service lasted almost three hours. But the amazing thing was it didn't seem to be more than thirty minutes.

There had been about ten people at Bible study, mostly women. There was one man there, a Mr. Isaiah Brown. Phillip had never felt the power of God as strong as he had as Mr. Brown prayed. It was something about this man's ability to open up the gates of heaven, or so it seemed. It was a very different type of service. It would appear that it was about to end when all of a sudden someone else would start a prayer. This one may be a prayer of thanksgiving. The next person may pray a prayer for repentance, the next one a prayer for deliverance; and so it went around the room and back again. It was doing that prayer service that Phillip began to feel a strong pull on his being, a desire to go after all the evil that was in the world, not just this town but the world as a whole. He could feel a presence or presences all around him. It was during this service that he believed he had gotten a glimpse of one of the little imps. Was he actually losing his mind?

After locking up the church, Phillip decided to take a walk, just to pray and sort out some things. As he walked, it was as if he was being led. Like a tour guide was showing him certain places, objects, and dwellings. Before he knew it, Phillip had walked to the other end of town and was standing in front of the Wesley United Methodist Church. The building was dark and deserted. What was God trying to show him, or what was he trying to tell him? Looking at the church building, Phillip had an eerie feeling like someone or something was being held hostage within the walls of this building. Standing there, looking at the building, Phillip began to pray a prayer of deliverance for the church, the pastor, and the members.

⚡

A message went out to the sons of darkness immediately as Phillip began to pray that someone had invaded their territory. This news went out through the demonic ranks as an electrical volt. Belial shot through the ceiling of the church with a fury unmatched. Gabriel was fully expecting to pull the hordes of hell out of hiding. This was his purpose in bringing Phillip to this spot. The angelic host was powered up to the uttermost; they were carrying so much power at this time, their physical statures had tripled in size.

Flying toward Gabriel with a fierce determination, Belial swooped down within inches of the massive archangel, hurling a fiery ball at him. Gabriel shot up into the air with the speed of light, chasing Belial through the elements. Belial shot sideways just in time to avoid Gabriel's heavy sword. Giving another flap of his mighty wings, Belial hurled himself straight up into the sky at Gabriel. As he was in flight, he heard the sound *swoosh* as an arrow from the mighty bow of Ariel caught him right under the left wing. With only one wing, Belial was flapping out of control, trying to escape the mighty swords and arrows of the angels.

Carmuel was circling around the church, swooping low and then ascending high up in the air to catch the attention of the nasty horde as they found their way out of the building to join in the battle taking place. Carmuel continued to fly down among the demons and then ascend high up in the sky. As the demons would try to pursue him, they would be picked off one by one by the mighty platoon of warring angels. Their deflated and listless bodies were strewn everywhere. They were lying in streets, in trees, and on top of vehicles. Green slim was running into the gutters as the demons' life force drained from their bodies.

Phillip, completing his prayer, turned and started toward home with Gabriel right by his side, leaving the warring angels to continue in battle.

With the demon forces defeated, Carmuel stationed his warring angels within the church and at each entrance. This property was now secured and ready for service. The strongest stronghold of the enemy had been captured and overrun.

Now it was only a matter of time before the sons of darkness would be defeated and cast out of this town with change the ultimate victory. However, as the angelic host knew, it was *not* over yet.

XXVIII

Now that the prayer warriors had been activated and there was a strong prayer covering, Mamie knew she could begin the task of bringing about change to Evansville. She could reveal some things that needed to be brought out into the open. First, she had a couple of people to talk to. She would first go and talk with Jack Sims. This had been a long time coming. Now the time was right; the truth had to be revealed. She would need to sit down and explain some things to Cherish. Mamie believed that Marge would be very helpful in this area. She knew then it would be time to break open the corruption that was brewing within the borders of Evansville. Those that were involved would need to be exposed and brought to justice. Once these things had been accomplished, Mamie knew her mission would be completed.

She had a strong sense of peace knowing that Phillip Fields would be a strong leader in fighting the forces of evil and bringing about good out of any type of evil. It was just a matter of trusting, listening, and then doing. If he would just trust God, listen to His instructions, and then do what He instructed, Phillip could be a very strong force against the sons of darkness. He would always have a strong backup, and any battle could be easily won with time and patience.

Pulling up in front of the One Stop store, Mamie determined to accomplish the goal she had set. Jack Sims was opening boxes, preparing to place the shipment of coffee creamer on the shelves as Mamie walked in. Jack had made a positive effort to avoid Mamie for years.

It had been Hank and he that had started the rumors through town that Mamie Webb was a witch. They had concocted the story that they had seen her out at the old well house on the east side of the Perkins place chanting and burning something. They said they actually heard her casting spells on certain people in town. They knew that if people believed she was a witch, they would not pay any attention to what she had to say. Jack was afraid that someday Mamie was going to confront him, and then the town and the people would know the truth that he and Hank had told a lie. Today was no different than any other; Jack was going to avoid Mamie. Whatever she needed, Michelle could help her. He would just keep doing what he was doing.

Turning to get more creamers out of the box, a pair of legs that he knew belonged to Mamie was standing right in front of him.

"Well, hello, Jack nice to see you back in the store. I do hope you is feeling better."

"Yes, I am. Thank you, Mamie," Jack answered, never looking back up but instead continuing to stack the creamer.

"Jack, now it is time that we have a talk."

"Have a talk about what?" he said, not wanting Mamie to sense the fear he was feeling.

"You know about what. Do we talk here or do we talk in private? The choice is yours; it doesn't matter to me if you want other people to know your nasty little secret right now. Or do you want to let them find out later? It is up to you, but they will find out."

"I don't have the slightest idea what you're talking about. Besides, everybody knows that you are touched in the head. Who's going to believe you? Now go away. I'm busy."

"No, Jack, I'm not touched in the head. You, more than anyone else, knows that. I know that you and Hank started that story, and I know why. Do you want to talk about a certain young lady out on a deserted road on a hot summer night right here or somewhere private?"

Those words sent terror through Jack. It was all beginning to come back to haunt him. It was going to destroy him. What could he do? What could he say? He needed help, and he needed it right now. Michelle watched the interaction taking place between Mamie and Jack. She couldn't hear anything they were saying but could tell it was something very important. Jack looked like he had just seen a ghost.

"Let's go into the office," Jack said with a tone of surrender.

Closing the door behind them, Jack motioned for Mamie to have a seat. It was going to be a very awkward situation. *What was he going to say? What exactly did this woman know?* It was Mamie that broke the silence.

"Now this has been something that I have held for a long time. Now is the time I need to let it out," she began. "I know about that night. You see, I had some things on my mind, so I just decided—or at least that is what I thought—I had decided to take a walk. Now I know I was being led to that place. I saw you, Hank Wilson, and a girl. You all were sitting on the car, drinking. I didn't recognize the girl. After a while, I heard her telling Hank to let her go. So I stood by the bridge and watched. The girl started to try to get away from Hank. He was real drunk. You both were."

The scene from that night was going through Jack's mind. A scene he had played over and over these last nineteen years, a scene he only wanted to erase.

"Hank finally caught and had his way with her. After he had finished, she just laid there on the ground, crying. I then heard Hank telling you that it was your turn. Yes, Jack I saw what happened next. The girl started to fight you. She spat in your face. That is when you started to hit her and hit her, and you kept hitting her. When she no longer moved, you stood up. Hank and you stood there and looked at the girl. After a few minutes, you both ran, got in the car, and sped away."

Jack was sitting at the desk, sobbing uncontrollably as Mamie related the details of a night he so badly wanted to forget. After a few minutes, Jack, in a weak, strained voice, managed to ask, "Why didn't you come forward when your son was being tried for the murder?"

"Because I wasn't sure exactly who had killed that girl."

"But you just said you saw the whole thing."

"No, I said I saw what you did. I didn't say I saw who murdered her."

This was making no sense to Jack. Mamie related word for word what had happened that night. Now she was saying that she didn't know who killed the girl. Wasn't it pretty obvious what had happened? He had killed her by beating her to death.

"I wasn't going to stand up and say that Jackson Sims had killed that girl when I didn't know who killed her. You see, I saw you and Hank leave, so I went to the girl. She was not dead at that time. She was really bad beat up, not dead."

Those words brought Jack's head up with a start. He couldn't do anything but stare at Mamie.

"I helped her up, offered her to come to my house to get cleaned up. But I guess she would rather have taken her chances out in the dark of night than accept my offer. That is the way it was in those days. So she snatched her clothes from me and told me to get lost. She could take care of herself. So I just left her sitting there, half naked, beat up. The next day I hear that they found a girl out by the West Bridge, murdered. No, Jack, you did not kill that girl."

A feeling of guilt swept through Jack. All these years, he had downgraded, slandered, and belittled Mamie. And she was the only person alive that knew he had not committed the crime, which even he thought he had. Jack had been the one that had accused her son Joshua of killing the girl. He had said he saw him standing on the bridge that night. He had said he saw Joshua talking to the girl as he and Hank drove out to the Rollins house. Lies, lies, all lies—just to protect himself. Now this woman's son had been killed for a crime he didn't commit. Jack was so ashamed he couldn't look at Mamie.

"You didn't say anything. Even when I testified in court, you still didn't say anything."

"What could I have said? I could have told them what I saw, but who would have believed me? The mother of the man accused coming in, accusing the son of the storeowner? I knew I couldn't say anything at the time, but there would come a time that it would all come out in the open. Everyone would know the truth, and my son would be vindicated."

"Mamie, I am so sorry. I am so sorry. I only wish I could go back and change things."

"There is nothing we can do about the past; it is the future I am worried about. Now it is time to change the future." Mamie got up without saying anything further; she left Jack to his own thoughts and conscience.

She had accomplished the first part of her mission. Now it was time for part two. She knew that Jack would call and tell Hank about their conversation. She would let him come to her. This would have been of grave concern a few months ago, Hank Wilson coming to talk to her about anything. But now Mamie knew she had a hedge of protection, and there was nothing he could do to her.

⚡

Cherish had a bittersweet feeling she had finally found a person that she felt she could share her life with. But now her mother was in the hospital because of her father's cruelty. One thing she had learned was that if she just believed and trusted, all things would work out.

It would be another three or four days before her mother was released from the hospital. The question then would be where she was going to go. Mamie had called and told her she needed to talk with her after she got home from work today. She had sounded as though it was very important Cherish couldn't imagine what it could be about.

Now Mamie had to decide in just what direction she needed to go with the last step in her mission. She decided on talking with Pastor Fields. She knew he would be at the church in his office, so she headed to the church.

Knocking on the door of the office, Mamie, with a determination she had not had in a long time, anxiously awaited a response from the inside. Hearing Phillip's invitation to enter, Mamie quietly opened the door.

"Pastor, are you real busy?"

"I'm never too busy for you, Mamie. Come on in."

"Pastor, I feel that I don't have a lot of time, so I need to work fast."

The sound of that statement made Phillip feel a little uncomfortable. Was she telling him that she was going to die or something? This could not be the case; he needed her there. There was still so very much that he needed to learn, and she was the one that he felt could teach him those things.

"What is it that is so urgent, Mamie? And why do you feel that there is not enough time?"

"Pastor, I know when things are coming to a head. Now it is of the greatest importance that some things be exposed."

Listening to Mamie, Phillip was indeed intrigued with the mystery she was laying out before him.

"For the last several months, I have been watching as large expensive cars and big cargo trucks go out the Rollins place. One day I got a glimpse at the men in the car. They were not what you would call *upstanding citizens*. They looked like the men I saw in that movie *The Men in Black*. Not only that; I have also seen Hank Wilson making a lot of trips out to the Rollinses.' The one thing that lets you know that there is something wrong, most of these incidents happen at night or late in the evening and usually always on Saturday."

"What do you think is going on out there, Mamie?"

"Not real sure, but whatever it is, it is nothing good."

"What do you think we can do about it? We don't have any legal rights to interfere with these kinds of things." Phillip was more than a little apprehensive, but he knew Mamie well enough by now to know she had a plan of action already laid out.

"One thing I know we can't do is go to Hank Wilson about this, because he is tied up in the middle of whatever it is. We need to talk to somebody that has more authority than he does.

That is where you come in. Nobody will listen to me, but if you would talk to somebody, they would be more likely to listen."

"How long did you say that you had been noticing these activities?"

"At least four to six months."

That was before all the strange happenings had taken place in Evansville. Could there be a direct connection between what was happening in the town and to the citizens and the activities out at the Rollinses'? Phillip wondered. "Before I can go to anybody, I need to have a general idea of what is going on. What can you tell me about the Rollinses?"

Mamie began telling Phillip the complete story about Nolan Rollins and his family. She told him about their illegal production of moonshine. She told Phillip about Nolan's abusive behavior toward his wife and family. She informed Phillip that Marge Rollins was currently in the hospital as the result of his physical violence toward her. She even told him the story about Cherish and how she had come to live with her for almost four years. The stories reminded him of the stories Sherri had heard about Evansville from her grandfather.

"Maybe I need to go out and pay the Rollins family a visit. After all, I am the new preacher, and I need to introduce myself," Phillip said with a look of deep concentration. Looking at his watch, Phillip said, "I might as well get ready and go out there later this afternoon. It is about twelve thirty. Maybe I will go out there around two. Before I go, I think I need to go into prayer and see in what way God wants to handle this situation."

"That is the best first step. Let's pray together right now."

After they had spent about thirty minutes in prayer, Mamie got up to leave, allowing Phillip some time to figure out what his next step would be.

The thought of going to the authorities was not one that Phillip relished. He had never been one to get involved in this sort of thing. He had a hard choice to make. What should he do? Should he just ignore this, or should he actually get involved? There were so many questions but no answers for Phillip. What if there really wasn't anything going on? He would look like a fool.

The last thing Mamie had to do was talk with Cherish. This was the thing she dreaded the most. Cherish had become like a daughter. There was no other way except to tell her. She would go home and wait for Cherish.

Manny was more excited than Jason had ever seen him. Even when he had told Jason that he wasn't going to Evansville.

And if things were not ready, he knew what to do. This was the happiest time in his life. He had just signed the largest contract that he had ever negotiated. Now it was only a matter of time before Rollins Royale would be on its way across the country. However, Manny had some serious concerns regarding those hicks over in Evansville. Once he had taken possession of the bulk of the produced whiskey, he was going to have to eliminate them. Understanding how moonshine was made, he could then put his own boys out there to make the stuff. He would have to come up with a plan to eliminate that Rollins and his imbecile boys. Then it would only be a matter of what to do about Hank Wilson. Wilson, Manny felt, would not pose too much of a problem. All Manny had to do was to make him feel like he was important. If Manny could just offer him a job somewhere else with the prospect of a higher position, Wilson would fall like pecans in autumn. Once Wilson was out of Evansville, the Rollins thing would be no problem.

⚡

Cherish would not be riding home with Shelly today. Instead, Randy had volunteered to come and pick her up. That, he said, would give her a little extra time to spend with her mother. Randy had even volunteered to watch Hope for her since this was his day off. Stepping out of the hospital, Cherish surveyed the parking lot for Randy's black Silverado pickup. Seeing the truck parked in the employee parking, Cherish made her way toward it. She was very happy. She believed that Randy had an interest in her, an interest that could or would lead to a permanent arrangement. Cherish did not want to rush things;

she didn't want to take anything for granted. It was after all a little early for that. She could only hope.

The ride back to Evansville was very relaxing. Randy felt comfortable with Cherish, and Hope was such a good little girl. He felt the same feelings now that he felt back in high school. He was not going to let his future go up in flames because of what other people thought.

⚡

Phillip read the clock on the wall; it was one forty-five. He knew he had told Mamie that he would be going out to the Rollinses' around two.

Fear was creeping up on him like a fungus. He got his Bible and headed out the door to make his trip. A trip he prayed would prove successful.

Phillip had never been in that part of town; he had never ventured across the West River Bridge. It was foreign territory, a territory that he soon would learn was uncharted by anything good.

⚡

The demonic hordes began to shriek and squeal as the threat of danger came looming into their domain. Cold yellow eyes were peering from the underbrush along the road leading to the Rollins farm. Demons were coming from every direction, attacking the vehicle with a vengeance, trying to gain entrance to the car and Phillip.

The warring angels assigned to protect Phillip were in full combat with these vermin. Michael and his platoon of angelic host were stationed high on the hill overlooking the

Rollins farm. They could see the activity below, as the sons of darkness proceeded to wage attacks against Phillip. The clarion call went forth as the heavenly host charged into war. Phillip had the distinct feeling of danger and harm as he made his way through the wooded area toward the Rollinses.' He prayed as he continued that the Lord would please take care of him. He still wondered if he was doing the right thing. If not, it really was too late now; he was headed straight for the entrance to the Rollins farm.

Nolan Rollins was not the friendliest or the most receptive person Phillip had ever met. He would not listen to anything the young minister had to say. Instead, Phillip was informed that if he didn't leave right now, he never would. This was a threat that Phillip knew full well would be carried out if he didn't leave. Before he left, Phillip had seen Samuel and Brent loading barrels of what he assumed was whiskey into the back of the trailer of an eighteen-wheeler. The trailer was unattached to the truck but was positioned to be ready to move at a later time. Maybe Mamie really was right after all. Phillip turned around and headed back to town. He knew now what he needed to do and he had a revelation of who he should go and see. Michael knew the time had come, time to end this thing once and for all. He headed into town alongside Phillip.

⚡

Mamie was sitting in her favorite chair as she saw Randy Baker's truck pull up to the curb and Cherish exit the front passenger side. She opened the rear door of the extended cab pickup, and out jumped Hope, running up to Mamie's front door. Mamie was so happy for Cherish. With Randy Baker, she knew that Cherish and Hope would be just fine. Randy would come to terms with the circumstances that surrounded the conception of Hope, and he would love them both unconditionally. It was now time for the final step in the plan to unravel the darkness that was surrounding Evansville and to destroy it once and for all.

XXIX

Entering the old building, Phillip remembered the first time he had crossed this threshold. It was a time in which he had so many doubts about coming to this place. He remembered the look of distrust and downright suspicion that he had received from Mabel Williams and Mayor Hanes. He also remembered thinking there was something wrong with the mayor. Now here he was, coming in here to talk with the very man he had originally suspected of corruption. *This was a very strange turn of events.*

Walking up to the counter, Phillip could see that Mabel was sitting in her usual place; this time rather than talking on the phone, she appeared to be reading something, something that had her undivided attention.

"Good afternoon, Ms. Williams," he said.

Looking up from the material she was reading and placing her finger in the spot she had stopped, Mabel answered, "Good afternoon, Rev. Fields. May I help you?"

"I was wondering if Mayor Hanes was in this afternoon." Once again, Phillip had put out a fleece before God. He had asked God that if he was not to talk to the mayor, let him not be in.

"Why, yes, he is. You just caught him; he was talking about going home early today."

"I don't want to stop him if he is going to leave." Once again, the fleece came back neither wet nor dry. The mayor was in but was getting ready to leave. *Oh well,* Phillip thought, *God must surely have a sense of humor.* He would stop trying to fleece God.

"I don't believe that will be a problem. He was only going home because he had nothing to do, but now that you are here, he does." Mabel smiled. This was the first time Phillip remembered Mabel ever smiling. He tried to remember if she had smiled on their first meeting. But he could not remember.

"Just a minute, I'll let him know that you are here." Calling in on the old intercom system, Phillip heard mayor Hanes say for him to come on it.

The mayor's office was not unlike the rest of the city hall that Phillip had seen. The furniture was antiquated; two walls were covered with shelves that held a complete law library, and the leather chair that sat in front of the mayor's chair showed fading on the arms from years of use.

"Have a seat, Reverend," the mayor offered. "What is it I can do for you? If you are looking for a donation, I need to tell you that we just don't have the funds available to make any monetary donations at this time."

"No, Mayor Hanes, I am not here for a donation, there is

something else I need to talk to you about. I know that I am a newcomer here, and I am not real sure how to begin."

The mayor sat up, interested in what the new preacher had to say. "Go ahead, Reverend," he urged.

"This may sound a little crazy, but here goes." Phillip explained to him what Mamie had told him, only conveniently leaving out who had told him.

He then told him about going out to the Rollinses' and what he had witnessed with the trailer and the barrels of whiskey. When Phillip had finished telling his story, there was what seemed to be a long period of silence on the part of Mayor Hanes. The mayor finally reached over and hit the intercom and told Mamie not to let anyone disturb him and Reverend Fields.

"Rev. Fields, I understand that you, being a man of the cloth, understand the importance of confidentiality, so I am prepared to share something with you. I have gotten the word that there was something; a very large-scale operation was going on right under our noses. I have tried to find out in roundabout ways what it is but until now have not been successful. I have asked the sheriff to look into it, but he still hasn't returned with anything."

"That is something else, Mayor. My source also said that Sheriff Wilson makes a lot of trips out to the Rollins place late at night, sometimes on the same night that the big trucks come in. That is why I came to you. I didn't want to risk going to the sheriff in case he had something to do with this whole thing."

"I am not surprised. I also have seen Hank going in that

direction at night. When does your source seem to think that the next time the truck will be coming through?"

"They say that lately it is usually late in the evening or at night on Saturdays."

"I want you to know, Reverend Fields that I truly appreciate you coming in. This just might be the break I have needed."

Phillip stood, shook hands with the mayor, and left, praying that he had done the right thing and hoping that it hadn't made matters worse.

After Phillip had left the office, Mayor Hanes picked up the phone and dialed a number he had in memory.

"Jim Jackson please," Mayor Hanes said to the person that answered.

"Hi, Jim, this is Harve. About that little project we discussed, I think I have what we have been waiting for." Listening to the person on the other end, Mayor Hanes ended the call with, "Yes, I will call and give you the details. Today is Thursday. I will call you tomorrow. Do you think we can get everything we need by late Friday evening? Great! Talk with you tomorrow. Bye now."

⚡

Cherish had a lot to think about. After her conversation with Mamie, she was so confused. Cherish had been around Mamie long enough that she knew she would never tell a lie, even if it meant saving someone from something terribly bad. Cherish needed to talk to her mother, and she needed to talk to her right away. Calling Randy, she asked him if he could take her over to Hugo to visit with her mother. She explained that is was very important. She couldn't tell him what it was right then, but she would when the time was right.

That night sleep came hard for Phillip, Mamie, and Cherish. Jack Sims had his own demons to deal with. He had to figure out a way to make this right with Mamie, not just for her sake but for his as well. He knew he would have to tell Rachael the whole gory details before it became public knowledge. He made up his mind that he would sit her down tomorrow and tell her the whole story, everything.

He had tried to call Hank to tell him what Mamie had said, but he didn't answer the phone and had not returned his message. Looking through the cabinets, Jack remembered that there were none of the Rollins Royale left in the house or the store. It was probably for the best.

Mamie had called for a special prayer service on Friday evening, but there didn't seem to be anyone that was able to come. She guessed it would have to be her, the pastor, and the pastor's wife. The Bible said where two or three are gathered in His name, he would be in the midst. It also said where two agree as in touching whatever they asked shall be given. Mamie had a strong unction that there had to be a prayer service on Friday and again on Saturday. No matter what, she was going to be obedient!

So on Friday night, she, Phillip, and Sherri gathered at the New Life Fellowship and prayed. They prayed harder than ever. There was urgency in the air, an urgency that said,

"Pray hard." The group decided to meet at the church on Saturday around five. Maybe more people could be there.

※

Saturday morning the sky was overcast. Thick black clouds were looming overhead. A strong storm was brewing. The wind was blowing through the trees, sending debris flying through the air. It was one of those days that no one wanted to do anything but lay around.

Phillip had a feeling of forlornness. He had not heard anything from the mayor; he couldn't help but wonder if he had made a mistake in taking his information to him in the first place. What if Harvey Hanes was in on the plot? All Phillip could do now was pray that everything would work out according to the will of God.

Ricardo "Manny" was giving last-minute instructions to Jason and the driver. He didn't want any screw-ups or excuses from those backwoods inbred hillbillies. He wanted the product delivered and ready for shipment by the end of next week.

Cherish knew that she had to confront her father. Talking with her mother, she had learned some very shocking information. She had to let her father know she knew everything. There was something else she needed to tell him, something that would change a lot of things.

She had told Randy part of the story, coming home from the hospital, but there was still something she hadn't told him. She had asked him if he would drive her out to her father's house after he got off work on Saturday. This was a confrontation that had been a long time coming. Now the time had come to bring everything out in the open.

Jim Jackson had taken all the appropriate steps for Saturday. He and Harvey had devised a plan that would take everybody by surprise. Checking his equipment, he found everything was in working condition and ready for use. Taking a head count, he was assured everybody was there and ready for action. Jim and five carloads of his handpicked, well-trained associates headed toward Evansville.

Mamie, Phillip, and Sherri gathered at the church to pray. No one else had shown up, so they prepared to continue where they had left off on Friday. Then as they started the prayer service, the door to the sanctuary opened; there coming through the door was a weak Diana Whitaker.

"The Lord sent me a message that I needed to be here," she said. "I know there's a major warfare in progress, and it takes all the ammunition we have to beat the enemy." They other three were elated, to say the least. There was always strength in numbers, a strength that was definitely needed at this time.

⚡

The driver made his way down up highway 69 toward the Indian Nation Turnpike. Billy Ray Cyrus' "Ready, Set, Don't Go" was heard coming from the CD player.

All he could think about was picking up this load, taking it back to Dallas, and getting home. He believed he would be back home by no later than ten o'clock. Jason, wanting to get there first just to make sure everything was ready, passed the trucker and sped toward Evansville. Jason was secretly tired of this. He was tired of following orders from Ricardo. He was smart enough to run his own business. After this gig, he was going to leave Dallas. He would go somewhere like

Memphis or maybe New Orleans and do his own thing. It was time he went out on his own.

Jim Jackson and his convoy of associates also were headed toward Evansville; they had to remain incognito as not to be discovered until the right moment.

⚡

The King of Darkness sat up on the roof of the city hall, seething, his army of beasts standing at attention, waiting for a signal to charge. This war had been disastrous for the sons of darkness. They had been defeated at every attempt. He was ready for a full-fledged battle that only the strongest would be able to withstand. He was going to call Michael out. This was going to be his ultimate victory. He would defeat and destroy Michael, and the rest of those angelic do-gooders would then be his spoil.

The angelic host and their crews of warring angels, where gathered at the cave behind the Rollinses,' also awaiting a signal to charge. It was their goal to bring the sons of darkness into their territory and away from town. Michael and the other archangels were well aware that the King of Darkness, his kingdom in such danger of being defeated, was going to be coming out for this battle himself.

Receiving the go-ahead, Carmuel flew toward town to lure the hordes of darkness out to the angelic host's location. This would not be difficult; they had a habit of going off half-cocked. They would follow without a second thought.

The large armored beast, sensing the present of good, immediately flew off the roof in pursuit of Carmuel; the other beast, princes, and powers of darkness followed behind.

Carmuel zigzagged across the sky with rocket speed, leaving a long trail of light behind him. To the human eye, it would have appeared as a comet.

The beasts of darkness, flying with all the strength and speed they could with the heaviness of their armor, were spitting balls of fire toward the archangel. Carmuel shot upward just as a fiery ball brushed past him. Within a matter of seconds, the sons of darkness invaded the hill behind the Rollinses.' There awaiting them were the mightiest angels in the arsenal of heaven. Swords flashed through the air as the two forces met head-on. Raphael and his warriors stood, silently awaiting their time for intervention.

Sneaking up from behind, a slimy black creature crept up the rocks, making his way to the top of the hill. The warring angel, distracted by the battle in front of him, suddenly felt the piercing pain as the creature jabbed his sword deep into his body. Turning to face his assailant, the angel, with one motion, slashed the demon with his heavy sword, sending him sprawling down the hill to land in a heap at the bottom. Instantly, Raphael was at the wounded angel's side. By placing his hand on the wound, it miraculously closed, and the angel was again ready to fight.

Gabriel, in the heat of battle, suddenly got that unmistakable odor; he knew that Belial was somewhere within close proximity. Turning just in time, Gabriel flew sideways, barely avoiding the two-edged sword that was being welded by Belial.

With the battle in full swing, Michael was on the lookout for the King of Darkness. It was no secret that he liked to use the weapons of deception and the element of surprise when he entered the battlefield. Michael knew that wherever he was, he would play dirty, so he had to be on his constant guard. Michael could not allow this horde of evil to get him distracted allowing their king an advantage. At that moment, the hill began to tremble as a dark cloud ascended over the land.

Smoke was bellowing from the pits of the earth; as it cleared, there standing on top of the hill was the vilest of all creatures, the King of Darkness. For this battle, he had changed his methods of operation. With a wave of his hand, the demons ceased their fighting and rose high up in the sky. The sky became dark and threatening with their darkness. The angelic host stood at attention to one side as Michael and the King of Darkness faced off.

⚡

Looking up at the threatening conditions of the sky, Cherish was nervous as she headed toward her old home. Randy had assured her that he was there with her in case anything happened. Cherish was truly grateful for Randy's support and understanding. But at the same time, she did not want Randy to get involved in this and possibly get hurt. Pulling his truck in front of the Rollins house, killing the engine, Randy prepared to get out.

"No, Randy, you stay here. I need to go in there alone."

"Are you sure?" Randy asked Cherish, sensing her apprehension at returning to the place from which she had fled almost four years earlier.

"I'm sure. I have to do this, and I have to do it now or I never will. It will be all right. I promise," Cherish replied, softly caressing Randy's hand.

Entering the inside of the house, Cherish found it in an utter mess. There were dirty dishes and clothing scattered everywhere. Flies were all over the kitchen table, making themselves a feast on the open jar of jelly and plate of half-eaten eggs. There was a strong smell of urine throughout the house and empty bottles of Rollins' Royale were strewn everywhere.

Being satisfied that no one was in the house, Cherish started toward the barn. Randy patiently watched each step she took. She could hear her father cussing as she approached.

Samuel, Brent, and Nolan were working, feverously filling barrels with the newly cropped moonshine. It was Samuel and Brent that saw her as she entered the barn. Samuel stood, staring at her as if she were a ghost.

"Well, the dead has returned," Brent announced.

Nolan stopped what he was doing and looked up to see Cherish standing in the door of the barn.

"Papa, I need to talk to you."

"You going to come in here all high and mighty and tell me what you need. I don't have time for no bull crap right now. So I guess you just better turn around and go back where you came from." Nolan's voice was hard and cold

"Oh, I believe you do have time for this, because if you don't, maybe I will just go to the police and tell them what you are doing out here." Cherish found a courage she never knew she had as she confronted her father. "And then I can also tell them how you beat Mama so bad she is laying up in the hospital."

From the truck, Randy could see Hank Wilson coming from around the south side of the barn. Not sure what to think about this, he thought he ought to get out; something just didn't set right about this whole thing.

Nolan Rollins was looking at Cherish with the look of pure hate and disgust on his face. He was trying to think of what needed to be done about this, when the problem was instantly solved for him.

"That's very noble of you, girl. You won't have to go far. I'm right here, so why don't you just go ahead and tell me what Nolan is doing and how he beat his wife." Hank laughed as he walked up beside Cherish.

A rage that she had not felt in years was rising up in Cherish as she looked at Hank. A quick flashback of pain and torment instantly entered her head, a flashback of a night, a night so dark that it was impossible to run without falling, a night that had changed her life forever. Turning back to her father, she saw Brent and Nolan both had a look of satisfaction on their faces. Samuel, on the other hand, was looking at the ground, not looking at Cherish or Hank.

"Now let's just see, little lady. You say that you would tell the police about what?"

"Papa, I guess you are going to stand there and go along with this pervert. Well, maybe I should tell you something else, something I have never told anyone else." Cherish started glaring at Hank Wilson. "You always wanted to know who knocked me up. Maybe I ought to tell you about a night four years ago. A night I was coming home from working for Mrs. Whitaker, a night that Sheriff Wilson was 'making his rounds.'"

"Shut up!" Hank said as he pulled his revolver. "That is enough." Nolan, understanding what Cherish was implying, started toward Hank with the winnowing fork in his hand.

With the gun now pointed at him, Nolan had to gain Hank's confidence to get up on him.

"Hold on, Hank," Nolan said. "Maybe I need to hear what she has to say. Not that I will believe everything."

"You just get back over there and continue working. What she has to say is not important." With a smug look, Hank told Cherish, "You best count yourself lucky. You could have ended up like that other girl, and you know, Nolan, the one they found by the river in eighty-nine. It could have been the same way. But in your case, nobody would have known what happened or who did it.

"I would doubt that anyone would have even cared. You could have been a long-forgotten memory by now, missy." Hank laughed as though he had just told a funny joke. "Now that other girl, she was a feisty little thing. She just kept trying to fight and run away. Not like you, who just lay there, crying. Not her, no sir. She wanted to be a hero, so she had to die."

Randy, coming up behind Hank, had heard the whole conversation, but before he had a chance to grab him, Hank brusquely swirled around. Now the gun was pointed at Randy.

"Oh, I see you and the little lady here got something going on. Just take my word for it. She ain't that great," Hank mused with a sadistic laugh. Samuel, not being able to stand any more, lunged at Hank. The gun went off, hitting Samuel in the stomach, and he fell to the ground. The sound of gunfire rang out through the woods.

⚡

Michael and the King of Darkness continued in their battle. Lightening could be seen flashing across the sky as Michael flew into the king. With a loud rumbling clap, the king would be knocked to the ground. With a mighty blow of Michael's sword, the king of darkness went flying toward the ground. He hit a tree with a loud explosive sound, the impact so strong, the tree split, burning down the middle. Everyone at the Rollins farm jumped at the sound and stared at the tree.

"All right, everybody get inside now!" Hank ordered after the tree split.

⚡

Jason wanted to hurry and get out of these forsaken woods before a tornado hit; he sped through the gate on to the Rollinses' property. *There were way too many vehicles here*, he thought as he got out of his Escalade. Making his way across the yard to the barn, he was startled at the scene being played out on the inside.

"Come on in, Jason," Hank invited, waving his gun in a motioning manner. "The boys here were just about to finish loading up the trailer."

Not really knowing the situation, Jason made a move to reach into his shoulder holster to retrieve his .357 Colt revolver.

"I wouldn't do that if I was you," Hank warned. "Now you just be a good boy, get back into your fancy new car, and go tell Manny everything is under control." The sound of a large diesel engine was coming down the lane. Hank nervously motioned for Cherish and Randy to get against the wall, the gun still pointed at Randy. The driver whipped the truck cab into the yard, maneuvering it around into position so that the trailer could be hitched up. After aligning the hitch, the driver got out and started to connect the cab to the trailer, unconcerned with the activity in the barn. His only objective was to get this stuff and get home. He could care less what was going on in the barn. Jason's SUV was in the driveway, so he knew he was around somewhere.

⚡

Harvey Hanes was at the edge of town as planned, waiting for Jim Jackson and his boys to arrive. When the convoy got to this spot, Harvey would get into Jim's vehicle and ride on out to the Rollinses.' It had been a long time coming, but he finally had Hank Wilson where he wanted him. Looking up, Harvey could see the sky getting darker and darker; lightening was flashing from all directions. The thunder was getting closer and closer. *Where could Jim be?* Harve thought. He didn't want to be stuck out at the Rollinses' in a huge thunderstorm.

Looking to the south, Harvey could scarcely make out Jim Jackson and his caravan approaching. This was it; time for the takeover. No one was going to run this town. This was Harvey Hanes' town, and no one else was going to come in and take over.

⚡

The four prayer warriors were in deep, heartfelt prayer inside the New Life Fellowship as the fierce storm was raging on the outside. With each clap of thunder, the prayer became more and more intense. There was danger lurking all around. It was the intercessors' place to divert it in another direction. Hadn't Jesus spoken to the storm? Were not they promised to be able to do the things Jesus did?

The caravan continued over the West River Bridge, gaining speed as the cars quickly approached the Rollins farm. As they crossed over the run-down cattle guard, the sirens were activated. Officers emerged on the property in full force. Hank Wilson, in a state of panic, rushed to the door of the barn and began to open fire on the approaching state troopers. A single bullet ricocheting off the corner of the house hit Harvey Hanes in his left shoulder as he attempted to exit the car, sending him to the ground. Another of Hank's bullets hit an approaching trooper as he ran for cover behind the semi rig. With perfect aim, a sharpshooter fired, hitting Hank in the right hand, sending his gun flying. Randy Baker, falling to the floor and rolling to avoid being hit by stray bullets grabbed the gun.

The troopers rushed into the barn to find Randy Baker holding Jason, Nolan, and Brent at gunpoint. Cherish was on the ground next to Samuel, holding her hand over the wound in his abdomen. Jim Jackson radioed for two ambulances to be sent to the scene. Then Nolan, Brent, Jason, and the truck driver were handcuffed and led away to waiting police cars. Hank sat under the glare of a state trooper until the paramedics could arrive and have his wound tended to; then he was carted off to the jail.

The King of Darkness, bruised and beaten, lay under the mighty sword of Michael.

"Go ahead. Banish me to my appointed place." He snarled up at Michael.

"Your time is not yet," Michael replied. "You will know when that time comes."

Withdrawing his sword, Michael motioned to his warriors that this battle was over. As the angelic host started their ascent, Gabriel, with one last swing of his sword, slashed Belial, sending him swirling to the ground. Before Belial could make contact with the ground, Gabriel lifted him up and sent him flying high into the atmosphere.

Randy, exiting the barn, glanced up at the clouds behind the barn just as a wall cloud dipped toward the earth and then lifted. *We are in for a mighty storm,* he thought.

⚡

It had been a week since the events out on the Rollins farm. The town and state were in a flurry of activity. The State Police had sent a sample of the Rollins' Royale to their forensics lab in Oklahoma City. There they discovered that the mixture contained a lethal amount of cocaine. The police knew that neither the Rollinses nor Hank Wilson could be the mastermind behind this operation; it was far too sophisticated. Putting pressure on Brent Rollins, he gave up the name Manuel Lopez. It was soon discovered that Manuel Lopez didn't exist. With a lot of persuasion and some intimidation, Jason finally gave up Manny's real name. Running the name 'Ricardo Almendarez' through the national crime database, the officers found he was the suspected kingpin for illegal drug trafficking into the United States from Mexico. He was currently under the surveillance of the FBI.

Hank Wilson was charged with conspiracy to distribute narcotics, the manufacturing of an illegal substance, first-degree rape, and shooting with the intent to kill. He was also charged with the first-degree murder of Misty Rogers, the girl found murdered in 1989. Jack Sims agreed to cooperate with the authorities and was given five years for being an accessory to the murder, three of which were suspended. He was ordered to pay $50,000 to the victims fund.

⚡

Phillip looked out the window as he prepared to leave the house for church; the sun was shining brightly, not a cloud in the sky. Birds were chirping in the trees, and the air held a "clean after the storm freshness."

This was a beautiful day, Phillip thought as he, Sherri, and the kids were leaving the house, heading to the church. Praise and worship was in full swing by the time they entered the building. Phillip was full of joy as he stood up in the pulpit. The church was filled with people this morning. Some he had never noticed or seen before. Marge Rollins was sitting with Cherish, Randy, and Hope. Mabel Williams was there, as was Harvey Hanes. Jack Sims' wife, Rachael, and son were also in the congregation. It appeared that the whole town of Evansville was at New Life this morning.

Phillip began his message with prayer, thanking God for his mighty power of deliverance of the town of Evansville.

"Turn with me to the book of Saint John the sixteenth chapter and the thirty-third verse," Phillip announced. "I will be reading from the King James Version," he informed the congregation as he began his message. "Let us read:

'These things I have spoken unto you, that in me ye might have peace. In the world ye shall have tribulation: but be of good cheer; I have overcome the world.'" Looking up from the Bible, Phillip was shocked; coming through the door of the sanctuary was Rev. and Mrs. Potter. This truly was a day the Lord had made.

⚡

For the angelic host, the battle of Evansville was over. The victory had been won. It was now time to receive their next assignment.

Ascending through the ceiling of the church, Michael and the archangels made their departure. Michael had assigned several warring angels to remain in Evansville to maintain the victory. The rest he summoned to follow him. He had received word from headquarters—there was trouble brewing in Missouri, trouble that could possibly turn into a full-scale war if not contained immediately.

The King of Darkness, arising from the roof of the now condemned warehouse that had served as their headquarters, shouted after the angelic host the warning, "It ain't over yet!" The sons of darkness, wounded and dejected, departed to a new destination with a new agenda already formulated.